R. B. Cumberland

How I Spent my Two Years' Leave

My impressions of the mother country, the continent of Europe, United States of America, and Canada

R. B. Cumberland

How I Spent my Two Years' Leave
My impressions of the mother country, the continent of Europe, United States of America, and Canada

ISBN/EAN: 9783337190101

Printed in Europe, USA, Canada, Australia, Japan

Cover: Foto ©Andreas Hilbeck / pixelio.de

More available books at **www.hansebooks.com**

HOW I SPENT

MY TWO YEARS' LEAVE;

OR,

MY IMPRESSIONS OF THE MOTHER COUNTRY, THE CONTINENT OF EUROPE, UNITED STATES OF AMERICA, AND CANADA.

BY

AN INDIAN OFFICER.

Dulce est desipere in loco.—Hor. Carm. IV. 12.

London:

SAMUEL TINSLEY,

10, SOUTHAMPTON STREET, STRAND,

1875.

Dedicated

TO THE CHERISHED MEMORY

OF ONE,

EVER BEFORE MY EYES,

WHOSE PURE CHARACTER AND NOBLE CAREER

ARE A FIT EXAMPLE

FOR MY LIFE'S IMAGE.

PREFACE.

I HAVE hid myself behind the name of "An Indian Officer," because it is so safe, and not easily recognized. Everybody is "an Indian Officer" belonging to the Service and coming from our Great Indian Empire. From the dashing cavalry Punjab Piffer —the B. C. S., which, by-the-bye, is one of the most honourable services in the world—to officers of the Indian Woods and Forest Department, all come under the category of "Indian Officer," whilst in England.

And now to say something of the book itself. It will appear incredible to some why I should have been so bold as to have attempted to publish my travels and experiences, which by the majority must be thought paltry and worthless. "Fools rush in where angels fear to tread." But my reasons are, that many of my dearest friends have expressed themselves differently, and have asked me to publish an account of some of the most interesting of my journeys. I have at last acceded to their very flattering request, and the following pages are the result. I only hope they will not be disappointed at the rough jottings of a practical man, whose only recommendation is that he has knocked about, and seen a great deal of the world and its five " quarters." I have refrained from publishing the names of my friends connected with my experiences in the following narrative, but they will have no difficulty in detecting where *they* figure in my encounters with them during my erratic movements.

In conclusion, I think it right to add that every incident and occurrence narrated in this work is founded on fact.

HOW I SPENT MY TWO YEARS' LEAVE.

CHAPTER I.

EARLY in January, 1873, I was on a visit at Lahore, with an old friend of mine, Suttan, of the —th Hussars, whose regiment had just gone home, and he had made arrangements to stop out, and was negotiating an exchange with an officer of a crack corps, ordered to India.

No one who has not spent several years in the trying plains of Hindustan can understand the morbid feeling one experiences when a regiment or a dear friend leaves you in the lurch behind "for home." It takes a long while before the soothing hand of time allays the "blues."

It was one of those lovely fresh mornings, peculiar to the Punjab, when, strolling off after breakfast to the Lahore Club, I hinted, for the first time, to my friend, that my papers for leave to Europe had gone in, and I expected to hear in a few days when I might be off.

"By Jove! you going too?" exclaimed Suttan; "I wish I could see my way clear. What a number of fellows have left, or are going home before the hot weather sets in. Have you heard, by-the-bye, that Hanton is going on furlough at once?" he added. "I don't know him myself personally, but I have heard you speak of him so often, and know your great friendship for him, that I should think it would be a good chance if you went together."

This was news to me. Hanton was my dearest chum; he had not written to me of late, and I fancied the poor fellow was unwell. Suttan proposed to drive me over to his diggings after reading the "gup" of the place at the Club. Suttan informed a few of the fellows we met that another "beggar" was off home, and pointed across to me. As is usual, they sighed on receiving this intelligence. Some sneered, and one or two congratulated me.

The Club was not so full this morning. The beauteous cynic, in all his splendour and magnificence of figure and dress, using the most soft and lady-like expressions, which come so naturally to him, was also talking of "going whome!" So also was the Scottish chief of a royal line. Our learned and gifted young Judge, Mr. Pucca, was talking "shop" to that mighty magnate of the law, Plunger, in the most cold-blooded manner possible settling a weighty and technical point of Punjab law. That very soldier-like individual, who looks as if he had swallowed a poker, is unusually stern and commanding this morning. The truth is, he drank too many "pegs" last night over whist, and lost a heavy bet in wrongly quoting 'Baldwin and Clay' to Touchstone, of the Gunners. That keen, sharp-eyed, knowing-looking Machiavel, is in the Engineers, holding a capital Staff appointment. He thinks it due to the official position he holds to appear troubled and absent—that is calculated to show his importance and a great mind. He is a good-natured sort of fellow at heart with all his petty failings, although somewhat dogmatic outwardly. There is Straws, of the Artillery, better known as "the gentleman," who is the greatest turf celebrity in every station in Upper India; Feckles, of the Highlanders, a would-be sportsman; the meek and mild Jesuitical barrister, Tomkins, who drives the fastest trotter of an evening to the band; the "Gorgeous Juvenile," in a fiery new necktie, cracking a big whip in the verandah, as he marches forth to hail his syce; the fastidious Blowup, of the Railway; and Farewell, the merchant.

What a conglomeration! And yet there are not half the unkind things said here which are concocted at Mrs. Curry's Badminton fights or Mrs. Flareup's *conversaziones*. Our padre is *so* good, such a nice man,—thoroughly enters into and understands all the talk of the ladies. To look into that pure innocent face, with upturned eyes, sweet though rather elongated mouth when in the pulpit on a Sunday, you would never forget it, reader.

I. don't believe he even *thinks* naughty things. Our padre sometimes patronizes the Club, but I don't think he quite likes it.

Well, after reading a cracky, supercilious leading article in the *I. P. O.* on some new appointment connected with a frontier command, and a clever hit in the *Pioneer* on the *coming* Bengal Famine, I take my departure for Hanton's quarters. I find him still in his pyjamars, in his bed-room, looking very wretched about something he tells me has long been on his mind. The worthy doctor, Manners, has just left, and advises him to go up, and pass the Board without further delay. I told Hanton of my intention to leave on seeing my name in orders; and, if possible (if he is not going home in one of those sea-hearses of troop-ships), to engage our passage per P. and O. This he agreed to do. I return, and have a night of jollification at Suttan's house. Buttons, of the Police; Ursie, of the Canals; the dazzling Adonis, with several funny stories ready to amuse us; Tomkins, Rattling, Poggle, Sala, and others. The following day, I received orders to go north, and report myself to ——, stationed at Badpoor, prior to proceeding on leave to Europe.

The Punjab Government generally does uncommon things. Perhaps it is because its chiefs and rulers like to be unlike other local Governments in all their dealings with the law and those under their authority. But the Punjab is to be congratulated on the demise of most of its old women and its fossils. Those who have taken their place are principally of the new school; may be, they are somewhat too confident in themselves, but they display greater energy and intelligence. Oh, shades of military-civilians of a score of years back! what would ye not say if ye knew the things which are done in these days?

The ghosts of the departed promoters of that *espionnage* system, do they ever hover over Government House or the Punjab High Court?

CHAPTER II.

It was a week after my return from Lahore, that a heavy dâk was brought me. I tore open the "Gazette," and found my leave in orders, also Hanton's, our Colonel's, Brown's, and half-a-dozen others'. A letter from Hanton informed me I was to meet him at Jubbulpore; failing that, at Watson's Hotel, Bombay. As Hanton will be my companion in most of my travels, allow me to introduce him to the reader. He stands six feet high, of a powerful frame, has already knocked about the world, and seen high-life and low-life in all their various vicissitudes. He glories in adventure, is the boldest sportsman it was ever my lot to meet, and is a perfect horseman and swordsman, as many a kandu could vouch for who had escaped his strong arm in the trying times of the Mutiny of '57. He is cool and calculating in times of emergency, and has a noble nature and gigantic mind. The women-kind, who know him well, rave about him, but he is impervious to the soft seductions of the gentler sex. Charles Hanton is one of nature's noblemen.

I was in raptures, of course, to think I should

have such a companion in my travels. We had often talked of going a trip together through Europe, as we had over many of the Colonies of Australia, Africa, and the Islands of the Southern Seas, to say nothing of our rambles in Cashmere and the Himalayas. I don't remember ever having had an angry word with Hanton. Of course, as he is over ten years my senior, and every way my superior, I naturally enough look up to him and make him my guide. Although there is this disparity between us, otherwise, in all things, we are like brothers. I had known Charlie ever since I can remember, and he was like one of our own family. When I went to College first, he was just leaving. We were educated abroad, so had many ideas in common, as is not unusual when you are trained by the same masters. We both had the taste for travelling and roaming about the world. I heard Charlie had gone out to India to join the Service, but I never thought that at my first station in the " blessed country," I should find him settled in the best bungalow in cantonments, acting for the Brigade-Major, who had gone to Nynee Tall for the season. He had an army of orderlies and servants about him, and talked the language like a native,—so I thought at the time. But no one has the proper pronunciation, so I found out afterwards, who has not been brought up from a very early age in the country. Craunies and the like speak the lingo as well as they do English, but our officers seldom do.

It was a great boon meeting Hanton again in this way. He put me up to no end of things, and helped me considerably in my green days of "griffin-hood," although I was often the subject of his jokes.

I invited Hanton up to a series of farewell dinners which were to come off at our mess before so many of us left the station for home, or for the hills, or other places for the season:—Our dear old Colonel, Browns, Peters, *alias* Knajjo, an Irishman famous in the Punjab for his extraordinary stories; poor Agnos, since dead, an exceedingly clever fellow, with a prodigious intellect, cut off in the prime of life, with such brilliant prospects before him. In spite of his ungovernable temper, he had already made some considerable stir in his branch of the service. Whykham was there full of unheard-of schemes for the re-modelling of the Punjab Forces. Nancy, of the Engineers, a splendid fellow of some celebrity as a man of the world; he excelled as a sportsman, and was deep at *finessing* at whist. With the ex-ception of Joe Gunner, I never saw a man who so gloried in the noble game. With Joe whist was a perfect religion. He had the greatest respect and adoration for a man who thoroughly under-stood the game. I believe with him such a man would rank next to the Premier of England in importance and dignity. Some half-a-dozen other fellows, principally officers of the Goorkas, formed

our party on the evening Hanton arrived. I was
president of the mess, and had to do my duty in
proposing the health of our Colonel. The dear old
gentleman in returning thanks was quite moved,
and before sitting down was kind enough to mention my name, and I was once more on my feet.
The toasts were numerous and a great night we
had of it. At last the time came for me to leave,
and I bade them all good-bye with a full heart.

CHAPTER III.

I HALTED for a time at Amritsur on my way down country, and had a lively time of it at the Club and Fort mess. Spanner was stationed here; and as he was rather disgusted at the manner Colonel Booregar had treated his well-planned schemes, was bent on returning to his regiment forthwith. Captain Bouncer had, for his own purposes, agreed with Colonel Booregar, and thrown cold water on everything of Spanner's which *he* did not consider feasible. Hence it is there is so much ill-feeling and petty jealousy in many of the Departments of the Punjab, because it is not in the power of those in authority to rightly understand the working of the officials under them, and the proper application of their administrative capabilities to all that makes a well-organized service honourable and efficient in its dealings.

At the Club, I heard that our old friend, Captain Bidder, of world-wide celebrity, was about to take to himself a wife. This astonished us, as he was considered by all a confirmed bachelor. The renowned Gordon had been promoted and sent off to Calcutta to astonish the weak nerves of timid councillors. Nancy, of the manly chest, was in

orders for the Camp of Exercise, to swell the ranks
of the gifted and the gay. Portly, of pun notoriety,
had returned from England in all the freshness of
youth, with a vigour for work which was truly
astounding. I had a most affectionate parting
from the pair of rose-buds, the dark Jewess, that
most sprightly specimen of her sex, Miss Juldee, of
Lahore. The Collegian, Mrs. Mota, of Peshawur,
was here on a visit, and made herself very amusing
at the nimble game of Badminton, to the delight
of all bystanders. That funny, active little man,
Mr. Rawbones, the ladies' doctor, was engaged in
a most important operation, so I did not see him
when I called. Also Measles, Sharpe, Dingy, and
that most promising of youths, Lowman: all were
absent.

At Amballa I stopped for two days with Freckles,
to play in a great tournament-match at polo, with
those overpowering fellows of the Irregulars, who
invariably won every game they played. The
Sutlej and Beras bridges were still in the same
chronic state of being enlarged and rebuilt. I
doubt whether—if all the stories reported are true
—Government is not more to blame for this signal
mark of failure than the talented engineers who
planned and are carrying out these everlasting
bridges. Proceeding on my way down country, I
broke the journey at that most cleanly of north-west
stations, Meerut, and stopped with my brother,
who is in a regiment quartered there. The mess-

room is most tastefully decorated with some grand specimens of horns of the ibex, bara singes, &c.— trophies from the sport of some of their officers in Cashmere and the far-off perpetual snowy peaks of the mighty Himalayas. In the evening we witnessed Byron's burlesque, 'Il Trovatore,' performed by the theatrical company of the 15th Hussars. I never saw anything acted so well before by non-professionals. They deserve great credit for the way it was put on the stage. Subsequently we went to a grand *nautch* at the house of a cele-brated mahájun of the city, and were very much disgusted at the whole performance. It was under the distinguished patronage of the officers of the garrison; but I don't think any one stopped longer than ourselves, which was about half-an-hour. The scenes were, "A Sahib and his Servant," "A Snake," "A Monkey," "A Lover's Trip through India," dancing, "A Court-Scene, Trial before an English Magistrate," and more dancing.

The following day I went on to Allahabad, left Meerut by the 2·37 down train. The carriage I occupied was most comfortable, and fitted up with every convenience. There was an upper shelf, which, on being pulled out, formed a capital bed. There were places for bottles, books, a bath-room, and other arrangements, which become a necessity when you are days together travelling by rail. These carriages are only attached to mail trains. The 2·37 is a mixed train, I found out, and terminates at Ghazibad; so I had to wait there several hours. I travelled in company with one of the numerous and distinguished family of Skinners, of Delhi notoriety.

At Etawah I awoke so cold, I was obliged to wrap myself up in blankets and rezais, which you always take with you in India. During the day the thermometer went up to 93°. The heat below Cawnpore was intense. I got rid of my collar, necktie, coat, waistcoat, and for decency's sake stopped; but I felt I could have adopted Sydney Smith's idea, if it were at all feasible, with pleasure. I was much struck at the very marked difference in the crops of the north-west and those higher up the country, in the Punjab. In the Lahore districts, where they have the benefit of canal irrigation, they are in splendid order, some three or four feet in height, just coming into ear. Near Delhi they are much more forward, but very poor and scanty; at Cawnpore quite ripe; and as you near Allahabad the crops are all cut and ready stacked. This is not altogether due to the climate of these parts, but the advantage of irrigation is clearly perceptible below Loondla. How much of this waste, barren land might not be brought under cultivation, if a few judicious water-cuts were run through the country!

On arrival at Allahabad, I was met on the platform by my esteemed friend, Mr. Padday, who kindly took me off to his house. After some refreshment, and a plunge in the swimming-bath, we visited the many improvements which have lately been carried out near the railway-station:— the institute, the bath, theatre, grounds, gardens, &c. The railway officers, and those concerned in the promotion of these benefits for the *employés* of the East Indian Railway, deserve the greatest praise for the boldness of their designs against great opposition, and the energy and skill evinced in carrying out works of such immense and lasting importance for the use of those who thoroughly appreciate the kindness displayed by the thoughtfulness of these officials.

The next day I left by the early train for Jubbulpore, and I could hardly believe that in a few years such tremendous changes could have taken place along this route—the scenes of the first pioneers of civilization, British Civil Engineers. The whole tract of country bordering the line of railway,—the small colonies of once large and commodious bungalows, with their attendants of out-offices and juvenile villages,—have been swept away, and in the place of all this stands a shed or a hut for some *employé*. The once spacious houses have been dismantled, and are now in ruins. It made me quite sad to think of the past. What scenes of revelry and mirth, of squabbles and fights, have those old walls not seen! They now lie beneath those heaps of rubbish and stones, all buried, past, and done for! And the actors are either dead or scattered over the face of the world, carrying on the noblest of professions, engineering. The heat during the day was something intolerable, and lasted so till four o'clock.

I received a kindly welcome from an old friend at Jubbulpore, known by the nick-name of "Governor," as good a man as ever trod, with a wonderful stock of general information. A most beautiful girl glided into the room on my arrival, and came forward, laughing, to meet me. To my astonishment, she turned out to be a child of his which I had not seen for eight years. She had returned from England a perfect woman—accomplished, with a vast amount of knowledge of the world for one so young. She evidently had been thoroughly well-trained.

The following day I visited the celebrated Marble Rocks of Central India. To see these to perfection, you should go down the Nerbudda by moonlight. The effect of the light and shade on the stupendous marble heights fills one with awe and majesty. The river was in flood the day I visited it, and the roar from the surrounding falls added greatly to the beauty of the scene. The heat below Jubbulpore was something awful. At ten o'clock the thermometer read over 100°, and the hot winds blowing till late in the day quite exhausted me. We Punjabees must congratulate ourselves on our mild and even climate compared to the terrible heat of Central India. We had a great scramble for food at a road-side railway-station at two o'clock, and again at seven o'clock in the evening at Khanda.

My dearest friend, the great and worthy chief, was out in these jungles, at his old game, tiger-shooting, in company with two royal German princes. These latter were singularly unfortunate in not killing a tiger, but that renowned sportsman "bagged" his. Travelling all day and all night, and all day and all night again, brought us to Egutpoorah. Another violent scramble for tea, &c. "Every one for himself, God for us all." I gave up my place to an invalid lady going home, then to another, until I was hustled out bit by bit, and found I was too late to get any refreshment. The railway company ought to make better arrangements.

I asked permission to go down on the engine and the brakes over the great Ghauts into Bombay, which request was kindly granted me; and I had a magnificent view, as we descended from Egut-poorah, some 2,000 feet higher than Bombay. The gradient of the line is 1 in 32 for some miles. This is the greatest inclination of any line in India. Four brakes are attached to each train, to hold it in check, and a sand-pipe, which is continually running, is fixed directly under the wheels of the brakes. The official who accompanied me told me of a goods train some years ago, which ran away down this slope at something like

150 miles an hour, more or less, when it came to the reversing siding, which it utterly ignored, but went straight on into *space*, falling over 80 feet in a clear drop, killing driver, stoker, and guard in its fall. To prevent similar occurrences, they have adopted what they call " cat sidings," which run up the opposite incline, and are always open; so that the mail and other trains have to stop from time to time, after going through tunnels, and whistle down the signals, in order to show the pointsman they have the train well in hand and under perfect control ; if not, they are run on to the " cat siding."

After descending the Ghauts the air is cooler and damper, as it comes from the sea. In about an hour or so we cross an inlet, and are on the Island of Salsette, Bombay. The buildings of this city are the finest in India. There are some noble blocks. The Post-Office, Controller's Office, Government Offices and Secretariat, would be considered something even in London. Watson's Hotel is of iron, made in England. It stands five stories high, and is something after the American plan. The Parsees and merchants have it all their own way here. The Mall and the Row, situated on the edge of the sea, are magnificent. The inevitable Hanton joined me here, and in the evening we went for a ride with a party of charming girls. The following day we were nearly lost, on our return from Elephanta Caves, and had the greatest difficulty in tacking back from Butcher's Island in a tiny yacht, the wind blowing a gale. One of our party behaved with the greatest coolness and intrepid bravery during the worst of the time, when our rudder was carried away and the mainsail torn to shreds. Poor Kelley! he fell a victim to yellow fever during the Ashanti Expedition, for which he volunteered, in hopes of getting a C.B., which, however, came too late.

I found my esteemed and honoured friend, the sportsman, at the Byculla Club, and dined with him in the evening. This Club is considered the best in India. The spacious 'rooms are superb in style and finish, and, although it is very warm at times in Bombay, they never think of punkahs. I tiffed at Kerent's, at Parell, the next day, and drove down afterwards to the Exhibition, which was well worth seeing. The most beautiful thing exhibited was a covering for the floor of the Gaiwur, worked in diamonds and precious stones. It glittered and sparkled most brilliantly. Its cost was something fabulous, and fourteen lacs of rupees had been refused for it. No one was allowed to touch it, and a double guard of sentries, with fixed bayonets, were in charge of it. Some of the most valuable things were being stored away for the Vienna Exhibition.

My last day in India was a busy one. My agents, Grindlay; Bank of Bombay; P. and O. agents; Medical Board at 12 o'clock; to report my departure; to grant power of attorney; to visit

Secretariat, and attest copies; to pack luggage, get it weighed; secure what was necessary for the voyage home and over the Continent, and off by 4 o'clock, was no joke. I left Bombay quite disgusted at the barefaced impositions which were practised on me. It is a most expensive place, costs fifty rupees a day, somehow or other. I was heartily glad to get on board that splendid P. and O. boat, the Hydaspes, and to see the gorgeous East disappear from view as we steamed on, homeward bound.

CHAPTER IV.

Oh! how my heart leaped with joy when I began to realize the fact that I was at last out of that blessed country, India; for a time, at all events, clear of niggers, flies, heat, and duty; cutting along at twelve knots an hour towards the mother country. I saw everything in a different light, and took Hanton off to the cuddy to have a " peg," and drink prosperity to a voyage which would extend over fifty thousand miles, and include all the other countries we had hitherto left out. I don't know how many " pegs " we drank, and how often my trusty meerschaum was refilled on that glorious and never-to-be-forgotten night, as we sat in our easy-chairs on the broad deck of that noble Hydaspes, with a full moon shining forth on the halcyon Arabian sea. Hanton confided to me all and every-thing. I did ditto. We were such perfect friends, that we had no secrets from each other. I am afraid, though, I am slightly exaggerating on look-ing back, and think I must have kept a few of my escapades with some of the charming sex quite to myself; but that is a mere bagatelle, and I must apologize for this digression.

"Who are our passengers?" inquired Charlie, puffing away at his pipe.

"I don't know more than a few who were at our hotel," I replied. "That simple individual, with a ferocious-looking wife and eight brats, is a Colonel Benny, going home for good; and there are Dodson, Printers, of the Punjab, Wyllyams, Elliott, Scott, and Blazes, from Bombay, on leave."

"I know Wrighte and Boggle," said Charlie. "They are from Central India; and, if I am not very much mistaken, there is Jack Bangney, of the 16th; that extraordinary, lanky looking youth with the swagger belongs to Secundrabad; and Dunlope, of the C. S., is from Madras. I like the fellow because there's no nonsense about him. Do you see that bouncing, scraggy little man? He is a Yankee, I should imagine; in trade, possibly," whispered Hanton, as the individual alluded to passed us in company with a well-known civil official from Bombay, on whose company he had voluntarily thrust himself.

We were able to catch at the words, "Guess this is remarkably *elegant*," from the said little man, which went far to establish his nationality.

On awaking the next morning, without knowing exactly where I was, a *Qui hai !* was utterly thrown away, as no sweet voice replied to mine. For the first time for many years I put on my own socks, and entirely dressed myself without the assistance of any one. I felt quite proud and independent as I settled down, with a most extraordinary appetite, to eat an enormous breakfast for a poor invalid going home on two years' sick leave. I never get any sympathy, as I have such a brilliant complexion. But, then, only doctors understand my case, I tell my unkind friends, who taunt me with cruel jestings. Ah! and how many sick men are there in the same boat with me!

Colonel Benny, who sat next to me at breakfast, was very indignant at the way he had been laughed at whilst bathing. When, he said, he was in the bath first, and there were some half-a-dozen youngsters outside, he declared he had not been in but a few minutes when he heard rude remarks from the *boys*, as he called them; then they knocked, and, at last, one said to the other, "It's devilish hard lines waiting here all this time; to my certain knowledge, the old bloak inside has been washing himself for the last *fyty* minutes!" And another impatient youngster, "I've been timing him by my watch; three-quarters of an hour has he been *scrubbing* himself!"—"I say," at last, chorus of outsiders, "are you coming out to-day, or shall we tell them to send you in breakfast?"

"Good morning, old boy!" I looked up, and friend Hanton greeted me. "Do you know that there are no less than *sixty* children on board? I know what I should have done had I heard that little bit of intelligence at Bombay in time," said Charlie, looking very knowing. "You know how I hate children, unless they are fast asleep."

"We must pray heavens they won't all shriek at once, or the number of murders and suicides will be alarming," I replied.

"I have rather sold our friend Dodson," smiled Charlie. "Not having any books on board, I borrowed two from him. I read them, and, on hearing I could become a member of the Officers' Book Club by presenting two volumes, I gave Dodson's to their library, and I became a member, much to his disgust."

Life on board the best of ships becomes monotonous and dull after a time, although we had some very amusing and energetic passengers, who got up theatricals and games for the ladies. We—Charlie and I—remained faithful to whist, unless we were compelled to give it up, or failed to make up a table. The Hydaspes is one of the newest and best of the P. and O. boats. Everything is in perfect order, and so beautifully clean. The captain and officers pull so well together; the table is most excellent, and the attendance good. I don't think I ever spent a more enjoyable voyage than the one in this vessel from Bombay to Suez. As we neared Aden, we encountered Sir Bartle Frere's boat going off with despatches to Zanzibar.

On arriving at Aden, about a dozen of us went on shore to see the tanks, read the papers, and visit the cantonments. They have no wells in the place, and are entirely dependent on rain-water, which is collected in artificial holes in the rocks, under the low hills. These holes are called "tanks," and contain from 10,000 to 40,000 gallons of water, and are at different levels, so that when the upper ones are filled, the surplus water runs on to the next tank below. They have been very much improved of late, Government having spent five lacs of rupees on enlarging them, &c. The aborigines of Aden are about the best swimmers in the world; it is no exaggeration to say they can spend most of the day in the water. At least a score of them came out a good mile and a half from the shore to meet our vessel, and dived for silver pieces thrown promiscuously into the sea. They go down to the bottom where it is fifty feet deep, and bring up stones and shells, and fight with each other under the water: for a small remuneration they will nearly kill each other.

There is an apology for a Government Garden and People's Park, which is about the size of our mess-room. This is the only bit of green on the island, and is greatly valued in consequence. The inhabitants come here of an evening to feast their eyes on this patch of green brushwood and hedges. Aden is of volcanic eruption, and the cantonment stands where the last crater closed in. The whole place has a most miserable, God-forsaken appearance, with nothing to break the monotony but low barren volcanic hills and peaks. It is, indeed, *a den!*

We returned from a gallop across the frontier of Arabia (more to say we had been there than for anything else) in time for tiffin at the 105th Regiment, who are quartered here—a most hospitable set of fellows, who insisted on our using their mess while we were at Aden. We were shown over the harbour defences, tunnel, magazine, arsenal, and fortifications, which are of no use. I doubt if they would stand the shock of some of the larger pieces of artillery being fired from the ramparts without coming down by the run. There were a few modern pieces of cannon, but they were not set up. General Huyshe, R.A., who came with us from Bombay, was doing his final inspection.

A cavalry detachment is quartered beyond the Isthmus. The officer commanding was compelled from ill health to leave at once, and came on with us. Heavy clouds were hanging about Aden when we left, and all thought Providence would send rain—a thing which happens about once in five years; consequently, water is about a penny a gallon. It blew hard the night of our leaving, so we beat about till five in the morning, when we entered the Straits of Babel-Mandeb. A most cool and pleasant time we had of it for the Red Sea; the thermometer stood at 80°. The mail for Bombay passed us at 10 P.M., within half a mile of our good ship, and close to some rocky spurs. We threw up some blue lights, which lit up our steamer from stern to bow, and fired off rockets; these were answered by the Candia, the effect being very beautiful. Songs all round, and the ladies playing on the piano, generally kept us up to a late hour. It struck me that some parts of the Red Sea during rough weather must be the most dangerous navigation between India and England, particularly about the " Eleven Apostles' Islands." We sighted the two towns celebrated for coffee soon after leaving these islands: they lie on the Arabian coast. The colour of the Red Sea is singularly blue, and is only equalled by the Adriatic and Mediterranean. We passed alongside of the Island of Shajwan, that treacherous reef being distinctly visible on which the Carnatic was wrecked. Vast improvements have been effected at Suez. The new dock-works and harbour are very extensive. The dredging-machines, each 200 horse power, were at work, deepening and clearing the docks for larger vessels. We went up the canal in a sailing boat, the wind blowing fair, and returned by way of the town. Two young ladies accompanied us, and we considered we had a most important charge in showing them Suez. We had some refreshments at an Italian *café;* and we bade good-bye to the Mackinnons and Mr. Lloyd, who were bound for Palestine and the Holy Land on a long tour.

The inhabitants of Suez are principally of the Greek mongrel tribe, but there is a mixture of Turk, French, Arab, and Italian scum. It is a noisy, bustling, dirty place, and anarchy and strife reign supreme.   It would be difficult to find a more lawless Government than that which holds sway here.   Most of the inhabitants are armed, and use their knives without much thinking.   Strolling about, I lost my way, and had to reward a Turk for taking me back to my party.   We made inquiries about the death of poor Agnew, of the 16th Lancers, who had, only a few days previously, been killed by a scoundrel of a fellow, who stabbed him in a *café*.   They said it had to be hushed up, as it would create scandal, and implicate some naval officers.   Poor Agnew died forty-eight hours after he was carried on board the Golconda, and is buried in the desert, a day's run from Suez.   Only a very few of us came on by train across the desert. We left the good ship Hydaspes at Suez, as she had to return to Bombay.

CHAPTER V.

IT was arranged, in crossing the desert by train, that we should make up parties to keep together in the same compartment. A gallant Major and his wife entered their names, with a numerous family, in the list for a compartment, which was duly assigned to them by the Suez railway officials. But, before leaving, the inspector, who came up to see all was as it should be, was surprised to find the gallant Major and wife in their compartment perfectly at ease, but *minus* their children. The inspector, much concerned, inquired for the precious belongings, seeing they were not there, and the train just about starting. The Major, in the most unconcerned and unnatural manner, told him to run back to the vessel and see they were not left behind. The bewildered official searched everywhere for the children to make up the full complement for a compartment, and with almost tears in his eyes returned to tell the unhappy father and mother of the direful news of the missing ones, just as the whistle shrieked and the train moved on; but all the father was heard to say was,—" Well, if they *do* turn up, look after them, that's a good fellow!" I need

hardly say how delighted the gallant Major and his
wife were to have a compartment to themselves,
whilst we were nearly crushed to death, during a
terrible cold journey of twelve hours, from seven at
night till seven the next morning.

But I shall hurry over this uninteresting part of
the journey. Alexandria is a bigger town than
Suez, but dirtier, and the people just as much, if not
more, loathsome; they are more of the Turk and
Arab species. Cairo is cleaner, perhaps, but not so
important. There are a few fine-looking buildings,
which lose a great deal of their beauty and stately
appearance on approaching them. "Distance lends
enchantment to the view" to all these Egyptian
towns. The canal is a wonderful work, and will
live for ever as a monument of M. Lesseps's great
and extraordinary abilities as an engineer, in the
face of all opposition, even by English engineers,
who laughed and sneered at what they considered
impossible. All honour, then, to the great and
noble Lesseps!

There is a great sameness in all the Egyptian
houses, temples, buildings, and towns, and when
you have seen one you have seen all. The mosques
are much like those at Lucknow, and the country
before you approach the salt lakes resembles the
plains of India. The natives are a dirty and lazy
lot. I recognized the "padday" bird of India at
some of the filthy tanks, the Indian buffalo, and
other animals and things, which made me think I

was still in India. The primitive system of irrigation is very much the same as is carried on in the North-West and Central Provinces.

I will not rave about those stupendous, grotesque piles of rough-hewn Ashlar blocks known as the Great Pyramids, which are as unmeaning and singular as you could well dream about; but, on scrambling up and contemplating, it is a most uninviting scene, and causes one to speculate how they got there, at what time, and for what object. All rife historical works are contradictory on these heads.

Having bid the remainder of our party good-bye at Alexandria, Hanton and myself proceeded on a tour over the continent, taking the Simla P. and O. steamer bound for Brindisi. I discovered that it was in this very vessel, nearly a dozen years ago, that we did a part of our voyage from Australia in, on which occasion the Simla was then as far ahead in point of perfection of the P. and O. fleet as she is now behind them. On the said occasion she distinguished herself by breaking her main shaft and other machinery, and caused us considerable delay, when off Madras. This time she was greatly crowded with a very mixed lot of passengers, some from India and our Australian dependencies, Germans, Greeks, Italians, Russians, Japanese, and French from Algiers, Egypt, &c. The sailors are all British this side, and the Lascars and Arabs don't go on to Southampton unless the steamers go through the Canal.

In the afternoon we sighted Candia Island, and as the sun was setting we passed quite close to the coast, and had a fine view of its snow-clad peaks, which looked very magnificent against the sky. The sea is supposed to have peculiar charms about here, from its ethereal properties and purity of colour. I must say it did not strike me as being anything out of the way. We had a squall, common to the Mediterranean Sea, off Cape Matapan, and passed so near to the main land, that we could easily see people moving about on the shore. We ran close up to the Island of Zante. Hanton amused himself by concocting some extraordinary stories, and telling them to an admiring audience of the fair sex—that the great patches of discoloured rock here and there were currant-bushes. Had he said, in that solemn matter-of-fact voice, they were *cakes*, only too many of those pure, innocent, and unsophisticated darlings would have credited the same.

It is marvellous the nonsense and humbug some persons believe. Of course it all depends upon who tells it and how and when it is told to them. I remember an intelligent lady in India years ago accompanying me, with others of her charming sex, to a great fall of water, and on my remarking with what fury and dash it was *boiling* in a certain spot, asked me, in the most innocent manner possible, how it became *boiling?* It was a great chance for me to have told her something edifying for her inquiring mind.

The monotony of the passage is broken by the varied and interesting Ionian group of islands. We pass near Isle Clepotum, and under the white cliffs of Corfu. A large brig hove to, quite dismantled, her mainmast gone; and she had great difficulty in making any way, on account of the torn state of her sails. She had experienced rough weather off Cyprus. There were some casualties of ships reported, which we hoped were only a "shave." We were rather glad to arrive at Brindisi, and equally glad to leave after a drive round the town. Took the express for Foggia, and the six hours' grace between the trains gives you time to see this clean-looking town. The country is somewhat broken, and the villas on rising eminences, with tastefully got-up gardens, common to Italy, abounding in olive-trees, were particularly pleasing to the eye. The railway runs alongside the coast for a considerable distance. At Foggia they gave us a dinner, some of the dishes oily, for three francs, including a bottle of Vin Ordinaire, the wine of the country, and very nasty it was. I warn my countrymen from drinking any spirits in Italy; they are vile and abominable, and are only beaten by Yankee concoctions.

On our halting for a time at Bari, we had an opportunity of witnessing a religious procession passing along one of the principal thoroughfares. Anything more silly and childish I had not seen out of India, and could hardly credit Europeans behaving in such an absurd manner, but I had yet to see the English pilgrims of 1873, who have taken the lead of fanatics until eclipsed by the Yankees.

The scenery near Trani is very remarkable; some of the largest olive-trees in Italy are to be seen here. Beyond this to Naples the whole country is one vast garden. Hanton having imprudently telegraphed for accommodation at one of the leading hotels in Naples, they concluded we must be travellers of some note, and assigned to us the first suite of rooms, for which we learnt, when too late to rectify the mistake, that thirty-six francs per day was the charge. This was a lesson to us, which we profited by, and, with the exception of telegraphing for two beds at Vienna during the Exhibition opening, we did not again use the wire whilst on the Continent. This thirty-six francs for "rooms engaged by telegraph" did not include eating, drinking, attendance, or baths, for all of which they made us pay handsomely. "Happy thought," said Hanton, on looking over the bill on our leaving ten days afterwards; "don't let us engage rooms by telegraph again."

On the evening of our arrival, Hanton told the waiter we wanted a guide and some sort of a trap on the morrow to take us round the place, and, to our amazement, at the appointed hour, a carriage and pair, two footmen in gold livery, and a guide dressed like a consul-general, waited our commands. This was beyond a joke; and as they said that all the other carriages and carts had been sent out, we were compelled to take this one; and, of course, they had some story about the horses being too frisky to be managed by a single man. I mention all this in order to warn my countrymen how terribly they are imposed upon by these land-sharks; and so it is all over the Continent. There was nothing for it but to drive away.

We called, first of all, at the Chapel San Siverto, famous for its rich statues. The one of the dead Jesus, life-size, is a perfect masterpiece, and one of the wonders of the world. This is situated directly under the altar of the chapel. You descend by a circular flight of steps, and lights are always burning round the figure. It being one of their holy days, thousands came to " poorga." The other celebrated statue is the one of ' Modesty,' in the chapel. The bas-relief of the ' Jesus from the Cross ' is a most striking work of art; and the other pieces of statuary over the vaults and tombs are all worthy of notice.

We next visited the cathedral. High Mass was being performed; our guide, nevertheless, took us all over the building, explaining everything of importance in a voice which was heard half across the portals. The statuary and stuccoes are of a very high order, and the mosaics are by some of the best masters. The underground chapel is worth a visit. The place was lit up for the occasion. Hanton, in the most unconcerned manner, went up quietly, and sat down in a very solemn style in the cardinal's chair; the monks present looked aghast; he then marched off, with his head bent down, to a confession-box, and, much to their horror, pretended he was confessing, but talking the most unheard-of nonsense in Hindustani.

After this little break in our tour, we passed along corridors and passages, round and in and out, until we returned by the same puzzled outlet. I am sure you could be easily lost in this place. We then ascended the upper level, and drove off to the Museum. It is a place I could spend months in with great delight. We could but devote five hours of our time to it. The most important collections are the antiquities of Pompeii and Herculaneum, and Furnace House, also of Rome, Asia Minor, Greece, Egypt, and of all old civilized cities, and places of those *bad* past dark ages, "famous only for its age," said Hanton. But I was not quite of his opinion, and said I had no idea that the "old, bad times" were so far advanced in arts and sciences. Some one has said there is "nothing new under the sun," and this Museum affords some proof for the saying in many things.

We now started off by the short road for San Martino, which stands on a rising eminence, and overlooks Naples and its glorious waters and surrounding country, with Mount Vesuvius in the background, in a halo of angry-looking clouds, emitting volumes of fantastic white smoke, which contrasted well with the dark horizon. San Martino, with its far-famed chapel, forts, buildings, and well laid-out grounds, is of very ancient date. The statuary is, perhaps, the finest, on the whole, of any collection in Naples, and the mosaic marble work is of such an elaborate nature as to make it puzzling to the eye. The stuccoes are in the most inaccessible parts of the building, even to the roofs of the principal shrines. They are of the most magnificent finish and style, and were executed by the first talent of the land. The relics, paintings, and the highest class of work in every department of Art are to be found in the adjoining passages and chambers off the chapel.

The drive home from the top of the Grotto to the Promenade, along the Bay of Naples, is beyond description beautiful, and acknowledged as one of the most magnificent sights in the world. It quite came up to my idea of what I had heard. The scenery is so varied, that, at almost every turn and step, an entirely new view strikes you as even more interesting and perfect than the last.

The horses and carriages of Naples, with the exception of those at Paris, I thought were equal to any I saw throughout the Continent of Europe; and the buildings are, I think, far in advance of those of Rome.

We went to the Opera in the evening, and were much edified at the display of the Italian dancers. These beauties lack that bewitching trait known as

modesty.   The most extraordinary thing was, that
some of the very *élite* of the lady society who were
present watched a shockingly improper ballet with
apparently great interest.   But I have often noticed
that, much as the fair sex profess to disapprove
of suggestive performances, they cannot keep their
eyes from things which they are supposed to be
ignorant of when an opportunity presents itself.
Hanton and I strolled about by ourselves, exploring,
till quite a late hour.

The following day we rose very early, and, after
an eight o'clock breakfast, started in a carriage,
with horses three abreast, for Pompeii.   The morning was lovely, and the glorious bay looked its best.
We managed to persuade an elderly gentleman,
with a lively daughter of great personal attractions,
who were stopping at the same hotel as ourselves,
to accompany us ; and their presence added greatly
to our day's enjoyment.   We did Pompeii most
thoroughly, going over the whole of this most
curious of unearthed cities.   The excavations were
busily going on, and I managed to obtain some
valuable specimens of ancient pottery, and a queer-
looking iron ring, and some ornamental marble
work.   The stuccoes, which had for so many ages
lain buried underneath masses of lava, were as fresh
and clear as if they had only just been executed.
The marble baths and courts, columns of richly-
decorated architecture, and statuary of historical
note, were exhumed in an excellent state of preser-

vation. Whole streets, and long lines of buildings and residences of the famed chiefs of those times, are still intact, and, with the records brought to light, are easily traced and distinguishable. Hanton could not but express his astonishment at the very high state of civilization they must have enjoyed in those "*bad* old times," as he is pleased to call anything which relates to the past. I thought of Bulwer Lytton's ' Last Days of Pompeii,' and many of the beautifully told stories came back to me, as I sat on an overlooking pinnacle of the Amphitheatre, lost in thought, contemplating this once buried city. In many places along the pavements the marks of chariot-wheels are distinctly grooved in.

We did not encounter more than a dozen tourists in our rambles, but the place was guarded at every nook and corner by Italian policemen, who looked at every passer-by with a great deal of suspicion. The skeletons of human beings, horses, dogs, &c., are constantly being discovered, and petrified human remains are to be seen, in a most perfect state, in the Pompeii Museum. There is one in particular worthy of mention, of a woman, evidently in the act of running off with a young child (of some eight years old apparently), who must have been over-taken by the liquid lava and smoke, with a key in her hand. Just as she had reached one of the outer doors she fell, with outstretched hand grasping the key, the other holding the child. This is one of the best petrified specimens they have. Here is shown the skull of the soldier who stood firm to his duty at the principal gate of the city, and perished in the lava and smoke.

We were unfortunate, after a terrible scramble to the top of Mount Vesuvius, in not being able to see the craters, as the summit was covered with dense clouds, and smoke in thick heavy volumes was issuing from the principal cavities. The heat from the recently thrown-up lava was intense. There is a marked difference in the lava of this year and that of last; and a uniform wall in places between the strata of the 1848 and 1868 deposits, which are somewhat lower down.

The town of Naples extends without a break from our hotel to the foot of the mount, a distance of nine miles. The city of Herculaneum is midway, and is quite buried under a part of the suburbs. Only the Amphitheatre and other larger edifices to the left are to be seen. Flanking these buildings, which stand out from the excavations, is a densely populated township overhead. You are shown over the Amphitheatre by the guard on duty, who provides each person with a lighted torch, and you descend a flight of very slippery steps, until you reach the original steps of the buried theatre. The passage cut is about four feet wide, and high enough for a man to stand upright, and is hewn out of the solid lava, which, on exposure to the atmosphere, becomes as hard as granite. The density of the air in these lower haunts is very stifling, and you are

glad to ascend and reach the summit. On returning the guide showed us where some skeletons and
petrified human beings were recently discovered
imbedded in the lava. Two of the finest statues in
the Museum were taken from this place.

On our way back we witnessed a very gay collection of Neapolitans, driving, and cracking their
long whips in rather a careless manner. It being
a holiday, they turned out in great numbers all
along the road by the bay. They utterly ignore
the Sabbath here, and shops and operas are open,
and the business of life is carried on as usual. An
Italian gentleman said, "You see Monday is as
holy a day to us as Sunday. You extremely funny
English! You are behind the age in this respect,
and your worn-out ideas of what you once considered sacred and holy have not yet been put
right." Our Scotch friends, with their long faces
and sanctimonious looks, evidently thought something was wrong; and I confess I think so too.

We reached our rooms at the hotel by eight
o'clock, very tired, very hungry, and very thirsty,
and after dinner and a pipe, we decided on the plans
for the morrow's trip, when it was fixed we should
drive out into the country, returning by way of
Pompeii, to see some places which we found we
had missed.

What most strikes us, just coming from the East,
is the extremely comfortable appearance of the
inside of the houses; the richly-worked carpets,

enormous mirrors, which the Italians are so fond of, heavy chandeliers lit by gas, swinging couches, easy-chairs hung on springs and pivots, the decorations and massive hanging curtains. The bells are worked by electricity: pressing the nob once, summons the waiter; twice, a chambermaid; and thrice a *commissionnaire*, who is only a head-porter, but by his dress, style, and air you might think him a commander-in-chief. They wear cocked hats, and in their gold and silver uniforms are equal in get-up to senior officers of our services.

Here, as in *la belle* France, the people are most civil and polite. If, for instance, you tread on their toes even, by accident or otherwise, they will instantly turn round, and, with smiles, apologize most graciously! It is all scrapes, and bows, and smiles, and taking off hats. You touch your cap to the person behind the counter when you enter a shop, and bow all round promiscuously when you leave it.

We visited in our trip to Rome, Cancello, Caserta, Capua, Fondi, Pontecorvo, Ceprano, Velletri, Civita, and Lavinia. Walking long distances or engaging a sort of waggonette, in which we could stow our portmanteaus, we branched off and wandered about the beautiful country. We seldom used the railway unless we were obliged. At Ceprano, where we returned a second time, we took train to Rome. The younger son of the King, who was travelling *in cog.*, was not recognized till he was leaving by the ordinary train as ourselves. The Italians, I remarked, do not rush after Royalty as the English do. It was the wish of the Prince to travel quietly, and the people knew it, and did not, therefore, make themselves objectionable.

At Rome we put up at a most comfortable hotel, kept, as we were told, by a broken-down Count, who spoke English fluently, and was a gentleman of very superior attainments. The hotel afforded accommodation for one hundred and fifty people. The rooms were nearly all engaged, it being the height of the season; and for so full a house the general arrangements were very fair, and the management orderly.

The first day we were busily employed in visiting the Museum, Capitol, and Cathedral. At the latter place we arrived in time to hear one of the youngest and most eloquent of the cardinals address a very crowded congregation. He was a man of singularly handsome features, which were well set off by sharp, penetrating, dark eyes. It was a perfect study to watch him. His voice was splendid, soft, and silvery when he was not excited; then, suddenly being carried away in his powerful language, he would raise his voice to a tremendous pitch, throwing himself into the most theatrical attitudes, and gesticulating in a very unnecessary manner. And in this wild way, with fiery eyes, he would denounce the mass in extraordinary uncharitable terms, and threaten his hearers with very terrible things, as if he had the powers of the Most High entrusted to himself to do as he pleased with.   After this apparently wrathful attack, he would as suddenly assume his former placid air, and, with clasped hands, up-turned eyes, now becalmed, and his whole behaviour entirely changed, he would address Heaven in the most appealing terms. The voice of this well-trained cardinal was one moment like that of a woman's, the next like thunder; and his conduct and language, which had been of so violent a nature, frightened some of the weak audience into tears. Aside, in the smaller chapels and passages, the performances were of an entirely different character. We noticed some very innocent-looking and pure-minded damsels confessing away to priests of all their manifold sins and wickednesses.

Many magnificent paintings, statuary, and works of art are to be seen here. The monks and priests are in great force in this city of cities, and have it all their own way.

Hanton appeared greatly disgusted at their mode of worship, which is thoroughly idolatrous, and of the Hindoo stamp, worked up in all the error and superstition by which learned impostors, who have made religion a trade, are capable of dodging up worn - out sentiments and old women's stories into the most elaborate forms of creed and dogma, in order to hold sway over the masses of womankind and the ignorant, who are weak and silly enough to regard these priests, who have degraded themselves by such a contemptible occupation, as infallible, and true masters of their souls and actions.

I freely admit that their religion did not impress me with that awe and grandeur which I at one time imagined it capable of producing in a young, ardent, and zealous soul. The music and singing, at St. Peter's particularly, is grand, and of a very high order.

The Pope's illness, which at one time was of a very alarming nature, created quite a panic amongst his still numerous subjects, and the wildest rumours were spread by gossips and sensational writers of the calamity which was about to fall upon them. His ultimate recovery, however, occasioned still further stories and unheard-of speculations as to the future. Who will be the next Pope, I wonder?

We devoted an entire day to visiting St. Peter's and the Vatican. These together pleased me more than anything else in Rome. I was charmed with the *ne plus ultra* of magnificent buildings. No description I ever read of St. Peter's gave me any idea of its gigantic dimensions. It is, without doubt, in point of the highest conception of art and beauty, one of the wonders of the world. So much has been written about St. Peter's and the Vatican, that I will not attempt to describe what has been so graphically told by numerous *savants* in such appropriate, glowing language.

I paid a visit to the celebrated Monks' Cemetery,

underneath one of the principal chapels, where they have for many centuries buried these holy divines. A most curious process the corpses underwent. As soon as one of these sacred personages had shuffled off this mortal coil, they exhume the last unhappy corpse from amongst a preparation of lime, &c., utterly disregarding the state of decomposition the body may have arrived at, and place it in either a standing, sitting, kneeling, or upright position against the wall, with his garb thrown about his bones and fleshy remnants, grasping the inevitable cross. The skulls and other bones of from eight to ten thousand monks decorate the passages, sides, and roof of this underground chamber, and very considerable taste is displayed in the style and general get-up. There are arches of various curves and radii formed of skulls; pillars and columns bonded together from the leg-bones. The smaller bones are planned in curious devices on the walls and roof of the vault, and the effect of the decorations is as novel as it is revolting. There are whole passages and grottoes, crosses and archways of human skulls, done up with painfully exquisite fancy. Everything is kept remarkably clean and nice.

A monk, who had died at twelve o'clock the previous night, was brought here for interment. He was the very last of the monks who would have these delicate attentions paid his bones, as the Italian Government had issued very stringent orders on the subject of stopping all burials within certain limits of the city, and the order was to come into force immediately. The aforesaid monk was laid out according to ancient rite and ceremony. We begged permission to be allowed to see him, and were taken down a passage of skulls. On "interviewing" him, as the Yankee would say, I was struck by his apparent great age, and his calm and dignified appearance even in death; and you might have supposed he was merely asleep, from the serene look on his placid countenance, which was truly astounding. He clasped the cross, and lights were placed round the body. Of course he died a very happy death, so I was informed.

A young girl, of some eighteen or nineteen years, whom I had noticed walking about these vaults by herself, on approaching our party, addressed the guide in Italian, and on my coming up to the lamp, she spoke to me in English. She told me she once belonged to my country, but as God had shown her the light and the truth, she had, since her conversion, resided in Italy. She said she loved walking about these peaceful haunts by herself. It was a real treat to be with the great and mighty dead, every one of whom she knew to be in heaven. To come here reminded her of death, and she went away happy for the rest of the day. She invariably received the priest's blessing before taking her departure. She wished me good-bye, and, on regaining the upper steps, fell down before a monk and implored for his blessing, which was granted her.   She had a peaceful, resigned face, and her eyes were filled with tears as she left the place. She said she was happy, and she had received the blessing she had so much courted.

To see Rome properly, with its various galleries and churches, buildings, museums, public institutions, and environs, would take you the greater part of a year.   I contented myself, therefore, with seeing only the most important sights.   Some stray book I came across told me of the following, which I enumerate for the benefit of those who have but a limited time to spend in Rome: — Of churches, S. Giovanni, S. Maria Maggiore, S. Lorenzo, without the walls, S. Paolo, La Cappella Sistina, in the Vatican, S. Maria degli Angeli; the chapels, S. Maria, in Arocoeli, S. Moria, S. Minerva, S. Agotino, S. Clementi, and Santa Prasseda. You get tired of arts and science after days and days of this sort of thing.   These splendidly got-up churches and chapels, rich in architecture, contain some of the finest paintings by the best masters of all ages, as well as statuary, frescoes, and stuccoes, of the highest talent of all times.   The celebrated ruins of the Roman Forum, Colosseum, Palace of the Cæsars, the Pantheon, Buttes of Titus, Forum Trajan, the Catacombs of S. Calisto, Pyramid of Caius Cestius, Baths of Caracalla, Theatre Marcellus, the collection of antiquities at the Vatican, also that at the Capitol of the Lateran, the galleries of Barberius, Borghesi, Doria, Pamfile, and some private ones.

In the evening, Hanton and I generally amused ourselves by going to the Opera. At one of their fashionable plays I noticed that the principal actress was no other than the lady who accompanied us with her father when at Naples on a trip to Pompeii and Mount Vesuvius. She recognized Hanton at once, our box being very near the stage. Between the pieces she came round on the arm of her brother to see us, and then begged us to dine with her the following day, with a distinguished party of theatrical celebrities at the Hotel de ——. We will call this *prima donna* Mdlle. Biano, and I will give her the credit of being the most beautiful girl I met with in Italy. She was as charming in temper and manners as she was lovely to behold, and it is not to be wondered at that I was very much smitten with her. She accompanied us in all our excursions, and before a week had passed she and I were so fond of each other's company, that I really began to think I was falling in love with an angel of a creature I was not worthy of. I shall never forget our parting. Poor Biano!

A deep-laid scheme had been planned to trap me one evening by some jealous Italians; and had it not been for Hanton, perhaps my fate would have been sealed ere this. We were accustomed at times to stroll about and explore on our own account when the excitement of the day was over. It was on such an occasion that I had been enticed away to witness some extraordinary performance. Without thinking, I allowed the man to lead on, and soon arrived at a well-known music saloon. I saw what was to be seen and heard here in a few minutes, and curiosity prompted me to see a gallery I had heard spoken of which was in the neighbourhood.

I followed my exceedingly polite guide to the passage, and, after several turns, and mounting innumerable steps, and closing of doors, I found myself alone in a dark room. The very polite guide had increased his pace, and passed through some door which I could not find. My stock of Italian was but limited, and I called in vain to him to return. I then knew some mischief was meant, and I suppose I must have remained in this awkward predicament for some ten minutes, when a gross-looking Italian made his appearance on the scene with a light in his hand. He inquired what I wanted, and my business in his chamber. I was not to be fooled by such humbug, and I told him to show me the way out. He hesitated, and on my approaching him he blew the light out, but not until I had caught hold of him and came to a second door, when he got away from me. From this door I saw a dim lamp burning in a passage some distance off, which I passed along, and arrived at a big doorway securely fastened. I attempted to unlever the cross-bar, and in doing so heard voices outside, and recognized Hanton's far above all others. I called to him, and we soon came to an understanding. Without difficulty he procured a powerful bludgeon, which he used to some effect on the barricaded door. At this juncture my Italian friend showed up, and with many apologies and barefaced falsehoods, finding his plans had been frustrated, said he would let me out and show me home, provided I would stand on one side, and would not do him any injury for the mistake he had committed. Such stipulation I felt I was not bound to grant even at this crisis. I ordered him to unbolt the door, and we would hold a council of war outside.

Hanton was furious at this insolence, and I had some difficulty in making him keep his hands off them. I knew together we were a match for a dozen of these rascally-inclined Italians, and I took care never to go sauntering by myself again in such questionable places. I found out afterwards why they were so anxious for me to go with them to their den, and I must congratulate myself on a wonderful escape.

The following day, to our consternation, we found that our previous night's escapade had created some dismay at certain houses and hotels, so Hanton proposed we should show ourselves that day as much as possible, and leave for Florence on the morrow. This I assented to, and Hanton, who was engaged with La Belle Helen and her party, to Belvedere at the Villa Medici, pleaded indisposition, and, not waiting to hear the result, accompanied Mdlle. Carlotta and Biano and myself to the Pincian Hill, the Corso, and Appian Way. This ended our doings at Rome, and we moved forward to Florence the next day, not mentioning our intentions to within half-an-hour of starting.

Hanton proposed we should change our names, as a list of tourists was published in many of the English papers which appear at Continental hotels, for the curiosity of scandal-mongers. We therefore took the name of Smith while in Italy, Brown in Hungary, Robinson in Russia, and Jones in Austria, and remained so until we got to France, when we adopted the name of Robinson once more. And we found thus altering our names of very great advantage to our progression from place to place. It certainly was awkward when we encountered friends and people who knew us, but we managed to elude impertinent questions and pass on our way rejoicing.

Everybody, of course, knows that Florence is a remarkably pretty place. Nature has done much to add to the picturesque appearance of magnificent villas on the south of the Arno, and its drives, and promenades, and gardens on the rising ground overlooking this fair city. The principal places of interest are S. Croce, S. Maria Novello, Palazzo Vecchio, and Pitti, with its unequalled splendour. This magnificent structure, the residence of different mighty sovereigns, with its superb collections of loot and legitimate plunder, together with its costly furniture and massive and gorgeous decorations, all in perfect order, is one of the sights of Florence. It seemed rather too absurd that such a modern palace, complete, even to the kitchen utensils, with gold and silver ware, guarded by royal troops, should not be made some use of. Passing on, we did the usual tourist's round, visiting Riccardi Palace, Pretorial Feroni, and Palazzo *non fineto*, and others of the private palaces; the Uffizi Gallery, Feroni, Hall of Painters, of the Flemish and German school, also the Dutch, Italian, Tri-buni, Tuscan, and the Ancient Masters. The Duomo Cathedral and Museum, with its elaborate sculpture and paintings of superb style and order, took up a great deal of our time. The wax-works and other rich collections of the three reigns of Nature, of Physic and Natural History, the Egyptian, Galileo, and National Museums, private galleries, libraries, &c., were worth much more time and study than we could devote to them. Its drives—one in particular, to that lovely spot Verna, just out of Florence, and Camaldoli, where there is a convent—will live for ever on my memory.

We took a circuitous route, halting at Prato, Pistoja, Vergoto, Imola, Bologna, Modena, Ferrata, Este, Padua, Mestre, and Venice, which we made our head-quarters, after many days of marching. We crossed the Apennines by rail in the middle of the day. We passed through several tunnels, and

I noticed that the gradients were very stiff, and the curves of a sharp radius.   The scenery of the mountains lacks trees to make it grand, but there are pretty places to be seen where vegetation abounds.   The villages are dirty, and the people of the agrarian class untidy and indolent.   Some fine crops were being raised, and the gardens of the wealthy and gentry, I noticed, were splendidly kept.   The system of irrigation is regular, perfect, and under the surveillance of the provincial governments of the country.   There is nothing new, though, in discharging and regulating the supply of water, which is not common in France and other countries.

Little attention is paid to the breed of cattle, with the exception, perhaps, that here and there one meets a philanthropic gentleman of means who may have a hobby for improving the breed of horses; but they don't, as a rule, take to it kindly, and allow a matter of such universal importance to take its course.   An Italian gentleman of property has not a single taste or pleasure like our country gentleman, unless it is beautifying his garden, and adorning his house with pictures.   Very few Italians I met care for riding, driving, hunting, shooting, yachting, or games of cricket, whist, football, rowing, rackets, billiards, or athletic sports. Fancy an Italian gentleman boxing!

I met some very distinguished men of science and literature amongst them, men of varied intelligence, and agreeable companions and right good fellows at heart; but as a nation, they are a despicable lot, deceitful, cringing, and fearful exaggerators of truth and fact. They are proud, haughty, and self-conceited, with all their ignorance and vanity, and still imagine their race first in the world as regards power and civilization. But they don't stand alone in this respect; Persia and China are each of the same opinion; and unhappy France holds some queer notion that most countries save its own are in a state of semi-barbarism, particularly Germany. Of course, I speak of them as a nation. A well-cultured man of the world may come from Japan, America, Scotland, Italy, or Russia,—it matters little to me what his nationality may be,—if he conducts himself properly, I meet him and value his friendship equally with that of my own countrymen; and I believe most Englishmen think as I do in this respect who have travelled and seen anything of the world.

The Italians, naturally enough, have a great antipathy to the Austrians, and are so foolish as to show their strong prejudices by insulting them in some petty way or other whenever they have an opportunity. Now it so happens that, although I am an Englishman to the back-bone, my own countrymen are often deceived as to my nationality, due, no doubt, to my cosmopolitan ways. It is not to be wondered at, therefore, if Italians should take me for an Austrian, seeing that in many respects I take after their race. Hanton's height, figure, fair complexion, light hair, and blue eyes, were enough to stamp him as one, particularly when he was in my company; and at Venice we had to put a few of these Italians right who were bold enough to suppose we were anything but English. Besides, the Austrians, we told them, were our pet friends, and any such insult to ourselves we were determined to resent. Strange to relate, we were unfortunate more than once, in Paris, to be taken for Prussians, and I decidedly object to be taken for one of King William's subjects. I prefer being a ruined Frenchman to a victorious Goth by accident.

We had a very curious adventure at Bologna, on our return to that funny old town from the Cathedral, two miles off. We were passing through one of the arcades, when I asked a gentleman, in indifferent Italian, the way. He answered us in English, and, to our surprise, we discovered an old Punjabee friend, Colonel Putler. Our delight was immense at meeting in such a place.

On another occasion, in the great Cathedral at Milan, I asked some English tourists who were near me certain information, and recognized dear old Toby, of Murree, who I thought was thousands of of miles away. We embraced each other there and then, and he, quite forgetting where we were, introduced me to his beautiful bride. They had been on a tour together over the Continent, and were now wending their way to Brindisi to catch the next P. and O. steamer for India.

The Italians must spend nearly all their money, it seems to me, on cathedrals and chapels, and fitting up the same at an enormous cost; and the balance, after royalty has been satisfied, goes towards paying the soldiery. What a number, it strikes you at first, their army must be; and are they all on duty at once? Soldiers and policemen at every corner and bend in the street; and when there is no bend or corner, there will be a cluster of idlers, dressed up in the most gorgeous colours imaginable, blue buttons apparently looking after yellow buttons, white looking after black, and green watching them all; then there are red stripes and blue, silver lace and gold lace warriors, in cockades, strutting about eyeing the people very suspiciously. Great Powers of Italy, wherefore this continual brilliant display of your miserably-paid caricatures of soldier-men? Your ordinary "bobbee" wears a cocked hat and sword, top-boots, and spurs! A captain is a perfect lobster in colour, with epaulettes, enormous boots, unnecessary spurs, and a dangling sword, which he never forgets wherever he goes. At the *café*, promenade, at all times and seasons, he is never out of uniform. His pay is barely six shillings per day to back and support all this grand get-up. As a rule, they are quiet and orderly amongst themselves, and take things calmly enough; few rows, and scarcely ever an intoxicated man. At the *café* of an evening, perhaps, an old gentleman may get excited when discussing politics, but it is not often the case. The only drunkards I met in Italy were Englishmen, a Russian or two, and a queer set of Yankees, who were " doing " the country.

I was much interested in an Italian review of troops, which was supposed to contain the *élite* and a few of the most brilliant regiments in their service; but I was much disappointed with the whole concern. I never met such a poor lot of soldiers, so lax in discipline, and disgracefully deficient in their duties. This under-sized mob of soldiers marched past talking in the ranks, some in angry tones, others laughing, not keeping step, and saluting in a careless, slovenly way. Even our militia would have put them to the blush. I learnt that sixty per cent. could neither read nor write. Their officers, as a rule, are of gentle birth, but very defective in drill. Their examinations are light and superficial, with any amount of ". suggestions " liberally offered and readily taken. Favouritism is the order of the day, and "interest" an acknowledged indispensable —a state of things I regret to find the flower of the French army is reduced to. Not so with matter-of-fact Germany.

The Italian cavalry are a mere show. The manœuvres were wretchedly distracting, and large squadrons were thrown out by the inability of their officers to give the proper command. The men are poor riders; they have neither a firm nor elegant seat. The artillery were massed together in sub-divisions. They seemed to be better up to their work than the other branches of the service, but they are wanting in that smartness which you would necessarily expect from picked men. I never came across officers of any civilized country so slack in their drill, and utterly ignorant of the first rudiments of their profession. What a state of things for the Roman soldier to have fallen into! I won't say they are wanting in moral courage, but such an undisciplined mob of an apology for soldiers could be' as easily dispersed as *pandies* with half—nay, a quarter—their strength of well-trained troops.

I cannot find words to describe how terribly disappointed I was with Venice. I had always heard it spoken of as " beautiful Venice,"—a second Paradise! Poets have set the fashion, and raved about a place which is frightfully over-rated. My humble opinion of Venice is (and I know it is heresy to say so) that it is a horrid hole, filthy in the extreme. I hate the unnatural and only mode of locomotion, the arrangement of going about in gondolas. The big canals are all very nice in their way, but the back water-lanes are, in point of fact, stinking places. All sentimental ideas on beholding Byron's residence or "The Merchant of Venice," the " mansions," and other dilapidated " palaces," on which so much poetry has been wasted, vanish from surroundings of foul water and putrid atmosphere. The open sea, I must say, is truly delightful and refreshing after the interior of densely-populated hovels and narrow, winding streets of water, which are receptacles for all the filth of the city. The San Marc Square is, for its kind, the finest in Europe, and of an evening is truly a beautiful sight. Its queer towers and far-famed church are well worth seeing.

We visited the cemetery, chapels, churches, galleries, and museums, all containing celebrated works in oils, and mosaics, stuccoes, frescoes, statuary, and various fancy works. Some of the palaces are well deserving of mention, and the collections of antiquities are a perfect study in themselves. The view from the tower top is very magnificent in the early morning. We patronized the opera and theatre, which are a sad falling off from Naples and Rome. Having settled our plans for a tour through Hungary, we left after a few days for Trieste.

CHAPTER VII.

ONE of the most glorious sunsets I think I ever beheld we witnessed after leaving Nabreshina. From the summit of the Julian Alps, overlooking the bewitching waters of the Adriatic, fell this magnificent sight. The clouds had been hanging in heavy clusters during the afternoon, and, when the sun sank beneath the horizon, the whole heavens were lit up by the most dazzling gold tints, surpassing in beauty the sunsets of the mighty Himalayas, which I had hitherto considered unsurpassable.

From Trieste we travelled with Lord and Lady C——, who had come round by the Mediterranean in his yacht, which he had sent back. Lord C——, a young man of free and easy habits, was in the Guards, and delighted in excitement and novelty. Lady C—— was a sweet woman, and with very engaging manners. They were bound—after a tour much in our direction—to Vienna, in order to be present at the Exhibition opening. As they expressed a wish for us to join them through this wild unsociable country we gladly did so.

Hungary has many advantages over Italy,

Germany, and France, inasmuch as you are quite off the beaten track of the cockney snob, shoddy Yankee, and purse-proud, vulgar, tourist, who overrun the Continent, and whom you meet at nearly every turn. The English who frequent Hungary are of a very different stamp to the ordinary sightseer elsewhere. They are chiefly sportsmen, men of the world, and very far removed from "suspicion" of any kind. Some most agreeable acquaintances we formed here. We broke the journey at Agram, Pesth, Grau, Kremnitz, Kiagenfurt, Marburg, Gratz, Gloggintz, and Baden. The country is very varied and broken, barren and fertile, plains and hills, rocky wastes and rich lands, all jumbled together. It is exceedingly lovely in many places. The railway runs through a hilly country, broken by the most exquisite scenery, resembling the Highlands of Scotland. As you ascend the mountains the temperature changes suddenly. Below we found it unpleasantly warm, and on ascending the Semmering Pass Mountains snow was lying in patches, with a cold, chilly wind blowing, which we wretched Indians felt terribly. The people we found hospitable and courteous, of very cleanly habits, and remarkably honest, but the majority primitively disposed and easily satisfied.

The strong winds of Hungary are a caution to railway trains. Massive walls of great height, supported by battering abutments of ponderous dimensions, run parallel to the line of railway, and are for no other purpose than to protect the trains from being blown off the rails. I mentioned this fact to a Yankee in his own country once, who evidently was not acquainted with the power and violence of the winds of Hungary, and he treated my story with incredulity. "Was a remarkably fine story, Britisher; but he was blow'd if he could take in such a 'winder' all at once!"

The majority of the Southerners of these parts are Roman Catholics, if they are anything. They appear to be very fond of the image of Jesus in sundry devices, and wherever they can find a place for one. In public thoroughfares, at every niche and corner, in the open fields,—even cartmen and carriers have a picture of the cross let into the woodwork of their conveyances. The practical American of the sceptic order is rather out of his element in a Catholic country given to bigotry. I heard a story here of one of these worthies which rather amused me, although, I am told, it is now trite. Yankees, after a little intimacy, would address John Smith as J. S., using only the initials. "Well, I declare," exclaimed an American, on beholding a magnificent (life-sized) picture of the Crucifixion, "here's my old friend, J. C., again in the same uncomfortable position!"

We put up at a new hotel in Vienna, situated at the corner of the Shotten Ring and Ring Strasse, which promises to be the finest street of any city in the world. The Hôtel de France is one of the most complete and comfortable on the Continent. It is an enormous building, and its thorough good management is only equalled by its cleanliness.

Having some time on hand before the Exhibition opening, Hanton proposed a trip to Russia, visiting Warsaw and Moscow, in order to get some insight of the people and the country. We accordingly had to make hurried preparations, and started *viâ* the Carpathian Mountains route forthwith. The tour was purely a skeleton one, and we only broke the journey at a few of the most important halting-places; and, as we were quite novices in these parts, many of our plans fell through, and we were unable to accomplish what we originally intended to carry out on starting from Vienna.

Our mode of travelling was various. We used the railway wherever we could, and were glad to get a rough sort of spring cart when away from civilized parts. Occasionally we were reduced to very rude conveyances and small scraggy ponies, which took us over hill and dale great distances. The longest journey ever ridden in one day was ninety-two miles; but the animals which accomplished this feat were of the highest breed and of very powerful make.

I wish to mention the marked civility and hospitality we received from Russian officers, particularly those of the scientific corps of the service. They treated us like brothers, in the most handsome manner possible, putting their houses, in some instances, at our disposal, and showing us every attention possible. Nothing was too good for us, and there was that cheerfulness and readiness to help us in obtaining information of one of the most down-trodden and oppressed of civilized nations. Of course there is a wide gap in the immensely superior position of the aristocratic classes and the illiterate, poor, forsaken, servile mass of the people. What a contrast between the lower classes of England and the lower classes of Russia! As vast a difference almost as the scientific men of their army are over ours. I don't think their ordinary foot officers of line regiments are as well educated as ours, nor have they the same amount of general intelligence and *esprit de corps* amongst them; but I do maintain that their engineers and artillery officers, as a body, are the finest that any army can boast of. Their theoretical training, which is of the highest standard, is only equalled by their varied practical knowledge, in which the majority of our scientific officers are so terribly deficient; matters which they consider beneath their notice.

I have only to point to some of the sad blunders which have been enacted of late years by that boasted corps. I have had frequent conversations with our own officers high up in the service, and they do not hesitate to state their inferiority to the Russians. The stuff we have; but our system is at fault. The British private gets us out of our scrapes. If the art of war is to be carried on with success, adopting all the many recent inventions science has achieved, we must discard all our old women of Generals, much as they may dislike it. The stupidity displayed by officials high in authority, who have nothing to recommend them but their length of service, must be very disheartening to the lover of a profession of such renown as the British army. I know scores of smart officers of known repute who have been compelled to throw up their commissions because they could not brook the daily arrogance and insolence of their commanding officers. In any trivial matter these proud-of-spirit would assert their dignity and infallibility, to the ruin of zealous officers who would have been ornaments to their noble profession.

We had to rough it very considerably along the Russian border; but I shall never forget the unbounded kindness shown us by officers of the Russian army. By some oversight, our agents had forgotten to send us our passports, but we had no difficulty in travelling in Hungary, Russia, or Austria. Simply declaring ourselves Englishmen, we were allowed to pass without further inquiry. Our heavy baggage we had sent *via* the Canal and the long passage to Southampton, and had only taken just enough for our trip. We were not even asked by the Customs officers to open our portmanteaus, whereas their own people were subjected to the strictest scrutiny, and were eyed with a good deal of suspicion. I mention this little incident to show the respect and courtesy extended to Englishmen, which is worthy of note.

Returning, we visited the battle-field of Austerlitz, and stopped at some other places of importance, *en route* to the Austrian capital. We had many curious adventures on the way, but none equal to one at a certain place on the Russian border, where Hanton, by some mistake of an angry father, was suspected of playing with the affections of a very beautiful girl, whom we had heard much about, and curiosity prompted us to make her acquaintance. I was happy to be able to serve friend Hanton as he had once served me when in Italy.

Vienna is situated between two ranges of mountains, which renders the city accessible to terribly cold blasts of high easterly and north-easterly winds. I don't think I ever experienced such cutting winds anywhere else. Vienna may not have the power, nor the great wealth, nor the overcrowded population, but I consider, for its size, it is unequalled in architecture, harmony, and splendour by any city on the Continent. The most comprehensive view of Vienna is indisputably from the top of St. Stephen's steeple, although, surveyed from the heights of the cupola of St. Charles, a more extensive view presents itself. The noble groups of buildings, churches, palaces, and other magnificent edifices, whichever way you turn, are all of recent date. In fact, Vienna is quite a new city.

Owing to the enormous enterprise and perseverance displayed by many of the leading commercial men in pushing on at too rapid a rate the vast improvements of this town, Vienna is greatly beggared, and the Exhibition will only add to many of their calamities. The place is too young for such a gigantic concern, and the principal financiers will feel it terribly after a year or two.

There is much to admire in the race of Austrians of the present day. They are very philanthropic, honest, and manly in all their dealings,. and are likely to profit by past experiences. " El Dorado," which was their characteristic of former times, is now considered utterly expunged from them as a nation. They certainly enjoy the good things of this world much more than any other people, save our own, but the business of life is not neglected. There is an earnestness and deportment, refinement and polish, not to be met with in the coarse German of the period. It is a very singular fact that street mendicity is quite unknown in the metropolis of the Austrian empire, which is no doubt due to the well-organized institutions of Vienna.

Some of the principal churches contain very beautiful paintings, by the greatest talent of the times. A miraculous picture is in the Mariahilf; St. John's is famous for its ornaments of frescoes ; St. Salvator's, just completed at an enormous cost (one million and a half of florins), is to commemorate the providential escape of the Emperor from the hands of a murderer, who was about to stab him near this spot, in 1855. The various chapels and churches are very numerous, and contain some superb works of art worthy of note. I forget now all the palaces, remarkable edifices, galleries, museums, institutions, libraries, gardens, suburbs, and environs I went over. I have mixed them up together, and so have rather a confused idea of all the fine arts and sciences, lovely sights and merry-making of Vienna. I know I thoroughly enjoyed my visit to those agreeable, happy people, the Viennese. I shall long remember with pleasure the delightful days I spent in their society.

A few letters of introduction are absolutely essential to get into society. Ours were to some friends at Court. One in particular, an officer in the Guards, who was on the Emperor's staff, was most kind and charitably disposed towards us poor pilgrims; and it was through him we managed to make many friends, and see something of Austrian life.

The Orpheum is just such another place as the London Pavilion, and the Sperl not quite such an aristocratic resort as the Alhambra. But, of course, there are better places and worse ones than these in Vienna. I was agreeably surprised to find it such a moral city, for the reports I had heard of it were certainly not to its credit. I have seen nine-tenths of the capital towns of the world, and there is not a city can vie with London in this respect. Perhaps it is a sign of civilization that the more advanced a nation is the greater the immorality.   Is it not protected to some extent by a paternal Government?

We were most anxious to see the Exhibition some few days before the opening, on an occasion of a general meeting of the Commissioners, when only exhibitors were to be admitted on this auspicious day.   Failing to obtain a Commissioner's card, Hanton suggested my going straight in without a pass.   I was to provide myself with a number of rolls of drawing-paper, carry a big stick in the other hand, which I was to be continually twisting round and round, speak in a loud voice, look very important, and pass the different guards and sentries without taking the slightest notice of any of them. My mild companion was an exhibitor of high reputation.   This arrangement proved successful. Hanton had not the slightest doubt about his passing himself off as a Commissioner; he was concerned about me.   But my not returning assured him of my having effected an entrance without the least bother.

It was only when inside, passing from the French to another department, that we were molested by a number of sentries, who demanded to see every one's pass.   Of course, I pretended to rummage in my pockets for mine, and by this time my companion, who came on, was asked to produce his, which he did, and, while it was being examined, I walked slowly on, and arrived at the next department.   It was a splendid opportunity to see this enormous building, with its gigantic rotunda; and there was no crowd to interfere with your seeing the various national departments, which to-day looked their best. All were busily engaged in pushing on the completion of the different sections. Of the nations that had the greatest show on this occasion, and who were most forward in order, were England, Austria, Belgium, America, Germany, and France; but an immense amount had to be done, and everything was not set up for a long time after the official opening. The British Mechanical Department challenged the world in ponderous machinery. But I learnt, on a visit to the Chicago Exposition subsequently, that the American agricultural implements and machinery generally,—engines of great power, lifting apparatus, cranes, &c.,—were lighter, and actually displayed greater ingenuity than John Bull's massive style of work. But if England had the best show here, and carried everything before her in the machinery line, it was simply because other powers shrank from vieing with her in this particular branch.

On leaving we were very kindly invited to see the cottage intended for the use of the Prince of Wales, which was in the enclosure of the grounds of the Exhibition, and fitted up, with every requisite, in superb taste and elegance, by a well-known London house. We were joined here by Hanton, followed by an officer of foot and two keepers. What had happened? My fears were soon quelled when I heard my friend ask a string of inquiries, which were promptly answered by the officer, who addressed him by a title which certainly was not his. Hanton, coming up to me in a very unconcerned manner, said, in English, "It has pleased these worthies to take me for some one of importance connected with the Exhibition, why or wherefore I know not; it does not hurt me, and I have had the run of the place and seen everything in consequence, which has been most kindly explained by this officer,"—and he introduced me to a good-natured, jovial-looking Austrian, who asked Hanton if he would see that everything was as it should be in the cottage prepared for the reception of His Royal Highness during the heat of the day. Hanton, on inspecting the place, signified his entire approval of the arrangements which had been made for the Prince of Wales.

On quitting the building, and arriving at one of the chief gateways, we were challenged by the sentry, "Messieurs, veuillez exhiber vos passeports." "Les voici," cried my companion, producing his, when Hanton and I passed out, the officer explaining there was no necessity to make any inquiries when such distinguished visitors as ourselves were pleased to pass.

On taking our leave, Hanton thanked the Austrian, and invited him to dine with us at the Munsch the next day, to meet some Russian officers who had just arrived in Vienna.

The following afternoon, in company with an officer on the Emperor's Staff, we visited the Military Riding School, and saw some good horsemanship by troopers from various mounted regiments going through a course of drill at the Academy here. We visited the Imperial Arsenal, containing a large collection of arms and Krupp cannon. Practising was going on in the space. The shooting was not very extraordinary. The workshops, with a dozen engines of 150-horse power, gave occupation to 3,000 mechanics for the fabrication of fire-arms and ammunition. We next visited the soldiers' barracks for infantry, the Francis Joseph Casern, a magnificent edifice. A block of stately-looking buildings is at Mariahilf, Caserngasse. An Academy of Engineers, the Cavalry Lines, Artillery Quarters, Military Train, Gendarmes, Military Police, and the Court Archers Guard, together with the Trabant Guard, were each gone over. The exquisite neatness and order preserved in every branch of the service in all its entirety are deserving of remark. The general good conduct of the men, the high state of discipline maintained, a thorough knowledge of their duties, and the gentlemanly bearing of their officers, place the Austrian army on a footing — which it has for years been aiming at—as one of the first in the world. The Austrian service is more assimilated to ours than any other.

The " goody-goody " people of England dislike the Austrians, because the majority of the intelligent of them are what they improperly call infidels and sceptics. I have a strong objection to the scoffing German theologian, or the impious Frenchman, who laughs at any idea we may cling to as sacred and dear. But we don't know the Austrian sceptic. He is a lover of truth; and will honour and respect your views, although he may not agree with you. As a nation they are manly and honest, and much more so than the generality of my own countrymen, who, to their shame and disgrace, believe one thing and think it pious and prudent to say another. I regret to say this dishonesty of thought, which prevails to such an alarming extent throughout England, is due to the teaching of a half-educated clergy, who can only think in one particular groove, and carry with them the mass of the ignorant, who are incapable of thinking for themselves, and the weak, who have not the moral courage to speak their minds.

We may learn many useful lessons from the Austrian sceptic of the day. The very fact of his being a sceptic shows his appreciation of truth, his value of justice, and of what is good and noble in man. It must be a very narrow-minded, silly person who thinks another wrong because he does not have the same identical views as himself on matters pertaining to religion and politics, the two most important subjects concerning ourselves we have any idea of. Good government is for all, or for none, and religion ought not to be made a quack trade of any longer.

I admire the Austrian race for producing so many straightforward, honourable men of intellectual capacity, who are slowly but surely dragging error and superstition from out the minds of their fellow-countrymen. God grant the day is not far distant when England may exert herself in this respect! and as the great mass of the people look to the clergy for instruction, Heaven help them to use their influence to some purpose by annihilating this thraldom, and giving their congregations some idea of a glorious reality instead of a contemptible caricature !

After some joyous days spent in Vienna, its suburbs, and its beautiful environs, and seeing all that was worth notice at Schönbrunn, the Imperial Palace of which contains 1,500 rooms, we were not sorry, after the opening of the Exhibition, to get away from the crowded metropolis, and were anxious to see other countries and people. We had a final parting from our Austrian and Russian friends at the Hôtel de l'Europe. The dinner was very *recherché*, and superior to anything we got in Italy. The wines, too, were sound and good, for a wonder; and, after many excellent speeches and songs, the party broke up towards the small hours of the morning. Our luggage, which was already packed, had only to be called for, and we started for the station, in time to catch the first morning express for Prague, in Bohemia.

CHAPTER VIII.

THE great drawback we experienced was changing our money. English gold is always at a premium, which, however, fluctuates according to the whims of the supporters of the Bourse. Paper currency is reckoned at par; but it is not so when you have an excess, and wish to exchange it for other German base coin, which is quoted according to no authority; and its management lies entirely in the hands of swindling money-changers, of the lowest type of humanity, who live by their wits on the ignorance of Englishmen and Yankee travellers, whom they consider legitimate prey. We were swindled to an alarming extent by one of these " catchers."

The trains move slowly, are not regular to time, and are generally overcrowded. Hanton wished to try his luck at a well-known " hell " in Prague with some superfluous cash he had won in Vienna, which he kept in order to lose again. By an extraordinary fluke his chances at pool écarté were in the most flourishing condition, and large sums were offered for his closing game. He refused; and, as if the cards were bewitched, he lost steadily. I fancied the men might be sharpers, and demanded new cards, taking the odds for a small amount. Hanton stood by me; and the luck set-in all in my favour. I won enough to satisfy these men; and Hanton a second time accepted their challenge, but demanded new cards each turn, much to their surprise. I rejoice to say, Hanton cleared them entirely out. It was delicious news when we were told we had been playing with the celebrated Brothers Fischer. I don't like gambling; but we were anxious to see what these places were like, and to try our luck. Our experience in this line paid us well.

The scenery of Bohemia is very delightful, and the people mild and considerate. Prague resembles Pesth in many ways. It has some magnificent buildings, fine streets, and a rising trade. Crossing the border and the mountains of Erz Gebirge, we reached Dresden, which deserved a longer stay than we could afford; but it was too cold for us, and we pushed on to Berlin, and put up at the Hôtel de l'Europe, not a little glad for a few days' rest from trains.

Berlin greatly disappointed me. Perhaps it was the people, who are so much absorbed with their late victories over poor France. The lower classes are eaten up with conceit and their superiority over a crushed nation. They have set up Bismarck as their God, and delight in worshipping him; and as to the Emperor, he is considered immaculate. Never was there a game played with such subtlety as the late war. Bismarck's plans were only too successful. He knew it was a great game; and he

was ready to risk all for what he achieved. But
what is very evident, the minor powers will never
again be fooled into joining anything so foolish as
a war for Prussia for her own aggrandizement-and
glory. Ask Bavaria what she thinks of it now,
after her finest sons have been slain as bolsters to
protect Prussian soldiers? Luckily for Bismarck,
there is no occasion, at present, to call the allied
powers together to fight for either Fatherland or
Grandmotherland.

France, under a good leader, with a well-organized
army, has made a Prussian host fly; and what
France has done she may yet do, when she is
dragged out of the quagmire she is in.

France, at the time she was attacked by Germany, had no leader that the army looked up to.
The wretched state of the whole service—badly
educated, badly fed, badly organized, of no discipline, without trustworthy, intelligent officers—was
no match for greater numbers of well-trained troops.
It was not that the German forces were so superior
to other armies, but to the low state into which the
wretched French soldier had fallen, from not being
well looked after, that their successes were mainly
due. But France, considering all things, has got over
her defeat better in a year or two, and paid up an
unheard-of cruel indemnity, than Bismarck thought
her capable of for fifty years to come.

France had no idea how weak she was, and how
powerful Prussia had become; and, what is very

certain, France is bound, ere long, to be revenged for her losses; and she will be prepared this time as she never was before. It will be a universal, popular war. The hatred they bear the Prussians is increased a thousand-fold, and age will never wipe it out. Had Germany, when she proved victorious, not been so grasping, France would have forgiven her. When something like order is restored in that benighted country, we must be prepared for a war which will be even more awful than the one we remember so vividly; when every son of France will jump with joy to grapple in deadly combat the followers of a Power which has been so exacting and unjust in the hour of triumph.

From Berlin we travelled, *via* Brunswick and Hanover, to Frankfort and Mayence, down the Rhine, the scenery of which is tame, and absurdly overrated. People, particularly Cockneys, rave about it, who have never been out of England before. The Hudson, in America, is far grander than the Rhine, and I will show scenery just as beautiful in despised Cornwall; and, as regards the Lakes of Geneva and Lucerne, what are they compared with Lochs Ness and Marie in Scotland, or the Lakes of Ireland and England? My countrymen seldom see beauty in anything English. Perhaps because it is the fashion.

From the Rhine we came down through Switzerland, and, after seeing the Tyrol and the Alps, returned to Munich. The cold nearly finished me;

and had it not been for constant relays of hot-water foot-pans I should have perished. We got a through-ticket to Paris, halting wherever we liked. I am not exaggerating when I say this ticket, or rather, series of tickets, must have measured nearly five feet in length; and it seemed to me that, between every station or so, a fierce-looking guard entered the carriage (train going all the time), and brought with him a cold blast of wind, to inquire if I was provided with a ticket; and, on my producing the string of tickets, he would pull off a bit, or a bit and a half, as he felt inclined. These guards worried me so, that I at last fastened my roll of tickets to the hat-rack, and, when one of these suspicious gentlemen made inquiries about my ticket, I pointed to the waving piece of paper which answered that purpose, telling him to help himself, but not bother me.

Hanton generally was fast asleep when he saw one of these fellows approach; and they would get vexed and leave him when he snored. On one occasion, the light having nearly gone out, Hanton pretended that the wretched guard, who entered our compartment very stealthily, while the train was in full motion, was some desperate individual. He frightened his wits out by grasping his throat, and asking him whether he was a thief or a devil. The poor man did not understand such treatment, and was only brought round by a long pull at Hanton's flask.

All Munich turned out the day we arrived to do

honour to the Heir Apparent and his young bride, a daughter of the Emperor of Austria. The young couple had just returned from their honeymoon. The procession was very gay; the soldiery lined the streets from the railway to the King's palace. The Prince and Princess were seated in a most gorgeous gold chariot, drawn by eight horses, with a regiment of the King's Body Guard, and the principal officials of the city preceding. The Princess is quite young, and certainly very beautiful and amiable. She bowed repeatedly right and left to her new subjects. The Prince looked happy and pleased with everybody and everything. Several picked mounted squadrons brought up this brilliant spectacle, and the streets for some hours afterwards were so densely crowded that locomotion was impossible.

Some of the Bierhalles in this part of Germany are well worth a visit of an evening. But I defy an Englishman to stop for any time in these places. The smell of the beer, together with the stifling atmosphere of smoke, is more than any civilized creature could stand for any time. It seems to agree with these coarse, sleepy beer-drinkers, who are everlastingly smoking. The most delicious beer is the Vienna beer, which is light and wholesome.

After seeing Munich we went to Strasbourg. The country along this route is somewhat dull and uninteresting. Of course we could not pass Strasbourg without seeing its wonderful clock and cathedral.

The place affords some interest to any one who cares to go over the scenes of the late Franco-Prussian contests. Metz will be regarded as one of the most extraordinarily fortified towns in Europe, and its late defence will be read and better under-stood in times to come than now. At Bazaine's death, perhaps, some light may be thrown on the whole mystery. I certainly think that, as a soldier, he was compelled to fight. With such an army he could have cut his way out, and saved his honour. Now he is disgraced, and it would have been better for himself, poor man! and all parties, if he had been shot at the time of his trial. He is useless as a leader, as the army would never put trust in him again. I have read a great many sensational paragraphs about his doing the proper thing in surrendering. By choice he was a soldier, and by accident a leader of an army of some pretension. Soldiers in peace are like chimneys in summer. But for Bazaine at this crisis it was stern winter; and he was in duty bound, for the honour of the French army, for the glory of France, for the main-tenance of peace, and the suppression of anarchy and plunder of his boasted capital, which he was supposed to guard to the death, to show himself as the chief of soldiers, who merely wanted a head to perform any daring. In this matter he failed. Away with all sentiment and nonsense! This is no time to look at things in a different light. We have to do with hard, practical questions. Whatever is worth doing, is worth doing well, even to defending Metz.

I halted at Nancy for a couple of days, in order to see two young girls in the convent there, daughters of a French naval officer, now in the British service in India, and a particular friend of mine. It was his wish I should see them, and tell the parents how they were, and the progress they had made.

The fact of my being an Englishman, and a supposed Protestant, was quite enough to damn me in the eyes of the nuns of the convent; and it was by a curious and roundabout way we were admitted. Sisters of Charity came for me on my presenting a letter of introduction. I shall not easily forget the shriek I was greeted with on the opening of the convent-door. I took Hanton as my friend. The lady abbess evidently expected to find an elderly gentleman, instead of two larkish young men, who were somewhat bent on mischief.

We waited some time before the two girls made their appearance. When they entered, in company with two elder Sisters of Charity and a nun, who spoke English for my edification, I was quite charmed with my novel position, and I begged to be allowed to see the young ladies' drawings and study-books, expressed a wish to hear them play the piano, and see the place. All this was granted me, and it was surprising how forward they were in their studies. Their drawings were from models, never from copies; they were well up in Euclid, and had a smattering of the sciences; were well grounded in arithmetic, and played the piano with dash and good touch.

We were shown over the convent, and got rather into disgrace, when visiting the chapel, by making some remark that there was no occasion to have made any excuse for the state of the cleanliness of the chapel, because everything was in the most perfect order. The look of horror the nuns gave me! With a hissing sound they placed a finger over their mouth to sign me to be quiet, and leave this holy place. Our fellow-travellers would not believe we had been allowed admittance to the convent, not even when I assured them on my word of honour. But some people are very disbelieving. All I can say is, that what I have narrated is not in any way exaggerated.

Nancy, at this time, like most of the frontier towns, was occupied by Prussian troops, and to show their contempt, I presume, for the French, they had got the smallest little soldiers in the service to strut about doing sentry over the railway station and principal buildings in the town. They are constantly having rows, and occasionally a German soldier is missing. He is not generally discovered. They hate each other like cat and dog. The strong arm of Prussia usually settles all such disputes in favour of their own side. At present not a single instance is on record of a German soldier having done anything amiss; and they are very unanimous on this point. At the Hôtel d'Angleterre we witnessed a great demonstration on the part of some French medical students, who had imbibed freely of large quantities of claret, which excited them to a tremendous pitch. I am sure they were fully prepared to march, there and then, and take the citadel, and drive the Prussians from the town. But on coming out the cool air worked extraordinary changes in their proposed plans, and they had some difficulty in propping each other up and keeping the pathway.

The country through this part of France is varied and pretty, and has some loveable villas and châteaux. We got to Paris during one of those noisy electional explosions. M. Thiers was at the time President, and Gambetta was exciting the ignorant rabble to strife and rebellion. Everybody had a grievance. All appeared terribly wild and clamorous about the very last bit of political news. Whenever it came, or whatever it was about, mattered little—they were bound to get excited. All were talking, no one was listening, and everybody wanted to be *master*. *That* was really their grievance, if they had any.

That evening we had a disturbance in the Parisian *café*. A gentleman we were playing with broached the subject of politics, and we were asked our opinion, which we gave against the adventurers who are seeking office. At this juncture a few questions were asked by an outsider, who, as we immediately discovered, was a detective police-officer. We finished our game, and then left, followed by the spy; but on nearing our hotel (Le Grand) we suddenly turned off, and walked down Boulevard Strasbourg. Getting tired of street-walking, we made for a well-known place of amusement, and there discovered my old friend, Madame M. Barthélemy. She was under a different name, and was considered the finest looking woman in Ryde. She drives the prettiest turn-out, with a matchless pair of ponies. Hanton was introduced to the woman he had heard so much about, and was all anxiety to see her people. Her brougham being here, we were able to elude our follower. The following day I was the object of curiosity in my drive with the charming Maria, and we finished up with the Opera. The Tuileries and Hôtel de Ville were not completely wiped out, and they were busy rebuilding these in great haste. Paris, considering the siege, is wonderfully well preserved; and, with the exception of the above, the Column, and one or two other places, little damage has been done by Prussian shot and shell to this superb city.

The comic opera, 'Madame Angot,' was being supplanted by 'Giroflé-Girofla,' which was such a rage in Germany when I left. The Londoners are generally a year behind the Continental people in music.

We visited the Palais du Louvre, and noticed that all pictures of the late Emperor were turned to the wall, or had a black cloth drawn over them, to show dislike to the late ruler; Notre Dame, Palais de Justice, Napoleon's tomb, Hôtel des Invalides, Champ de Mars, Rond Point de l'Étoile, Arc de Triomphe, Parc de Monceaux, Place de Havre, and Versailles, which took us a fortnight. The fortifications round Paris, which at one time were considered impregnable, we found in a sadly dilapidated state. The French, though, will not be long in rectifying the mischief done by Prussians and Communists. They are determined to obliterate the past without delay — to forget reverses, live for the glorious present, and an imaginary millennium!

The gay portion of Paris, bent always on continual excitement and amusement, was enjoying itself as is its wont, caring little for politics, which did not concern it, and for the state of the country, which had so recently emerged from a great national calamity.

Wendell Holmes says, " All good Americans, when they die, go to Paris."   If so, I think Yankee angels of the period must be somewhat falling off, judging from the specimen we met at the Grand Hôtel.

Hanton's uncle and cousins were over here on a short visit, and we were very glad to find them out, and get a few invitations to some delightful balls and dinner-parties. The uncle was a fine specimen of an English gentleman. He had been in the army, and retired from the command of the Rifle Brigade a short time before Lord Cardwell's rough order came into operation. He had now, while comparatively a young man (forty-eight) settled down to enjoy a country gentleman's life in Sussex; and, although he had sold his racing stud, he still kept a fairish stable, where one could always reckon on getting a mount to hounds, of which Colonel Hanton was master. Charlie's cousins were pretty and clever, with thoroughly English habits, and of very refined and elegant tastes. What Elysium was ours! We were in the seventh heaven! The Colonel had a box at the Opera, but which, he said, was quite out of his line, and was at our disposal, if we cared for that sort of thing. Of course we did, and so did Charlie's cousins.

It was on the last occasion at the Opera that that beautiful demon, Maria, discovered us. She was in company with a young Baronet, a terrible black-leg, who was cut by every gentleman of his Club in Pall Mall. I have generally found it the case that if a fellow is disliked by a whole regiment, or his Club, he must be a very bad lot, because in a club or a regiment there are men of many minds and many tastes, and if they all go against a poor devil, depend upon it he has not many redeeming points. This young Baronet I knew at one time intimately;

but he treated me shamefully, and I said I would have nothing further to do with him. Now Maria was perfectly acquainted with his disreputable conduct; and I told her that she was to make up her mind quickly which of us she intended to retain as a friend. When, on the present occasion, she signed me to come over and see her, I refused to go, and took no further notice of her. Whether it was jealousy on her part, my being in company with Charlie's cousins, I know not; suffice it to say, she, together with that young black-leg, tried to work my name up into something like scandal, in order to have her revenge; and, on retiring from the Opera, sent for that beauty who followed us that night from the Parisian *café*, gave him the name of our hotel, and said it would be as well to inquire into our conduct, and search our boxes, as we were in Paris under two different names, which looked suspicious. Anyhow, she made a good story out of our case.

On our return to the hotel, after seeing the ladies home, we were met by a lady in deep mourning, in a thick veil, which hid her face from us, but on her addressing us we discovered the wily Maria. She demanded an explanation of our conduct to her. She was even more furious with me than with Hanton. I was aghast, and surely required an explanation if any one on earth did. Hanton asked her if she had taken leave of her senses. At this her passion was beyond control, and then she

threatened me. I, not wishing a scene, walked on
and up the staircase. She followed me at a rapid
rate, saying she would ruin me unless I consented
to her proposals. I told her not to further annoy me
or I should be compelled to send for a *gendarme*.
Imagine my astonishment when I heard her declare
I was her husband trying to evade her, and then, in
company with our old friend the detective officer,
who made his appearance on the scene at this
moment, they marched up to my rooms, Maria
throwing herself on a sofa in a passion of tears; and
the officer, touching me on the shoulder, said,—
" Monsieur Robinson, you are my prisoner ";
adding, " Veuillez ouvrir les valises, les malles ? "
—" Faites lever même; nous nous reposerons en
attendant," said Hanton. The officer was now
joined by some others, and our boxes opened and
searched ; and several sweet things in love-letters
were taken charge of as evidently of a very suspicious nature. " Ah ! ne mettez pas tout sens dessus
dessous," cried out Hanton.—" N'importe. La loi
est précise, et nous devons veiller à son exécution,"
said the stern-looking officer, who considered we
were very dangerous characters. We had spoken
with contempt of the ruling powers in a public
place ; had changed our names for some bad intention ; and, as a married man, I was trying to escape
from the woman who claimed me as her husband!
We were on the point of being marched off, when
Charlie got very determined, and said he would not

move until his uncle arrived, who was well known, and would explain matters; that Maria, in a fit of rage, had imagined the whole story, was plain enough. A letter was written to Colonel Hanton, who hurried down, and was greatly horrified to find us in such a predicament. He appeared vexed we should have changed our names as we did, but in a few words fully satisfied the detective who we were. And then the dear Colonel was so amused at the whole thing, that he laughed till tears came in his eyes. He was greatly astounded at seeing Maria, whom he recognized as his wife's companion at Ryde, and French governess to his elder daughter, before her beauty was known and her charms won her such renown in certain circles of London and Paris life.

This created a good deal of speculation and talk on the following day; and, as we were watched by gossips and old women, we thought it prudent to leave Paris. We bade farewell to the dear Colonel and his lovely daughters, promising to spend many happy days with them in Sussex, and when they went up to town, expressed a hope they would not exclude us from their balls and parties in Chester Square.

In Belgium a little incident happened which will show how our countrymen are appreciated and thought of by some people. Hanton and I, talking rather loudly in English, were assailed by a mob of ruffians, who shouted after us, "Oh, you roast beef

John Bull; Got dam!" We only had to stop and advance towards them, when they took to their heels and ran for their lives.

Travelling through Belgium, we returned to Boulogne, and made our way to London just in time and temper to begin everything afresh, now that the height of the season was on.

CHAPTER IX.

HANTON was unusually high spirited on our arrival in the dear old country, and what he had long promised to do on reaching home he carried out on landing at Folkestone, viz., to drink off at a draught a quart of half-and-half, which he did in a most business-like way.

My first care was to proceed to my tailor's and have a decent lot of clothes made forthwith. Everybody is acquainted with the story of a certain rough old Bengalee, " Qui hai ?" who made straight for Poole's on arrival in England, and asked to be turned out a gentleman. The story goes that the forward assistant replied, " Turn *you* out a gentleman, sir," eyeing him from head to foot, with a shake of the head; "that's impossible, sir!" I thought my tailor looked at me with a dejected air, and considered my case a most hopeless one. And although much sentiment has lately been wasted in a public journal on " what constitutes a gentleman," a great many are indebted for that appellation to the ingenuity and consideration of their tailors. We Indians, after a sojourn of some years in that benighted country, are ignorant of the burlesque we figure on arrival, to the amusement of the London dandy.   I was somewhat ashamed to be seen anywhere until I had got decent things to appear in, so returned to my hotel.

After reporting my arrival, I made for Kensington, to see my people.   Of course, they were delighted to see me, and I engaged lodgings near them in Palace Gardens Terrace.   Everything was new to me; I was in a perfect whirl of excitement.   Hanton had gone to see his people in Belgravia, and had taken lodgings near Victoria Station, so he telegraphed me, and I was to meet him that night, when he would introduce me to his governor, an old club bird.   His brother was also coming in from Woolwich, so we should be posted up in all the news of the day.   I was very anxious to see the Underground Railway, Albert Hall and Memorial, then the Park; and encountered about a dozen friends, Indian and Continental acquaintances, at that wonderful meeting place, Hyde Park Corner, opposite the Duke's statue.

The dinner at the "Rag" was like all ordinary dinners, but somehow I never enjoyed a more pleasant evening.   There were four of us, but whist was quite out of the question, as little money would have gone out of the family; besides, we had so much to talk about, and Hanton's father was full of anecdote and racy stories, and was quite ready to initiate us into all that was going on in town.   We smoked some superb regalias, and, after drinking more wine than usual, the inevitable "peg," which has quite become an "institution" here, was introduced, and we broke up, all very well pleased with ourselves and the world in general.

What a melancholy day Sunday is in London! at least, I thought so,—and one feels the great quietude after a Continental tour much more, I think. It is an awful day for the gay French and German people here; all places of amusement closed, and the day spent in idleness or strolling in Kensington Gardens, doing "Vanity Fair," sporting your dress, if you are of the feminine gender, for the enlightenment of admiring women of every class, of various ages, of many minds, and all of studied artificial tastes. It does one good to take a chair and watch the beauties pass to and fro. They have got themselves up, regardless of all things, to be seen and to please others, particularly to attract the notice of our poor dubious sex. It is certainly very kind and good of them to take so much trouble on our account; but I am rather inclined to think the sham is too subtle, and with at least fifty per cent. it is a losing game they are playing. Their ready wit and vast experience of what's what does not stand them in much need here; and the unlucky ones would be saving time and trouble if they would discontinue the practice of duping. Everything is false with the majority of them, as much so as the hair on their heads, the thoughts inside, their "soft nothings" of sayings, and the lie their whole life is. The fault is sometimes attributable to ambitious mothers, who are ever anxious to make good marriages for their daughters, either for rank, position, or money; hence the deceit they think necessary to adopt in order to attain their aim and end. Thank Heaven! all are not so base and contemptible at heart, and that there are some noble specimens of woman-kind amongst my country-women. God bless *them!*

London strikes foreigners as a wonderful place on the Sunday. They are astonished that an enormous city like this, with millions of a population, can be kept quiet and in order by a mere handful of police, and that all religions are so much respected. The various creeds and doctrines of over a score of worships, with as many branches, sects, and denominations as there are tints for ladies' dresses, all praying for each other, but in their hearts hating all who differ from their own class, with a "thank God, I am not as my neighbour," seem to get on very well on the whole. Although London is England's capital, it cannot be called exclusively English. It is the freest city in the world, and although you are not allowed to offend the people's national custom of keeping the Sabbath-day holy, in all other respects you can do and say pretty much what you like. If you are an Englishman or a Japanese, an excited Pole or a Yankee speculator, you are all thought much of a muchness, provided you keep a civil tongue in your head and pay your way as you go. You may be a Tory nobleman or an upstart red-hot Radical, a ritualistic enthusiast or a scoffing atheist, a libertine or a gentle saint, you fail to astonish the people of London. You can express your sentiments as you please, and you can do so unmolested, provided you keep in harmony with the views of the day. London is for men of all climes, of all shades of opinions and theories. In this sense it is the capital of the world, where every man finds his own level.

Of course I went the round of the operas and theatres. 'The Happy Land,' at the Court, and 'The Wicked World,' at the Haymarket, were quite the rage; and at the Opéra Comique, 'La Fille de Madame Angot' had just been introduced, and had taken the place of 'Geneviève de Brabant' at the Philharmonic. Some charming concerts were given at the Crystal Palace, Albert Hall, and other minor places, where occasionally Madame Nilsson and other great performers delighted crowded audiences, which were of the fastidious element, and where you could take your female relations and enjoy a very pleasant evening when you had to take your share of duty.

What a noted place the East Indian Club, in St. James's Square, has become as the rendezvous for Indians from the three Presidencies! It has taken the lead of the Oriental and Travellers in this respect, and a more respectable club is not to be found in London. I have enjoyed many happy days there amongst my various "Qui hai?" acquaintances. It was a very remarkable fact that I never visited that club without meeting some fresh Indian I knew just home; and, without exception, I don't think I ever walked along Regent Street or Oxford Street without encountering an Indian or foreign acquaintance. Sometimes you meet them at such odd, out-of-the-way places,—when travelling by the Underground Railway, or in situations where you would never dream of coming across any one you knew. The world is very little after all; you are constantly stumbling over people you fancied were thousands of miles away.

I shall not forget at a certain house in Kensington where I was dining, the topic of conversation turned on Indian affairs, and I freely enough entered into it, giving my opinion with more authority than was warranted, when my friend whom I was addressing said, "As regards the Presidency you refer to, I think you must be mistaken, as I was Governor of the province for five years, and I am not aware of any such proceedings having taken place in my time." It proved to be a distinguished Bengal civilian I was speaking to, whose face I afterwards recalled to mind.

" You meet these Indian *people* everywhere now," said a worthy leading member of the bar to another Londoner of importance. English people have a very vague idea of the relative ranks of our proud Eastern officials. They mix up judges and governors, commissioners and chilumchees, magistrates and punkah-wallahs, Indian colonels and brandy pawnees. The great majority have really very little interest in the country and the people, and imagine everybody coming from the East a nabob in wealth; but they don't know, and care less, what goes on. It was not so very long ago that when any Indian subject was to be broached in the House every member that could absented himself on the occasion, as they considered it such utter waste of time discussing anything connected with our vast Indian Empire. It is somewhat changed for the better now, but the ignorance displayed at times is more than ludicrous, it is lamentable.

I was present in the House on an occasion when a very noteworthy Under-Secretary of State, in referring to a motion which had been brought forward of certain substantial grievances which concerned an influential body of gentlemen, exemplified matters by analogies so preposterous as to give the initiated the idea that he intended what he said to be treated as a burlesque. With the exception of only one leading paper, the gross errors were passed over without comment. I remember it caused some to laugh, others to mourn.

When in Sussex, I attended a lecture delivered by the son of a late Punjab Lieutenant-Governor. It was on Central Asia. As no one present had been in any of the places he was full of, particularly Turkestan and Mongolia, he was quite safe in venturing forth in imaginary stories, and he was listened to with apparent earnestness, no one contradicting him; but when he came down in the world, and alluded to Affghanistan and our North-Western frontier, it was evident he was talking at random. I remember well one of his stories of the main roads of the Punjab, that their normal state was utter dilapidation, so much so, that they were beyond repair; and, as vehicles passing over them were continually breaking down from the shocking condition of the roads, the authorities had taken the precaution to hang up ropes on trees at intervals, for the convenience of a broken-down public.

Although this little delicate attention on the part of the thoughtful authorities was duly appreciated by an attentive assembly, I, knowing the circumstances, began to doubt my own senses, as I was under the impression the Grand Trunk Road, which extended to Peshawur, with the numerous branches of Macadamized "kunker" roads leading therefrom, were about the finest in the world.

By the kindness of General Sir J. Adye, Director of Artillery, I was enabled to visit Woolwich Arsenal, going over all the scientific departments, of which Professor Abel is at the head. I witnessed some very enormous guns being turned out, which was most interesting and highly instructive. The whole system of experiments, although costly, has been invariably attended with success. The working of the several branches is complete and uniform in all its details, and almost amounts to perfection. The great courtesy extended to any one belonging to the service who takes an interest in their gigantic notions of gunnery, is deserving of the highest commendation, considering how much of their valuable time is taken up in red-tape formulæ, and that the authorities are at the beck and call of countless subordinate departments.

I was in time to see the Engineers at Chatham execute some very creditable performances in earth-work defences and gun-cotton experiments, which were carried out with promptness and order. Subsequently I came here on duty, and gained many useful lessons in working parties of sappers and miners.

Returning to town, I attended all the lectures at the Institution of Civil Engineers, and, being an Associate, I was able to introduce my friend Hanton, who passed a splendid examination at Chatham whilst I was there on a visit at a relation's, who was principal over a class, holding a good staff appointment in the Royal Engineers.

It was about this time the celebrated Claimant's trial was going on, and, as I failed to obtain admission in the usual order, I was compelled to be "smuggled in" as one of his counsel, and adopted a barrister friend's wig and gown, and passed in with a score of the most learned and greedy. I acted my part exceedingly well, so I was told,— looked very sedate and engrossed while evidence of a most important nature was being extracted. After withdrawing my pocket-book and scribbling something, I thought I had stopped quite long enough, and withdrew, having seen the man who was the chief topic of conversation with half England. To me he appeared an intelligent man, but gross, and overbearing in his general demeanour, and had become hardened to his idiosyncrasy. The learned Doctor for the defence was, as usual, bold as brass, and making as good a case as he could of prolonging the agony of suspense. Any one who had followed the events of the proceedings must have known how it would end, and the mockeries and shams practised by the counsel for the defence make this one of the most absurd trials on record.

When the Derby Day arrived, a party of us left our club in a drag and four, well provided for a heavy day's campaigning. Eight of us started; three we lost there, and double that number of stray friends we brought back to town. What a glorious day the Derby of '73 was! The result of the Derby race is all you can think of on that day when away from England, and it has now become quite a national affair. How all the wires are cleared on the occasion, for the news flashes to New York and the great American Continent, even to the shores of the Pacific, to Europe, to India, to China, to Australia, and known in these parts the same day!

People who care little for horse-racing, and have never made a bet in their lives, will take an interest in knowing who won the Derby and the places of the other horses. Enough money changes hands over this race to meet the original national debt of England. A single individual once lost a quarter of a million to different parties by backing the wrong horse. I shall not easily forget the excitement that prevailed when the outsider, " Doncaster," distinguished himself to the world by winning the Derby of '73. I was on the Grand Stand to witness the race, and after it had been run the few bright, happy faces of the lucky ones were nothing compared to the despair and misery depicted on the countenances of countless gamblers who had staked their all and lost everything. Wretchedness henceforth would be their doom.

What terrible disasters this race brings to thousands of homes who have been bold enough to risk what was death for them to lose! It becomes a crime when a man gambles to this extent, and imperils the happiness and prospects of a whole family. He is quite at liberty to drink himself into the grave if he feels inclined, or commit suicide if he is tired of life, and finds he has made a blunder of all things. This is a free country, and you can do pretty much as you like; but it is an awful thing to drag others with you against their wishes into the mire of ruin.

Some writer has said of London that its vastness and magnitude are so great, that buildings, churches, parks, squares, and streets are passed by as nothing. And it is very true you give but a careless glance at some of the greatest buildings. What interest do you take in St. Paul's, or Westminster Abbey, or the Houses of Parliament, or that noble block of recently constructed offices in Whitehall (which, by-the-bye, is out of the square), or a thousand others, after the first hurried look? Minor things and great people, from the Queen downwards, are overlooked. Vastness alone interests you in London.

The mighty throng of human beings, in a fever of excitement, bent on business, pass to and fro, caring for and noticing nothing, so absorbed are they in their thoughts of amassing the god of this world—filthy lucre. If they live for anything, care for anything, it is money: from morning to night, and night to morning, they dwell on that one idea—money. And when they retire at last, and have enough of this world's goods, they aspire to rank—to be courted and sought by the noble of the land. A peerage at this stage is all they think wanting to make this life a paradise. It is to be hoped that those who do succeed in attaining their ambitious ends in this respect, fully appreciate their position and importance—rest from their labours, and are satisfied. The adventurer in Parliament and successful London trader are terribly selfish fellows at heart, and by their wits and sharp roundabout doings clamber over the mass of the people whom they have used as tools and ground to powder for their own aggrandizement and love of money.

Although I cannot sympathize with the working

classes when they become violent and insolent, still I think a great deal of the blame of the late "strikes," "union and indignation meetings," lie with the masters. They have no right to work these people to death as they have done, and then remunerate them in money barely enough to support life, caring not a jot for their bodies or souls, and treating them no better than cattle. A worm, they say, will turn, and it is characteristic of the nobleness of Englishmen that they "never will be slaves."

It is a crying shame on the wealthy manufacturer that he is so indifferent to the prayers of the wretched hirelings he gets fat on. They are ignorant, and have no idea of comfort, you say. Whose fault is that? With all our boasted talk of Christianity, justice, virtue, and other moral duties which our papers and old ladies teem with, what have we done in raising our great labouring classes, the working hands of England? Put yourself in their place, how would you like it, friend? Don't forget the old saying, "Do unto others," &c. I have visited most of the large manufacturing towns, and have inquired into their grievances, and regret to find it is only too true about the way numbers of them have been treated. For my part, I should be glad to see a man in Parliament to represent this enormous class of my countrymen—an intelligent, straightforward, honest man.

The higher you cultivate the mind of this powerful element and backbone of our country, the more truly loyal and staunch citizens will they become. But in common justice to humanity they have every right to be heard; and I honour them for having the manliness of character to resent the cruel wrong which has so long been theirs. I am not a Radical in the vulgar sense of the phrase, but I desire the rooting out of all error and superstition; of abuses of long standing, which have come to be looked upon as infallible and perfect by the weak and ignorant; and a general change or re-modelling of certain incorrect laws and institutions of the mediæval period. Of course, such a change must be brought about by degrees, slowly, but surely, as you work up a snow-ball. All would be the better for such grand alterations in established things, I feel convinced.

What a contrast this great city is at two in the morning, when returning home from your club! The noisy, bustling crowd is gone, the thousands of rattling conveyances which filled the streets have vanished, and only occasionally a "four-wheeler," or "Hansom," or carriage, darts by with some dissipated bird from his club or from a late train, or an editor of a newspaper, or a Member of Parliament; no one else, save a solitary policeman here and there, occupies the countless streets. London is wrapt in slumber; its millions of busy people are buried in sleep, weary and worn after their day's toil. As you approach the West-End, there are more carriages and people astir, owing to its being the nucleus of such things as balls and late invitations, and heavily-laden vehicles, containing the joyous fashionables, begin to deviate in all directions. And strings of conveyances pass every now and then, bearing homeward the merry party, until the world is all active again.

My friend Hanton, a most jealous advocate for truth and knowledge, was anxious to go the usual rounds, and see everything that was to be seen, from an interview with that most wonderful man, Dr. Lynn, and entertainments at the Egyptian, St. James's, St. George's, and Lyric Halls, and shows of Spiritualistic tomfoolery, to entering into the same at a certain well-known quackery assemblage not far from Bedford Square. It is surprising how many sane people are humbugged by these impostors and swindlers of so-called Spiritualists! It was at one of their private "*séances*" we were admitted, I must acknowledge, under false colours; not that we gave utterance to any untruths, but we passed in as "believers." Taking our seats in an ante-room, I made inquiries in which place the "spirits" would assemble, and then quietly "sloped," examining the sides, floor, ceiling, and furniture in the room unnoticed, Hanton being on the *qui vive*. I satisfied myself; I could discover nothing moveable, and retired, to follow, in my turn, round the table when the "medium" appeared.

After the usual formula had been gone through,

we caught hold of each other's hands, and the only light was put out by the medium. We were now in total darkness. I was seated on the right of Hanton, and next to me sat a brute called Smith, —a rough, coarse bully, who acted as a second medium, and he was assisted by two or three accomplices. Very soon the "believers" began to mumble something to themselves, and asked if lights were visible in certain parts of the room. I owned to not being able to see them for some time, when at last, sure enough, very brilliant stars floated about, and rested on the shoulders of some of the favoured ones. These asked some questions about Peter and John, and voices were distinctly heard in a squeakish sort of voice overhead. Then a music-box struck up "Sweet spirit, hear my prayer!" and floated about the room, dropping in semi-circles apparently, as it came to low and high notes. A guitar was now introduced, and played some airs. A bell was rung, and friend Hanton said, in Hindustani, "Don't appear astonished, but invoke the spirits, and they will speak to you." I then asked for Peter, in a subdued tone, to come to me; and a voice addressed me in answer, asking me when I intended giving *my séance*. I inquired if Peter would appear on that occasion, and the voice replied, "Perhaps I may." It said it knew me of old, was continually lamenting my disreputable career, and hoped I would reform.

Hanton was now holding a most familiar conversation with the spirit, spoke to it as " old fellow," and regretted Peter had not appeared oftener in his dreams. He questioned him as to the soul of Napoleon,—who the Claimant was,—what Gladstone's end would be, and a great many more things, all of which were most cautiously and guardedly answered, without being satisfactory. I now asked to shake Peter by the hand, and be on friendly terms with him, he previously having chucked me under the chin and patted me on the back. Smith, the bully, told me I was permitted to let go his hand, but on no account to let go that of my companion's, as it would break the spell; and I had, without his knowing it, been poking Charlie in the ribs, and telling him what infernal nonsense the whole thing was, all the time, in another language !

Peter now grasped me by the tips of my fingers, and lifted me up from the ground, then on to the chair; but I could not get sufficient hold of his hand, and, getting beyond my reach, I made a final snatch to retain the hand (whilst on the chair). Immediately I was struck in the chest a violent blow, the spirit calling me " a rascal," and the whole room thrown into disorder. I was asked how dare I attempt to do anything so sacrilegious as to seize the spirit? Having a lady friend with me, I was unable to revenge myself then, but I was determined I would smash some one for the blow I received. Hanton begged me to remember we were there as "believers," and on another occasion we would disclose the humbug, and bring a few to grief, but not now. So we contrived to fasten the principal medium in the cabinet. I was allowed to secure him; and if the knots were not tightened so as to prevent circulation, I hope I may never tie another.

Peter and John now appeared from beneath a cloud of lovely colour, and Peter addressed the company in very unbecoming language, I thought, for a spirit. Hanton called it every bad name he could think of in Hindustani, which it treated with profound ignorance and contempt. The voice said it was unable to understand that language. After a few more experiments we left.

Talking this over at our club some nights afterwards, we were determined to sally forth, a sufficient body of us, well equipped, and reveal the medium to the gaze of his weak belongings. Leaving our watches, card-cases, and purses behind us, nine of us, under perfect discipline, marched out to do for this place. We had engaged the services of a police-officer to be present, so that, in case of any rough work, we should have the law on our side.

We took with us proper dark lanterns and Pompeii lights. No names were to be used, only numbers. The fellows were to go in with the throng at intervals, but take up their position in places previously arranged upon. No force was to be used unless they showed fight, when, of course, they would be attacked, the lights put on, and, as we should be under the power of spiritualism, the chandelier, mantel-piece glass, mirrors, and window-glasses would be easily damaged;—legs of tables and chairs don't require much handling,—and we were to prove the whole arrangement was a gigantic swindle and fraud, and damage their cause so effectually that that part of London, at all events, should know them no more. The first time, by some blunder, it did not come about. It is simply disgraceful on the part of Government not to put down such places. Weak-minded men and women are beset by these impostors, who stop at nothing short of murder when they are attacked.

I shall never forget the amount of fun this caused. I have much pleasure in stating that my friends have taken the initiative, and disclosed more than one of these "shops" in London. Of course the spiritualists take good care never to bring the matter up before the law, so any one is perfectly safe in venturing forth in showing "mediums" off to an admiring set of fools.

It was at this time the renowned " Shar " was bewildering the London people to such an extent as to greatly interfere with the whole business of life. The metropolis was turned upside down on his account, and the Cockneys could think of nothing else. They rushed to see him in hundreds of thousands. They raved about His Majesty and his diamonds. This most contemptible and disgusting of mortals was thought more of than any living man. Such a panic, I believe, was unprecedented. Foolish John Bull must have something to occupy his attention, and he is quite as prepared to make himself ridiculous about a Shah's visit as he is to indulge in sentiment and talk of an odious character when he considers it necessary for his *prestige* and honour to burn a few huts at Coomassie, and slay some inoffensive savages on a malarious coast.

John Bull can be very plucky in clearing off Abyssinians and Ashantees when there is really little occasion to wage war for England's flag, but he thinks twice over an affair such as Slesvig-Holstein, even when his honour is at stake, if he can possibly get out of it. And when there is no Ashantee war (?), a sensational Bengal Famine, ten thousand miles away, will do until something better turns up. Meanwhile he must be engaged in getting rid of some of his superfluous money. The Bengal famine was over a country nearly the size of England, with a population equal to that of Great Britain; and, after months of ravages, the total number of deaths reported in His Excellency the Viceroy's telegrams are twenty odd. And no one is present to swear they did not die from toothache or old age!

To return to that most objectionable creature— the Shah. It is to be hoped the authorities have quite fumigated the halls of Buckingham Palace by this time. A dirty savage of a potentate, whose despotic rule has been the means of his accumulating all the revenue of his country for his own selfish lusts, treading on the rights of his people, encouraging anarchy and armed hordes of banditti to molest the weak and unprotected. Years of tyranny and oppression at last brought about pestilence and famine, and, while his people were dying the most awful deaths, he was grovelling in luxury and comfort, butchery and murder; and his court comprised all the rakes and flatterers in the kingdom. The country's revenue was used, not for the suffering multitude, but to purchase larger diamonds and precious stones for His Majesty's state, to add brighter damsels to his harem, and to enlarge his palaces and courts. The result of this was utter desolation everywhere but around his august person; and, wishing to get out of his country for a time, he sold his kingdom to a semi-English-German Baron, stipulating the most unheard-of demands and penalties if everything did not progress as he thought fit. And he meanwhile went away to enjoy the hospitalities of the sovereigns of Europe, and to fool the soft English with his diamonds and splendour.

Our kindness and hospitality were quite thrown away on a man who is as ungrateful as he is mean, cowardly, and ignorant. Persia could be of no use to us if we went to war with Russia. Her soldiery are out of date, and no match against the bold border forces. Ameer Shere Ali, for instance, at the head of his daring Puttians, would in a single encounter annihilate the tame Persians. The Affghans are a very warlike race, and, I believe, would help us when there is occasion. They are a people worth cultivating. They are manly, and, for a nation so backward in civilization, honourable, and faithful to their word. The Persian is treacherous, and does not understand what honour is, and in this respect resembles the Arab.

The military review at Windsor, naval affair at Portsmouth, and other absurd displays in the Shah's honour, or for his edification, were lost on him. He failed to appreciate anything but the novelty of seeing men in kilts, lewd ballets, and Madame Tussaud's wax-show. These are about the only things he will remember of England's name and glory.

But Londoners of a certain class are very partial in taking notice of any coloured man. Bengalee writers, Baboos, even some Khitmutgars, when in England, are considered Indian Princes, and are courted and made much of, particularly by the Exeter Hall stamp. Whether it is in order to show themselves off, or that they are carried away by fanatical ideas, or the novelty is of such a charm that they lose their wits when they are so fortunate as to have an Oriental to introduce to an easily pleased audience, I cannot tell.

What has been engrossing the minds of my weak country people for some time past is the unsettled, divided state of their religious belief, a goodly number preferring to adopt a ceremony nearly approaching Roman Catholicism in their form of worship, which easily attracts and pleases certain women.

In some parishes throughout this fair land religion has been its chief curse; families are divided and separated, envy and hatred are rampant. What will be the result of all this? A civil-religious war? But, if Protestant and Catholic have met in deadly combat to settle differences of religious creed and dogma, I see no reason why these two great hatreds (which surpass the old worn-out feud existing between Protestant and Catholic) should not be ended this way. God forbid! but they are going the right way to bring about a very serious national disturbance before this enlightened century is over.

Looking at Christianity in all its lights, never was there a religion such a lamentable failure. There is really no constituted order or authority for anything which is done. Then, again, witness the discussions which have lately puzzled the public mind respecting the infallibility of the Athanasian Creed. The Jew, Mohammedan, Hindoo, and Buddhist *have* laws and constituted rules, which do not occasion rankling and fighting. I have great admiration for the poetical beauty and highly moral code of this latter faith; and I consider it a piece of insolence for any Christian to dare to tell a Buddhist he is wrong and on his road to hell for not believing as he believes. As regards numbers, there are double the number of Buddhists in the world that there are Christians, and it is older by nearly a thousand years. Anyhow, it exists *now*, and for what it is worth. How would the Christian like a learned Pundit Buddhist to preach to him on the humbug of Christianity, and the weakness of believing in anything so preposterous and vulgar?

To look at these creeds fairly and impartially, you must place yourself outside the pale of all these formulas of faith. Don't forget you are by a geographical accident born in England, and it follows you are brought up to regard the Christian religion as true; but had you been born in Asia, you would have been something else, and would have denounced your present ideas with as much hatred as you do theirs. But one God created you all, and " is rich unto all them that call upon Him, for there is no difference between the Jew and the Greek," and, for that matter, between the " High Church " and the " Low Church."

I was very much struck at the varied services which are held in St. George's Hall on the Sunday. In the morning you hear the Rev. Charles Voysey, the noted " infidel," who preaches pure Theism; later on, Father Ignatius, blind and passionate in his language, who, unlike Mr. Voysey, is very intolerant towards anybody who does not think as he docs. I heard Ignatius more than once. He has a good voice, and has always a flow of vehement language at his command, but you need not look here for either sequence or logic. Surely Ignatius must only damage his own cause when he is so strong in denouncing Voysey or Gladstone, and the ruling powers of Government, in harsh and unnecessary language! Anyhow, how puzzling it must be for the people who attend these services of worship, as both cannot be right! Mr. Voysey's views are certainly liberal, tolerant towards all sects, and charitable and manly to a degree.

Mr. Spurgeon, I can quite believe, has worked considerable good. I should class Ignatius, Archbishop Manning, and Monsignor Capel as men of strong fanatical tastes, toned down by some amount of knowledge, rightly and wrongly worked up by ill-judged trainers,—unlike Dean Stanley, who is a most refined and polished gentleman and sound scholar, without being a vast or deep thinker. What extraordinary emotion Dean Stanley caused the orthodox by allowing Professor Max Müller to preach from the pulpit of Westminster Abbey! This was a step in the right direction; for although the orthodox make out the Professor to be an Atheist, they all admit of his profound knowledge, and clear, solid, reasoning capabilities.

Having joined one or two Scientific Clubs and Societies, I was able to become personally acquainted with some of the leading literary and scientific men of London, and I derived much information and a considerable stock of useful knowledge of all sorts from many kind members, whose thoughtful and considerate demeanour towards me I shall never forget.

Some of the most pleasant recollections of my London life are dinners I gave to my friends of opposite views, whom I brought together for a general debate. On one occasion, I collected as many as a dozen of the most extraordinary characters I knew, every man having extremely advanced ideas in his own particular line. They were all celebrated men of letters, and I took a delight in occasionally throwing in a live shell and seeing the effect thereof—an M.P. barrister of·the Liberal side generally coming off victor when he started an argument.

In both my works, ' Origin of Christianity,' and ' Preliminary Observations on the General Nature and Objects of Science,' I have attempted to depict facts, as represented by different people, of different nations, at different ages, in the form received by the orthodox of the day, for what they are worth. My sole object is to know the truth; and I have gleaned information from every available source in the old and the new world. I have for years past been in communication with some very talented men in various parts of the globe, who have kept me acquainted with the progress of the pioneers of truth and science ; and, although it has not always been in my power to grasp some of their advanced ideas, it has been the means of giving me an inkling of that nobleness of purpose which will one day take the place of ignorance and hypocrisy, the present rulers. of the civilized world. I have been compelled to write anonymously. My name and position are too humble to appear before the tribunal of a mighty Government; not that I fear Government; but individuals over you, who by accident have risen to high power and command, are capable of misunderstanding you, and injuring you by mean and unmanly actions. It is very praise-worthy of those who, by dint of perseverance under the most discouraging circumstances, have main-tained their rights, to the prejudice, of toadyism and sophistry. I have no wish to be spiteful, but many will bear me out when I say that several appoint-ments and preferments of distinction can be traced to that half-hour after dinner when the wine passes round, or to agreeing with your chief in some insane proposition or worn-out sentiment, which belonged to the fossil period. To please the old gentleman, you would readily acquiesce in his definition of things in general. The more distorted and absurd the statement, the more satisfied you would appear to be of its correctness. This may be somewhat bordering on what is commonly understood as hypocrisy, but rest assured your application for some special appointment which you have had your eye upon for some time will, if he has anything to do with it, meet with his approval and support.

A few years ago an uncommonly smart officer, a candidate for the staff, dining with his General, ventured forth in anecdote. He finished up by telling him of his latest scheme for re-modelling the service, which was to the effect that as soon as the authorities had discovered a brilliant officer, they should make him straight off a Field-Marshal; and the older and more imbecile he became, he should be placed down step by step in rank, until one day, if he lived long enough, he should attain his Sub-Lieutenantcy. The dear old General took it as a personal affront; and a few days after this, when the letter came to him to be forwarded through the usual official channel, he remarked that "there were some very strong grounds for his not being able to support this officer's application, as he did not consider he was fit for *any* staff appointment." Smart officer as he was, he was premature, and had to wait till the General's time was up and another took his place before his application was renewed.

Good stories and bad stories at mess have often been the making or damning of a man. It all depends on how, when, and where they are told; aptly related, they are all very well. Sharp officers have often got out of scrapes by taking advantage of the ignorance of those over them. An artillery subaltern, who had paid more attention to whist than his drill, was, on the occasion of the General's (an infantry officer) inspection, called out to put his battery through a few manœuvres. He was at his wits' end, and his orders were so confusing, that one-half the battery went off in one direction, and the other half scampered about in eccentric circles. Another command or two brought them together, when they were ordered to open fire—one-half blazing away at the other half. This looked so queer, that the General asked to have this particular manœuvre explained to him. The officer command-ing and some others were obliged to go to the rear for laughing. The witty subaltern replied, "I've got the enemy on a bridge, sir." The General then appeared to have considered it most admirably planned and successfully carried out, and testified to the drill qualifications of the said officer.

It is very strange how old service stories are dished up as new, and invented for and related of men,—"manufactured," perhaps, by their grand-fathers. How some fellows will bore you with the same story over and over again, or relate it to every person he meets, even when you are present, until you become sick of it! Such a man was a dear friend of mine, Captain Konar, who had a wonderful yarn about a brother officer of his when he was stationed at Attack, "gulling" a "griff" that if he would bring up Samson's name at mess he would tell a good story about the prodigious strength of the ancient Hercules. True enough, when there was a lull in the conversation, the "griff" thought it a fit time to introduce Samson's name, and inquired without further ado of some fellow sitting near him of his private opinion as to feats of removing columns and pillars *à la* Samson. As they had just previously been talking "shop," this remark was scarcely considered *à propos*, and they looked at him in blank astonishment with their mouths open, thinking he had either drunk too much or had taken leave of his senses. The officer who had suggested the story to Konar never took the slightest notice; and this poor "griff" brought up the name of Samson so often, that he was compelled to say at last,—"Not half such a strong man as you, my dear fellow, for you have dragged him into conversation without rhyme or reason half-a-dozen times."

Well, this wretched story I had heard so repeatedly, that I began to be weary of the very name of Samson, and I knew that every new guest would be sure to have it told him; so I was determined that when Hanton came I would put him up to the story, and make him relate it to Konar, which he did. Hanton began,—"I have a most amusing anecdote to tell you, Konar."—"Have you?" said he, and added, "I have one for you, too."—"But, stay," said Hanton, "let me tell mine first. It is about Samson."—"About Samson! How very odd, because mine was connected with Samson." And Hanton told him the story. Poor Konar shrieked out, tears almost coming into his eyes. "Why, that's *my* story! How *did you* know it?" I am glad to say Konar was twice the fellow afterwards. All was told him, and he never repeated it again, and got quite confused whenever the name of Samson was uttered.

After the Derby, I hardly know which great race to class next—Goodwood or Ascot. At the latter, the *élite* of the ladies turn out to grace with their presence the day's proceedings. It is much more of a holiday, and it is for the company they meet more than the actual race that the majority of people assemble at Goodwood and Ascot. Perhaps it would be difficult to find such a crowd of beautiful women, more superbly dressed, than at Ascot. They try to vie with each other who shall look the handsomest. At the Grand Prix, the French ladies make a good show; but they are not in such numbers, and the display of real taste is certainly in favour of Ascot. Apart from the artificial element, the class is decidedly very wide. I don't say that the generality of our English women *study* the art of dress and the adornment of themselves to such advantage as the French; but I maintain I prefer the somewhat stouter appearance, bright rosy cheeks, and honest faces of my countrywomen. Nowhere do English ladies dress so well and look more becoming than on the Ascot day.

The only drawback was the insufferable heat, which resembled India. Some will hardly credit it, that I have, on more than one occasion, felt the heat of London equal to anything I experienced in Australia or India. Perhaps it is because in the latter country you don't venture out when it is "killing." And in London you dress in a costume not at all suited to a temperature which reads by the thermometer 80° and 90° in the shade, or at an opera or theatre when the house is somewhat crowded, with no ventilation or a way for foul air to escape and fresh air to enter. Your dress is precisely the same as when snow is on the ground. A great cause of illness may be traced in all this. I took a box at Drury Lane Theatre the night after the Ascot, when 'Marie Stuart' was making such a rage, and on that occasion one or two ladies fainted away from the terrible heat of the house, which was greatly overcrowded in parts. Why can't managers start punkahs, and properly ventilate theatres and operas? Surely it would pay them.

Millais's pictures were creating a great sensation amongst the lovers of the brush at the Academy. I know it is heresy to say so, but I prefer some of the modern masters to the old ones; but I cannot see the harmony of colour in Millais's paintings. The hues do not blend unless you retire some distance from the picture. There is a species of coarseness, a want of skill in manipulation, and the beauty, fineness, and colour are either lost or display superfluity in parts. What I regret to find in the artists of the day is, that they leave too much to the imagination. We have great ability in many of our artists, but there is a carelessness in the handling of some of the highest powers of conception in the art, which is truly appalling to the connoisseur.

A successful picture at starting either makes or damns an artist. Too much praise or encouragement ill timed may set the brains of the most sedate on fire with excitement, ultimately proving his ruin. Again, a satirical criticism on the handiwork of an over-sensitive artist may work terrible effects on a promising career. Judging from my own experience, I can quite understand some amateurs not submitting their pictures to the Royal Academy. '

The other great collection of paintings of the season was at the Doré Gallery, 'Christ leaving the Prætorium,' being the first; and Mr. Holman Hunt's picture of the ' Shadow of Death,' in Bond Street, was drawing tens of thousands to see it.

Although I have never resided more than a few months in London at a time, I flatter myself I know it as well as most town men, particularly the West-End. I shall not forget going with a fair cousin of mine to see the British Museum, some picture-galleries, the Tower, and some other places in that neighbourhood, and being able to tell her the short cuts, and the names of certain streets she was not acquainted with. She appeared greatly astonished at my knowledge of localities, and re-marked, " You must know this end very well, for I have lived in London all my life, and am ignorant of any part but our own." She was more than astonished when I told her I had never been there before. I had studied the map of London, and had it in my *sanctum sanctorum* in India. Hardly a day passes but we Anglo-Indians, when abroad, allude to our London life, and give our experiences, for what they are worth, to attentive hearers; and with an enormous quantity of papers and literature of the day pouring in every week per overland mail, we are kept well acquainted with everything going on at the nucleus of the world—the acme of civilization—London.

Hanton and myself had both received permission from Her Majesty's Secretary of State for India to proceed to certain places in the United Kingdom for the purpose of reporting on professional matters, and making ourselves *au courant* with all the recent improvements in science in every department we chose to take up. This was exceedingly handsome on the part of Government, and was duly appre-ciated by their very dutiful and zealous servants— ourselves. I am rejoiced to see this privilege is extended to many officers of the Indian services whilst on leave in England; and I hope all will de-rive as much pleasure and enjoy the opportunities of seeing as much as we did. We combined pleasure and duty together in a very delightful way. We

independently submitted our plans, which wer
approved of and returned, granting us all or
proposed routes of travel. We were not idle
taking advantage of the kindness of a paterni
Government, and we shall return to India all the
more useful public servants, it is to be hoped, for
this and manifold other indulgences.

At a certain literary club not far from Waterloo
Place, a number of youngish men were sitting,
discussing some of the new books, and striking
articles of an original type in the leading papers.
When, with more warmth than usual, Hanton questioned the accuracy of an anonymous book which
had created unheard-of scandal in many fashionable
circles in the London world, we were beset with
doubtful speculations as to the rightful owner, when
a very noted man, Sir S. Hoote, remarked he was
of opinion that Professor Wonder's friend in tho
adjoining room was no other than the man whose
work half London was puzzled about. "Here is
the book," said Charlie; "ask him when he comes
into the room, whether he has read it, and then,
by his look or language, you may be able to satisfy
yourself." Scarcely had Hanton finished speaking
about him, when the gentleman in question strolled
into the room, eyeing every one in turn, until he
bowed to Hanton (who was in the habit of speaking
to everybody he came across, from prince to beggar),
and shook Sir S. Hoote by the hand. Smiling, he asked
him if there was anything very startling in the

papers that morning. "Nothing," said Sir Samuel, "besides a little Continental diplomatic intelligence for the Foreign Minister."—"Have you heard the last bit of gossip in the way of scandal," said the supposed author, " that a renowned nobleman has run off with a married woman, the charming actress who was engaged for this new piece brought out by the sucking Randolph?"—"Heard it! No, I never hear anything till I see it in the papers and it's days old; but I daresay it's only *canard*."—Charlie now made some observation *à propos*, when taking up the red-covered pamphlet, he idly remarked,—"*This* is a queer sort of production. I suppose the fellow who wrote it meant it as a burlesque, and to 'fetch' the sensational Londoners. Have you read it?" inquired Charlie, lazily throwing up his eyes, and meeting the eyes of his friend, who was quite prepared for the worst. —"Yaas," he drawled out, "I *have* read it, and think there is a deal of truth in it."—"Any idea who the author is? A dozen at least have denied having had anything to do with it, as I suppose *you* know?" asked Charlie.—"I know! why should I know? Oh, I see you have some idea, perhaps, that I am the author. If I were to tell you that your surmise is well founded, you would think yourself uncommonly shrewd, no doubt."—"Not exactly; but I think you attribute a greater importance to the book than I do. I feel convinced that you *are* the author, if you are so anxious to know my opinion." And Charlie kept his eyes fixed for a second on the gentleman, who did not like his inmost thoughts read by a man of Hanton's stamp. As we turned away, Sir Samuel strolled off arm-in-arm with Charlie, laughingly saying,—" You had our friend there. I had no idea I should find in you such a man of the world, with a power for reading character."

That evening we met under very different circumstances at the Botanical Fête, Regent's Park. I was with some lady friends, and, most strange to relate, Hanton and I, talking over matters afterwards, found that both our future careers depended upon that evening's appointment. A delightful ball at Grosvenor Square, where I met Fitzmore, and settled our plans for Ireland, and private theatricals at Colonel Hanton's, Chester Square, where Charlie figured as the ardent lover in ' Thwarted,' and I as the gentleman whose actions were invariably misunderstood (a piece written by Sir S. Hoote, in which he took the part of Madame Grundy), brought our doings in town to an end, and I left London rather exhausted and worn after an unusual bout of excitement, with a longing for quiet and rest.

CHAPTER X.

JOURNEYING alone to visit a few friends at Cheltenham, Bristol, and Bath, and the children of some of my old Indian companions at various out-of-the-way places, where they were at school, being brought up in the way they should go, I astonished myself by joining in their games, and making them happy by giving them the most simple presents, and delighting their young hearts. I was as big a child as any of them, and actually found myself seeking pleasure in picking wild flowers in the fields with young children. This sort of thing lasted till I left, and met Hanton and his uncle at Dawlish, and we went on a most delightful cruise with a party of his cousins. The weather was simply heavenly, and we sauntered about, calling at all the nicest watering-places.

Previously to leaving Dawlish, I dined with the father of a great friend of mine, Wykeham, a most promising young officer in the Punjab Police Force. I was charmed with Mr. Wykeham, senior. He was a gentleman of the most refined tastes, and had great powers of discrimination, and a profound knowledge of the world, combined with considerable learning. I took to him more, perhaps, because our views on things in general were nearly identical. He remarked, in a casual way, after dinner, that he had some notion of going on a trip to America; but how, when, and where, he had no idea, and it made no lasting impression on me, although I informed him of my intended visit to the States and Canada. Most strange to relate, I met him at Beaumont's English Hotel quite by chance, and discovered he had taken his passage in the same steamer as myself. But more of this anon.

Our party broke up at Torquay, some going on a cruise south, others bound for the Highlands. I halted at Plymouth on my way through, and met a great many of my people, some for the first time in my life. An auction of the estate of an old uncle, lately deceased, was being held whilst I was in Plymouth. I met the only child of my guardian and uncle, who was killed in Bhootan in 1864, when in command of the Artillery; and in the evening, with some cousins, attended the local theatre. The comic opera, 'Geneviève de Brabant,' had, at last, come to Plymouth, and was creating quite a *furore* there. I was greatly amused at hearing the Plymouth people aping at superiority. It is a cliquey place, and ladies go in sets, and have a strong objection to know some beautiful Mrs. Smith or fascinating Mrs. Brown, because they are not considered good enough for *them*. They tell you " So-and-So is not in society," and when you ask why not, their reasons are as childish and absurd as a sane person can well imagine. I have an idea that petty jealousy has something to do with it. The Plymouth people in this respect resemble the Bostonians of the United States. I met some dear, nice people in the Western capital, and a great number of very silly ones.

Plymouth boasts of a famous Club, one of the best of its kind out of London. It is select, quiet, and surprisingly moderate in its charges. The advantages to officers temporarily stationed here are immense. For a small fee you are admitted an honorary member, enjoying all the privileges of an ordinary member. I can quite understand Plymouth becoming one of the most important towns in England before many years; but it is a pity that idle gossip carries so much sway with the multitude, and that scandal is gloried in to the extent it is. I think I should prefer Plymouth when it is a little older, and is not quite so primitive in all its dealings. As to the lower classes, they are the scum of the land, and are unequalled in wickedness and ignorance in any place in England I was ever at. With all this there is a vast amount of hypocrisy and cant, sickening to behold.

Travelling on through Cornwall, I found rest for a time near Falmouth. My uncle met me at the station, and drove me half-a-dozen miles through a fine country to his house, where I received a warm welcome from a staunch household. I left Cornwall (which, by-the-bye, is my native county) when I was a small boy, twenty years previously, and this was my first return to it. I had passed through unheard-of dangers and vicissitudes in that short time to make many an older man's hair turn grey, or bring him to an untimely grave. I was, consequently, overjoyed to visit the scenes of my youth, and greet those remaining of my own blood who were near and dear to me; and I shall never forget the cordial reception I received from all my many belongings, both great and small, old and young, tall and short. I visited the place of my birth, Truro, and then on to the Cornish watering-place, Perran Porth, where I lived a week of rural enjoyment, and made some friends, true and loyal, who will last me for my lifetime.

Much as I like Cornwall, there can be no denying that, in point of civilization, it is very far behind the age. The people are honest and frugal, with pious, mild tastes, and easily satisfied; and as to Falmouth and Truro, they are as far behind the "*first*" of Plymouth as that ancient borough is behind London. People actually attempt to be particular in this out-of-the-way part of civilization! Perhaps they ape the Plymouth folk, speak of "cliques," and "sets," and "society," as something beyond my comprehension. I was always under the impression that if a man was considered a gentleman he was good enough for any gentleman's society; but they have adopted caste in these parts, and a series of different grades, which is most puzzling and ludicrous at first to a novice.

Devon and Cornwall are famous for the exceeding beauty of the fair sex. Plymouth is pre-eminent in this respect, and sports as fine a show of graceful maidens as any city in England. It is notorious for its illustrious charmers, and its superiority for women cannot be denied, nor is it exaggerated. The Cornish girls are not so unsophisticated either in worldly matters as one would naturally imagine in such an isolated part of humanity. They are keen, self-possessed, portraying diplomacy, with a considerable display of self-complacency, real taste, love of beauty, and are neat and elegant in their attire. As a rule, they are good tempered, bearing little envy and jealousy. The older the sex the more this is seen; but the very worst of them are bountiful and good-natured at heart.

Although there are some grand specimens of my countrymen, they are, take them all round, narrow-minded, obstinate and overbearing, fond of cant, soft-hearted, and not unlike the English characteristic in being manly withal. The lower classes, as a rule, are the most honest in all England, temperate in their habits, and courteous in their manners. You seldom hear of a labouring man addicted to drink, or using bad language. The local sailors and fishermen along the Cornish coasts are all alike in this respect. I attribute this state of things in a great measure to their mode of religion, which is simple, and quite what they can understand. The bad cases you hear of are generally of Church-going men. It may be hard to say so, but then it is the truth, and nothing opposed to it is the truth. Not that I care more for the Methodists, or ever attended one of their meetings, or know much about them beyond the facts here recorded. The common statement made by the clergy is, I know, at variance with what I maintain. But then they are prejudiced, and, if they thought differently, they could hardly be free to speak of what they know to exist. I am an unbiassed outsider, and, although occasionally I lose the esteem of some sterling good man, I cannot refrain from being candid and honest in my language.

The vulgar idea prevailing amongst many of my friends is that it is not genteel or fashionable to believe in anybody but their own spiritual adviser; and, without further questioning, they consider this individual immaculate, and his language in the pulpit infallible. It is a sign of palpable weakness or gross ignorance, when they consider it a crime to think and read out of the old, old groove. How much more noble and grand my countrymen might be if they were not grounded in a false doctrine, which is connected in some way with nearly every event of their daily life!

Then, again, how absurd it is to hear some influential country gentleman lay down the law, and assert his arrogance and ignorance of certain constituted laws of the realm, when he has never read a single line of Political Economy; and condemns standard works and the greatest men of logic and metaphysics this or any age hath produced! And when you ask him for his reasons in thus denouncing them wholesale, he can give you no reason; and, on inquiry, you find he knows no more about them than he does of the man in the moon.

CHAPTER XI.

AFTER making the acquaintance of some very nice people, old friends of the family, I left Falmouth for Dublin by steamer, and experienced a little rough weather in the Irish Sea. I met one or two extremely pleasant passengers, whose friendship I renewed, and we became fast friends. One in particular, a charming young widow of great personal attractions, and of an enlarged and culti- vated mind. We got to know each other so well from the fact of her husband having been a dis- tinguished Indian officer. There is a strong free- masonry running through all Anglo-Indians and their families, and you have only to declare your- self as coming from the East for Indians to receive you with open arms. I was invited to her father's house, a pretty place, just out of Dublin, and expe- rienced that open-handed hospitality peculiar to the generous Irish. The bright, joyous faces of dark- eyed Erin's daughters did much to endear me to the "Savage Islanders"; and I began to think if this was what they were like, I should get on admirably with a people so wrongly cried down.

At Kingstown I met Fitzmore, whose illness prevented him from carrying out his intended cruise; and he was ordered quiet and rest. I saw what severe dissipation had wrought for the poor fellow, and unless he were to give up his usual excitement, it would go hard with him. The American war-boat, "Congress," was lying off Kingstown, and a visit to see the orderly state of the vessel, and experience the civility of her officers, was not thrown away, and gave one an idea of the tone of the United States Navy. Kingstown is a fashionable place, with great attractions.

I was somewhat disappointed with Dublin. It certainly has many grand institutions, noble buildings, parks, and streets; but I expected something more. I was intensely amused to witness the profound contempt the authorities bore towards the Home - Rulers. These beauties talk wildly, and without interference on the part of the Police, provided they don't get over-boisterous and demonstrative in their zeal for liberty. Their definitions of the rights of freedom are absurdly extravagant. I am afraid if such privileges were extended to them, they would annihilate each other like Kilkenny cats before Parliament assembled. The wretched state of things existing is mainly due to their excessive ignorance, false religion, love of indolence, and whisky, which madden an excitable race like the Irish to commit the most awful deeds. They are a queer conglomeration of mixed people of mixed views. I have come across classes of men in Dublin I hardly knew from Italians,—their fine-cut features and mode of behaviour were identical. All this vanished, of course, when you heard them speak.

The middle and lower grades of society scarcely ever succeed in their own country. Abroad they rise to eminence and power. Some of England's greatest warriors, statesmen, scholars, judges, governors, and captains, have been Irishmen. The noblest specimens of the human race are to be found amongst the Irish, and also the lowest type of civilized humanity. What is to be done for raising this great section of our poor countrymen? Compulsory education, or expulsion? In their present state they are not only a nuisance to themselves, but to society at large. They have equal advantages with the rest of the people, but their stupidity blinds their reason. It is as humbling to the pride of human wisdom for the ordinary Irish agitator to discuss politics as it is for a clergyman to venture forth in theological argument.

Leaving Dublin by the 9 A.M. express, I reached Nenagh, after sundry changes and stoppages, about two in the afternoon. The speed of trains in Ireland is nothing extraordinary, and, as in Cornwall, they are often an hour or so late. As my people, living a few miles out in the country from Nenagh, did not expect me, I took a jaunting-car at the railway station, and, making friends with Pat, the driver, I was greatly amused at his wonderful stories of the different families in the vicinity, my own relations included. Pat had not the slightest idea who I was, and I did not conceal my being English, which put him off the scent.

"And it's to Allut yer honor would go? Sure there's not a *bolder* family in all the counthry round. And a great general the father was, and his father before him, and the present man's a darling and his dear lady and their happy family, and it's kind and good they are to the poor. Faith, you couldn't go to see better people."

It was satisfactory to know that they were all appreciated by the tenantry. I had heard most alarming stories of landlords and masters being shot from behind hedges, and occasionally the wrong man was "potted" for the landlord, and I own I was not at all ambitious to meet my death in this way. My Dublin friends informed me I was sure to be shot if I went to Nenagh; it was a most barbarous place for Fenians. I am able to say, though, I was agreeably surprised to find such contentment and happiness prevailing amongst all classes. I received a hearty welcome from my people, and I was soon quite at home with the whole household, which comprised, as usual, many visitors. The houses are very far apart in this part of Ireland, and you are dependent, to a great extent, on your own resources for amusement and pleasure. We accepted invitations to see a regatta at St. David's, on Lough Dergh, which commands a magnificent view of a wide expanse of water, and which resembled, on the occasion of our visit, a perfect sea. Some two hundred of the *élite* of the county were guests of the gallant Captain. The "Countess" distinguished herself a third year by coming in first, and, consequently, winning the cup. Amongst the guests was the notorious Lord Avonmore. The day's doings were brought to a very successful issue.

A day of great rejoicing comes once a year to Allut, when the young heir is petted, congratulated, and made much of on attaining another birthday. It was my good fortune to be present at one of these entertainments. Rows of flags, banners, and decorations lined the roadway leading to the house. The tenantry were invited for the day's amusement, followed by a sumptuous feast, which was duly appreciated; and when they made themselves scarce, the "gentry" terminated the carnival by dancing and other revelry to a late hour.

In Sussex I initiated the Hantons, at whose house I was stopping, into the mysteries of our Indian games, "Polo" and "Badminton." Here I started paper-chases and hockey, and rare fun we had at times. One run in particular I shall not easily forget.

Tipperary is deservedly designated the Garden of Ireland. Some delightful drives we took along the Shannon to beyond Killaloe, where we "tiffed" in the Bishop's grounds. The Cathedral adjacent is a quaint old place, of the twelfth century. On another occasion we went to Cloughjordan (pronounced Clockjudan!). The scenery is equally interesting, but of a different nature. The wet climate is Ireland's worst feature. But we were singularly fortunate, in a trip to the Lakes of Killarney, in having glorious weather for such a country as the Emerald Isle. We broke the journey at Limerick and Mallow, where there is a spa well, famous for its waters for consumptive people; and an abbey of some celebrity, with adjoining woods, stocked with deer, and prettily laid-out grounds; with a queer, old-fashioned dirty township stretched out below, similar, in many respects, to hundreds of other towns throughout Ireland of equal significant calibre! We reached the Lakes an hour after leaving Mallow, and put up at the Muckross Hotel, where there was an extraordinary collection of mixed people, Yankees predominating. The following day our party visited Muckross Island, Mr. Herbert's magnificently-arranged grounds, on which is the familiar ruined abbey, and noted views from the surrounding peaks and eminences.

On Lord Kenmare's property stands the far-famed Castle. Crossing the Big Lake, one comes upon a series of juvenile islands. We take a look at O'Sullivan's Well, some ruins, and an abbey of great antiquity, with very fearful legends attached to every sequestered stone of the dilapidated remains. A tree is pointed out which the Prince of Wales planted when visiting these haunts in company

with his much-lamented father.   The cottage the
Queen stopped at with the rest of the Royal family
on the occasion of her visit to the Lakes, a quarter
of a century back, is called after Her Majesty, and
an establishment is still kept on, and is quite
prepared for the reception of Royalty.   An auto-
graph book, containing the signatures of celebrated personages, visitors to these parts, is kept
in the Queen's bed-room.   " Victoria," " Albert,"
" Albert Edward," " George," &c., head the first
page, and dozens of the great and mighty follow.
Occasionally a Smith and Tomkins have forced
their imperial signatures in between those of dukes
and princes of the blood of every nation.   The
book is already valuable to people who have a taste
for collecting autographs, and should be taken
greater care of, as a leaf or two could be easily
removed.   Tomkins and Smith pride themselves
that their embellished names should be handed
down to a grateful posterity amongst the sovereigns
and potentates of the enlightened nineteenth century; and it would greatly disappoint these illustrious personages if they heard anything had
happened to the book in question, and that the
ages yet to come should be no wiser that they
lived, moved, and had their being.

The following morning we drove to Dunlow, and
walked through the Gap.   The scenery is wild, but
not beautiful.   There are huge, high spurs, devoid
of life, with nothing to recommend them but their

bleakness,—a most absurdly overrated, rocky, monotonous, uninteresting, walk; and I never wish to see the Gap of Dunlow again. A few Irishmen came out at different points along our path, and fired little guns, blew trumpets, and shrieked like lunatics to hear the re-echo taken up and repeated over and over again. I was told the most disreputable of them had made sufficient money to sell his post, and was contemplating retiring into private life. The women, dressed in the oldest style, follow you for miles, asking for money or wishing to sell you goats' milk, which all are expected to drink who visit these parts.

I met some very agreeable gentlemen in my sojourn here, who were leading Liverpool barristers. They accompanied us in our excursion round the Gap of Dunlow. We lunched on an island just above one of the upper lakes, where the scenery is remarkably varied and beautiful; and so it is down the several courses of water and lakes. Shooting the rapids is very pleasant, and one wishes it presented more of this novelty. As we passed the bridge spanning the only outlet to the big lake, the wind blew cold and strong.

Our guide, who had been trumpet-blowing the old familiar air peculiar to the Lakes of Killarney all the way down the channel, for the distant mountain-sides to take up the echo and resound it a score of times over, was now greatly fatigued, and so commenced talking. Every corner and spur we came upon was connected with some rambling story which we had heard before, and, let us hope, unfounded, as most of them were "quite too awful" for our lady friends to hear.

During our visit to Killarney, the Dowager Countess of Kenmare was interred in the family vault. It caused universal regret amongst all classes, as her Ladyship had been very philanthropic and benevolent to the multitude of poor which exist in these localities. The Dowager died a Roman Catholic.

We stopped at Cork on our return. Robinson's Theatrical Company were here, and created a great sensation. But, during the piece, ' Ours,' the band struck up 'The National Anthem,' which the savages hissed at, and, failing to stop the music, pipes and missiles came whizzing at the heads of the bandsmen. Such occurrences were put a stop to; but the people of Cork showed their abhorrence at anything loyal or national when an opportunity presented itself. Some nice houses are on the heights overlooking Cork. We visited Queenstown, and admired the view from many points on the rising ground to the left, where a more extensive sight presents itself. The scenery is, on the whole, exceedingly beautiful. We were well received by friends at more than one house in the suburbs of Cork, where we met with the usual hospitality and general Irish kindness.

The fame of the beautiful girls of Limerick has spread throughout all lands, and they are not behind their more numerous sisters at Dublin in point of grace and elegance. I was agreeably surprised to find it even exceeded all I had heard. Go out between two and five of an afternoon, and mark the lovely creatures which you meet in the streets! Every other one at least will be handsome in features, elegant, graceful and stylish in deportment, and sweet and amiable in all her dealings. English girls, as a rule, are a little jealous of their sisters of the Emerald Isle, and well they may be.

A lady at Tenby once told me, that in her opinion "real beauties were so uncommon in England, that it was not to be wondered at that when a girl was beautiful, and was admired, she lost her head, and became conceited and horrid. There are so few," she added, " compared to the numerous charming faces you meet with in Ireland. Take any dozen ordinary girls of both countries, in the same station, of life, and see which are the more advanced in accomplishments, duties, and beauty." We waited for our good host, but found he had preceded us; so we pushed on, and reached Allut, tired and worn. But a warm greeting did much to soothe our weary and exhausted party, which had become less from Cork.

I had some letters awaiting my return—one from Charles Hanton, urging me to leave as soon as possible for our trip to America, as the season for travelling in the States commenced in September. He wrote that he had come across one or two decent

Oxford men who were bent on a trip to America, and possibly his friend, Sir S. Hoote, would join us at New York or Quebec for a journey to California, and round by the West Indies. Of course I wrote, and told him "the more the merrier," and fixed the day and steamer per Cunard's line.

One of the happiest days I spent in Tipperary was at Michrond, where an assemblage of one hundred people were collected in order to play the delightful game of croquet, which, however, did not come about owing to a tremendous down-pour of rain, which kept us all indoors; and when the major part and old folk disappeared, a dance was talked of, which came off to the delight of all present.

The silver-mines in the neighbourhood would succeed admirably if properly worked; the whole process was most interesting, and we were much edified at our visit to the works.

Lord D. very kindly gave me the run of his preserves, and put everything at my disposal; but I found out afterwards, as in Kent and Wales, the shooting at home is but tame after India. Game is either very scarce or so plentiful that it is simply murder, and you can shoot down partridges and pheasants as easily as cocks and hens in a poultry-yard. What sport is there in this any more than in stalking tame deer, who, if they see you, will approach you for food? A year in Oudh would spoil one for shooting in Europe. In India you can get anything from a snipe to a tiger without much trouble, when in season.

Lord D. was in a terrible state of mind, as his only son, an officer in the Rifle Brigade, had been ordered to Ashantee, and he was not at all ambitious his son should join the Expedition. His fears for his health were quite unnecessary, as it turned out; for, although his Lordship went to Madeira to be near the seat of war if anything happened, his gallant son returned all the better for his trip— a renowned soldier, crowned with laurels, · to be honoured and welcomed by the whole county.

I was immensely amused to hear of some of my cousins at Allut, quite young children, having had some altercation amongst themselves, in which it would appear that in signing the terms of peace most of the blame fell to the share of their dolls, whereupon they sat in solemn conclave to adjudicate what was to be done to the delinquents, when two of the favourites were missing. This created a tremendous stir, and it was understood those present must have cruelly murdered them. They were immediately tried by drum-head court-martial, and the servant and governess going in, found the unhappy dolls hanging by their necks from the backs of chairs. Young Ireland!

I was anxious to see how justice was dispensed in this part of the Queen's dominions, so I attended the Court on the occasion of a full bench of J.P.s presiding. I was allowed to take my seat along with them. All was very grave when the proceedings commenced, but before long it became a very laughable performance. Every magistrate was divided as to the guilt of the unfortunate prisoner; some thought he ought to be hanged, others were not satisfied with the evidence, and begged a further cross-examination; others objected on the plea of its not being legal; while others spoke in strong terms of the man's innocence. The consequence was, he was sent up to be tried by the Sessions Court, where it is to be hoped he was legally dealt with.

The cases which were brought up on the occasion of our visit were two larceny ones, which were summarily dismissed, as nobody could agree. One of the prisoners was proved innocent of the charge brought against him, and yet some cautious magistrate warned him, and, in discharging him, told him not to do it again! There was an old stabbing case, where the man was allowed to go on bail, and was amongst the tenantry who joined in the festivities at Allut already alluded to. Two for selling intoxicating liquors on the Sabbath during the hours of Divine worship. The evidence of one witness, which was the most important, all hinged on his being able to see through a key-hole. On a little reflection, it was clearly proved impossible to see what was going on in a dark room from the street-door key-hole!

The low Irish of these parts appeared very partial

to have some trivial private matters arbitrated by a counsel of J.P.s. They displayed in their evidence the most gross deception, and vile, cunning traits possible ; and I never thought I should find any race so degraded in point of morals and truth as certain classes in India. Afterwards I visited the jail, in company with the Governor. Everything appeared cleanly and well kept, the prisoners were under good discipline and organization, looked happy, and at home.

A few more pleasant days with loving friends, and occasional pleasant excursions, brought my visit to a close, and I left Tipperary with many fond, sad longings, which will live for ever on my memory.

I stopped at Limerick on my way through, and visited the Cathedral and the principal places of interest in the town, and met a few old friends. On my journey by train here, I had the honour of travelling with two very noted Roman Catholic priests, who immediately made a dead set upon me. I am of opinion they must have taken me for some one else. They tried all in their power to convince me of the truth of their faith. Not thinking it worth the trouble to attempt to argue with them, I readily enough agreed to some plain propositions, which were put forward as arguments to build up their fabric of elaborate formulæ. They caught me fairly enough in a well-planned syllogism, and were so greatly elated at their small victory, that they devised a scheme to accompany me on, as they were sure their powers were beginning to work. I assented to their proposal, saying how glad I should be of their pleasant company. Finding I was not the individual they took me for, or I was not worth converting, they left me after many regrets, each exchanging cards. I am informed the Holy Romans have some of their most taking fascinating priests sent out on missions of conversions by different trains, to bring home an occasional lost sheep to their fold.

I had a most agreeable time at Cork, and had the pleasure of meeting some long-established acquaintances, and keeping up a farewell party at the "Imperial," till the time came round for me to be off to catch the train for Queenstown, to meet the "Algeria" from Liverpool. Charlie and I embraced when we met, and he introduced me to a few bright specimens of Oxonians bound on a three months' jollification to the States. Sir S. Hoote was also on board, and all things seemed probable for our having a most delightful trip.

Amongst the ships starting from Queenstown was an emigrant one; and although I was greatly rejoiced to see dear Hanton again, I could not but watch these poor Irish, who were leaving their native land, perhaps for ever, under the most distressing circumstances. The parting of parents from their children; brothers, sisters, lovers, wives, husbands, the young, who were full of spirits for the future, the aged and broken-down, looking forward to theirs, the grave!   A more sad sight I never before witnessed.   But it is a good thing for the low class of Irish to emigrate; as I have already remarked, they are generally discontented with their native land, and get on so much better when out of it.

CHAPTER XII.

OUR passengers were mostly well-to-do Yankees, who had been spending without stint the almighty dollar in England and on the Continent, and were full of new speculations and ideas of our country-men. We form very erroneous notions of the great element and backbone of the supporters of the American Republic. I am not carried away by any false sentiment on this head, but I affirm, for the sake of truth and justice, that we have a very wrong and one-sided impression of Yankees gene-rally. The people who speak so disparagingly of Americans have only met one or two bad specimens, and, from hearsay gossip, condemn a whole nation. Out of the scum of the United Kingdom, the refuse of society, rebels, villainous speculators, and the spawn of convicts, the most powerful and growing Government of the age is formed. She is quite in her infancy still; as a babe she opposed her mother, and went her own way. It has been all up-hill work with her. She has never met with encouragement from England, or from but few of her children. In a few short years she has, out of her own resources, built up a mighty nation, vying with the oldest constituted Powers of Europe.

If Americans have not in manners all that love of beauty and refinement, elegance and polish, of English gentlemen, they are not behind us in novelty and power of invention. Their schemes for the general improvement and welfare of mankind are beyond us in many respects. They grasp the most prodigious ideas, challenging comparison with anything we have done, with a boldness equal to any emergency; and display unheard-of perseverance, ingenuity, and a nobleness of purpose in all things, which afford lessons to the world at large. I freely admit· I was at one time exceedingly prejudiced against Americans. I had been brought up in an atmosphere where I had always heard them cried down and abused, and I began to think there must be truth in the vulgar belief. I was more than agreeably surprised, I was amazed, to find some Americans actually *gentlemen!*—with tastes, inclinations, manners, customs, and ideas truly English, were profound scholars, and men of the most refined habits, who had travelled all over the globe, knew many languages and many nations. These quiet Americans pass through England without creating any notice. The noisy, shoddy class of " bagmen " poisons our minds against Yankees; but I doubt if this stamp of people are more objectionable than our London snob. And then we infer the dishonesty of Americans, as if there were no rogues in England! We should think it very foolish of Americans if they were to condemn Britishers because they have been unfortunate in believing in "Lord Gordon," or call them a nation of impostors, with "Sir Roger Tichborne" at their head! There is more wickedness perpetrated in New York, perhaps, than in any other civilized city; but, mind you, how much of our rubbish we have shot there, and cleared from our *own* doors!

It is wonderful, considering all things, that any order can be maintained in many great places in the United States. It only shows how vigilant the authorities must be at work to suppress anarchy and promote good government. There can be no denying it is not without its faults, and there is greater bribery and corruption existing than with us; but, then, see the stuff you have to deal with. Yet there are some very noble and sincere men at heart at the head of affairs, who work only for the public weal.

Instead of Americans being jealous of us, I think we have cause to be jealous of them. Anyhow, we have much to learn from them, with all our boasted ideas of constituted laws. I took a great pride in thinking such a people belonged so much to us, that certain of the spawn of convicts have so far reformed as to be most delightful companions, are called by many of our own names, believe in our national religion, speak our language, and copy us in various good institutions, and, I regret to say, too closely in many of our vices.

I had heard that the Americans gloried in funny

stories and relating pithy sayings, and, sure enough, before we were clear of Queenstown, that particular set of Yankees who delight in hearing themselves talk congregated together, and drew forth from each other an unheard-of string of amusing anecdotes.

"Well, Captain," said one of them, "did you ever hear of the skipper who picked up a boat's crew when crossing the pond from Liverpool to New York? These men were actually pulling over in an open boat for a wager!" And in describing the occurrence, a Yankee sailor present said,—"Wall, Captain, I couldn't credited that story if I hadn't been one of the crew!" The American slang is peculiar to themselves. They call crossing the Atlantic " sneaking over," and the ocean itself " the herring-pond." We generally make Yankees figure in certain of our jokes. They put Englishmen in where they want pig-headedness and foolery to figure.

A story goes how a certain worthy Britisher wrote to Mark Twain to know whether eating largely of fish was a good thing for the strengthening and developing of the human brain, and, if so, what quantity was it necessary to consume to bring this happy state of things about. Mark Twain, in reply, said he had heard fish was a most excellent thing for the brain; and, secondly, as to the quantity necessary to take, judging from the style of the composition, and what he knew of the Englishman, he should think if he took about two ordinary-sized whales it might have the desired effect.

A day or two after we were at sea it began to blow a bit; and one morning early, whilst taking our usual walk before breakfast, we noticed an uncommonly bilious Yankee, who sat perched up, looking dreadfully ill. We had compassion upon him, and asked him how he was getting on. He said "he really didn't know, but if he could only get hold of that er crittur who wrote them darned lines, 'A Life on the Ocean Wave,' he guessed he would chuck him overboard." A sick German here came forward, and said,—"There ish mash nawn-shence in sangs," and, for his part, he should like to see "Britannyer ruling the infarnal vaves better." He observed they were generally "ruf; all oversh de plase ven I comdsh to de vater."—"I guess it will be mighty fine day afore I'm seen sneaking the pond," remarked the sickly Yankee, catching hold of the sides of the brass capstan to prevent slipping away, as the ship gave a lurch, and a double cross wave struck her amidships, going clean over her, and wetting the whole of us. "What pleasure can there be in all this?" asked the Yankee invalid, looking more concerned than ever, as he firmly seized with both hands the railing, balancing him-self as he spoke. I could not refrain from laughing, and in doing so lost my hold. The great steamer, which was tossed about like a cork on the water, gave an extra lurch, and I was thrown with great violence against the sky-lights. I bounded off, as the vessel gave another roll and a pitch, and away I went the whole length of the deck, coming to a sudden stoppage amongst coils of rope and iron near the side hatchway.

On recovering myself after this very undignified proceeding, I looked up and found Hanton and a few Americans with hands extended, and kindly inquired if I was at all hurt. "No," I said, "not much; but I feel uncommon queer." When I came up to my sick Yankee friend, he grinned, saying,— "Well, stranger, you were in a tidy hurry to get over that last journey of yours. I guess all conceit was knocked out of you on landing in that er fashion. As neat a performance as ever I saw." I must confess I felt somewhat bruised; and Hanton suggested a "peg," which is a universal panacea with him for everything.

I had a long talk with one of our passengers, Mr. Gerald Massey, the poet, and author of some scientific books. He was on his way to lecture in America on various subjects. He is an original thinker, of some depth, but I cannot agree with him in some of his theories. In speaking of the development of the human race, he has some notion that he can trace all languages and religions back through the ancient mythology to a remote period in the Egyptian era. That as man worshipped "*ma*," so women, long before we can have any idea of time or origin, worshipped and did homage to man. Hence the idea of a plurality of gods.

In the evening the learned lecturer read us an original paper of his "On Wit and Humour," of which he has a very just appreciation. He is a good plain speaker in public, and reads without using auxiliaries. The amount of the collection was devoted to some Seamen's charitable fund.

The cold up to the time of our entering the Gulf Stream had been very severe. The difference of the temperature was most marked, and it was as warm now as it had before been cold. The cabins became suffocating, and I lived on deck as much as possible.

I became acquainted with a Mr. Carter, of New York, a most refined and polished American gentleman. He was very orthodox in all his views, and his visit to England had strengthened those ideas, which required balancing. Some Colonels of the United States Southern Army were of our number, but I was greatly disappointed to find that they were not the gentlemen the Yankees were. This I know to be contrary to the received opinion; but whatever the Southerners might have been, I did not find them equal to the New Yorkers and Bostonians; and it stands to reason that as most of them have lost considerably by the late war, they have not the means and opportunities of travelling, and keeping themselves up with the literature of the day, to the extent of the enterprising Yankee.

An ill feeling still lingers between the Northerners and Southeners. The officers of the army of the latter State, who fought against the Washington yoke, are men of a very inferior stamp to our officers of a similar rank. Those who held important commands were totally unacquainted with gunnery or engineering formulæ, and had but a rude smattering of cavalry and infantry drill. They invariably denounced our policy with regard to the Alabama claims, and considered " our action premature, due to England's weak ministers," who, had they held out for the original proposition, the treaty must have been adopted. At the period of their submitting their claims, they were, according to Southerners, " ill prepared to compete with Great Britain in a national struggle, and annihilation of every port and town along the coast, from New York to New Orleans, wherever the flag was opposed, would have ended another phase of the notorious claims." I have the firmest belief in our navy and our staunch little army, but I was not so confident of success as the unlucky Southerners.

The *élite* of American society never mix in politics. The country is ruled by the mass of the lower classes—the rabble, the mob. What refined gentleman would soil himself by coming in contact with such as these ? Their votes are bought and sold, and bribery and corruption have an easy time of it in many quarters. It is a great shame of the United States Government that they do not hold out greater inducements to literary and scientific men of distinction for offices of state. Although there are some pure-minded men in Congress, diplomatic adventurers are generally actuated by mercenary motives. It would be a wise step if public honours were awarded to great talents, and superior attainments were adequately compensated, instead of being excluded by the ruling powers. All stimulus to intellectual labour is practically ignored,—an evil which can only be remedied by supplying ins titutions for mental exertion, whereas in Prussia and Austria they are the greatest bulwarks of a nation's strength, nobleness, and power.

The Americans as a people are essentially a practical race. Very little sentiment they encourage. Complete emancipation of every kind of superstition they endeavour to aim at; they sneer at theories which cannot be turned to some account in the money line; and stop nowhere in their gigantic speculations in science and craft, always provided their prodigious plans and schemes will yield a fair return of the almighty dollar, which they dearly love—not more so, though, than certain Englishmen and Scotchmen love sovereigns.

It was a glorious day as we steamed in close under Long Island, and up the magnificent harbour of New York, its waters alive with crowded steamers, of ponderous dimensions, passing, crossing, deviating in all directions. Well-dressed, orderly throngs were to be seen moving in the streets. As I drove up Broadway to the Fifth Avenue Hotel, I should not have known I was not in some part of Oxford Street, if it had not been for the flag of the stars and stripes floating from every principal edifice, and I knew I was no longer in any portion of Queen Victoria's dominions, but in a Republican land, where every man was as good as his neighbour, and liberty, equality, and fraternity, those boasted words of no meaning, are the order of the day.

CHAPTER XIII.

If Americans excel in anything it is in their hotels, which are simply magnificent mansions fitted up with every comfort and luxury. Nearly all our friends preferred going to the Windsor Hotel, which is one of the most princely palaces in America, and very far superior to either the Clarendon or the Fifth Avenue. These latter hotels are somewhat larger than the Gloucester or the Langham of London, which will give some idea of their enormous size and gigantic arrangements for feeding a continued string of people from 6 A.M. to 12 at night without a second's break; though I cannot approve of their fare, which is generally execrable. But more of this anon.

Hanton ordered a "four-wheeler" to be ready at two, to take us to pay some official calls. The vehicle in question was an ordinary New York cab, but about a quarter the lightness of our conveyances, fitted up superbly, with a movable hood and front. The lightness of the buggy was only equal to its strength. Nothing was out of place or superfluous. It was drawn by a handsome pair of fast trotters, and the driver was neatly dressed, after the manner of our own men.

We paid West Point a visit, and delivered certain letters of introduction, which turned out to be of immense advantage to us. We were most kindly received by the officers of the scientific corps, and were shown over the Academy, similar to our Woolwich one. Their system appears admirable, and, in some things, I think I prefer it to our training. The practical mode of organization is eminently advantageous, and the vast superiority of their new officers over the old school is self-evident. Apart from the very high intellectual order of the cadets of the scientific departments of the services, the gentlemanly tone of the officers of this important branch of the army has undergone a complete change for the better; and the military engineers of the United States Government would be a credit to any nation, and certainly are one of the finest professional corps in the world. With their profound training, they have lofty notions of *esprit de corps*, are kept well informed of every new invention, and a love for their noble profession, which is very pleasing to behold.

The old officers of line regiments are, as a rule, I regret to say, rude, ignorant, and not worth cultivating. A few of the superior ones are well enough in their way, but nearly all delight to turn England into ridicule and contempt, which shows that they can be officers without being gentlemen. The more ignorant the man, the greater his hatred will be towards England. But not a word disparagingly of the mother country did I ever hear fall from an officer who had been educated at the Academy at West Point. They are perfect gentlemen, and duly appreciate the grand old institutions, masters, and scholars of Great Britain. If the American army makes as rapid reforms in the other branches of its services as it has done in the Artillery and Engineers corps, or in the ·Naval and Maritime departments, nations will look up to her with dread and awe as one of the first powers of the world.

Under the strictest discipline the Yankee loafers would make splendid soldiers if officered by men of the same mental calibré as their gunners and engineers. But the severest order would have to be maintained to rule and hold in check such a lawless scum as the general run of their lower soldiery. Never was there an army which required such weeding, such radical improvements, to make it at all efficient, and bring it up to the standard of some of the Continental Powers. And America could do this very easily, for she has money, talent, and advantages few nations possess, besides having the stuff in her rough supporters to work up into a great and mighty army.

In the evening we attended Booth's Theatre, and saw the celebrated actress, Miss Mitchell. She is considered by the New Yorkers one of the best actresses they have on the stage, but in London she would be thought only a third-rate one. The building itself is of good size, and remarkably well got up. At Wallack's Theatre, Sothern, better known as "Lord Dundreary," was making great running, and went down tremendously with the Yankees, as most London actors do. I thought he had somewhat fallen off in his acting, overdid it at times, and was slovenly in his style and language, to say nothing of unguarded expressions which he used to the prejudice of propriety and good order.

It is a common belief amongst my countrymen that the very fact of going to America or mixing with the Yankees must necessarily contaminate one. No one but a verysilly person could entertain such a notion for an instant. Of course, if an individual is so constituted as to prefer coarseness to refinement, ignorance to knowledge, baseness to manly virtues, there would be no necessity for him going all the way to New York to perfect himself in all that is bad and corrupt when he could attain such qualifications in his own immediate vicinity, in any part of the United Kingdom. A man who is inclined to adopt a rude, vulgar, brutal manner, will do so at home as well as he would by going to America; and a man who is a gentleman at heart will not do himself any harm by even coming in contact with the lowest of the low: his noble nature cannot be contaminated. "To the pure all things are pure."

After seeing everything of importance in New York and its environs, harbour defences and fortifications, we went on a most delightful trip up the Hudson to Albany, the scenery of which is magnificent, and far surpasses in grandeur the absurdly overrated Rhine. We returned to New York in time for the Jerome Races, which were very fair. The trotting matches which followed were entirely new to me. It is very extraordinary that the English do not encourage this sort of sport, which has become quite a national thing with the Americans, and likely to prove of utility in improving the breed of horses.

The Yankees most kindly made us honorary members of four of the leading clubs of New York, and we were able to see for ourselves the tone of the *élite* of their society, which is very select. They are most particular whom they admit into their circles, and never was there a class of people who courted rank and birth to such an extent as the fashionables of New York, Boston, and Washington. The " Upper Ten " pride themselves on being directly descended from the English, and love to talk about Paris, London, and Rome. The idea on which their nation is formed, " Equality," is nowhere more put aside than here. The wealthy, learned, and powerful of the land ape everything English, even to gorgeous liveries for their servants, cockades included. What does this betray? Simply monarchial propensities, Court indulgences, rank conferences, where pomp and show have full swing, and aristocracy is considered an essential necessity.

Of course the most truly noble, learned, and practical meet such notions with a grin and a shake of their head, as if such a state of things was impossible; but I feel convinced that the wealthy *élite* of America will never rest satisfied until rank of some sort is introduced to mark their present ideas of the value they attach to certain favourites of society.

The ladies, of course, have a great deal to say in all this; in fact, they are the prime movers in following up the mode of the fashionable world. Women are not such novices and nonentities in ruling mankind as is generally supposed. Nearly every woman has great power if she would but properly work it; and some do by clandestine or roundabout ways see their wishes carried out. Perhaps the savage despot, the surly sovereign, the determined minister and logical statesman, bigoted priest, and most obstinate husband, may be unconscious all the time of the web which an intelligent, deep woman is capable of entangling round him. The late Lord Lytton was once heard to say most women can understand men, but no man ever yet understood a woman! Instead, then, of their being the weaker sex, they are, in point of fact, the stronger sex. They allow us to carry on the technical and practical part of the business of life while they enjoy the fruits thereof, and reap the benefits of our labours. Poor men!

Nowhere in the civilized world is woman so

valued as in America. She commands, in proportion, more respect; has equal rights, if not greater ones, in her favour. All professions are thrown open to her. She is free and unfettered. Her word, if she has risen at all to note, is considered something of authority, particularly if she belongs to the barrister class; and, however preposterous or gross her views may be, she invariably demands attention. Perhaps the very worst of the advanced school is the notorious Mrs. Victoria Woodhull, who actually stood for the Presidentship of the United States. There is no disputing her talent; but her most ardent admirer would never be able to mistake her for what she is—anything but a lady in language, feeling, or manner.

But there is a wide difference in the class of women, from the gentle and refined *belle* of fashionable society, who studies everything English, and cultivates all that is beautiful in ethics, to the highly objectionable Victoria Woodhull stamp. And if there is this disparity in the minds of their women, there is a similarity in the men which is truly insufferable in the extreme class. I have no very decided objection to hear a man of intellectual capacity speak of " equality, fraternity, liberty," in the form he conceives it to be, in its purity and nobleness, but to hear a version of it from an illiterate brute, who has nothing to recommend him but his coarseness and vile baseness, is simply a waste of time, and an insult to the human understanding.

I met the great English Republican, Mr. Charles Bradlaugh, in my travels in America. After one of his usual monster meetings in New York, I had an opportunity of speaking to him. I told him I was an Englishman, travelling to see the country, and was ever ready to learn. I was anxious to know what would be the result of his visit to the States. He expressed his willingness to tell me all about himself and his mission generally, and was pleased to think I should take an interest in what he deemed of such vast importance. He spoke in very gentlemanly language, and was logical and manly in his theoretical views of universal suffrage. His ideas of religion are somewhat interwoven with politics, which is a mistake, and is likely to mislead the ignorant and vulgar, who are incapable of seeing beyond the surface of things, and who love misconstruing anything and everything which they cannot or will not look into. It is a line of action totally unfitted for him—premature, and wholly misdirected.

If I disagree with him in thus promulgating an anti-religious spirit in the minds of a dissatisfied people, aiming at a higher sphere, unsupported by mental culture, I denounce, *in toto*, his elaborate forms of government for the masses. His universal laws would never answer, unless the illiterate and ignorant were raised in point of knowledge up·to the highest standard of human wisdom. You would require the greatest perfection known to man to understand rightly his extensive code, to the minutest details, of a Republican Government. It certainly does work in a new country like America fairly enough, but that is no criterion to go by for England. We see the evils of it elsewhere in old established monarchial States like France and Spain. You cannot transfer the power of the land from the wealthy and educated to the ignorant and the rabble. Theoretically, it may read logically enough, but it would not answer practically. At all events, not for the present.

There is no country so free, so truly Republican, in the highest sense of the term, as England. And the labouring classes, we may rest assured, are much better off under the present *régime* than if a general scramble was made for offices. Surely a well-educated, sound man, of refined tastes, is better able to administer the affairs of the State than one of their own rough, untutored class. Educate him, if you will, up to the highest standard of mental culture, but don't put him as he is in a place of trust to rule his fellows, until he has acquired some elevation of nobleness. I do not think Mr. Bradlaugh can improve on our present system; and it is a pity a man of such undoubted ability does not leave well alone, and seek office with less preposterous notions. Once in Parliament, he would be all right; for there is no situation more trying to an ambitious man than the House, which brings him down to a proper sense of his own worth and use for the general welfare of his fellow-creatures. He is a man who might be of material good in advancing the rights of the labouring lower classes, and they would find him useful, hardworking, straightforward, and honest.

I had made arrangements with a well-known banking-house in London to draw on a New York bank. On my producing the cheque, the wily Yankee who received it looked at it very suspiciously, and said, " This is all right, but you will have to identify yourself."—" Identify myself!" asked I; " what do you mean?"—" This cheque is made payable to a certain person. I don't dispute that person, but I want to satisfy myself you are that person; and it will be necessary for you to have yourself identified."—" Which I am prepared to do," said a New Orleans merchant, who had escorted me to the bank, taking hold of a pen, and about to attach his name to the back of the cheque as he said so.—" Stop!" I cried. " Never! If you will not believe my statement, I will not be beholden to you for my honesty." And I certainly was rather offended at the banker's way of doing business. So off I went with my cheque, and came to a famed London house, and begged to see the manager, who was a Mason, as I had heard, high and mighty in the craft and of all the orders to the chivalry degree. For the first time in my life I saluted as a brother in distress a Knight of Malta. Behold! it was to some purpose, and I was greeted most affectionately. I then produced my cheque, and asked him if he would cash it. Of course he did so, and gave me a higher premium than that offered me by the bankers.

Freemasonry, then, has been of some use to me. I own I have not attended lodge for a long, long time, and once I was such a keen Mason, and took out every degree, Royal Arch and Knight Templar included, by dispensation, before I was twenty-two. But it was too hot to last, and I dropped it almost immediately. But my advice to my countrymen visiting the States is, become a Freemason, as it will be of immense advantage to any one travelling when far away from civilization, and when you least expect it. I met with the greatest kindness and attention from some leading Yankee Masons, and was received most cordially by various institutions and Grand Lodges throughout the country. I regret I was unable to accept all their invitations and use many of their letters of introduction. Nowhere in the world have I found Freemasonry so encouraged and supported as I have in America. It has become quite a national institution, and the good it does is immense. Much as I disapprove of many of the absurdities and ceremonies of the craft, the charitable part it maintains is not to be denied; and it is what it professes to be, viz., a beautiful system of morality veiled in allegory and illustrated by symbols, where politics and religion are not discussed, and fools and fanatics may freely enter and dispense their charity in hidden mystery.

I visited the far-famed Trinity, Grace, and Christ churches, and attended Divine service at each in turn, and I could hardly believe I was not in English churches. The only things which reminded me of being far away from home were certain passages in the Litany, and prayers for the President and the Government of the United States, instead of for our beloved Queen and the rest of the Royal Family.

In the usual round we took the Rev. H. W. Beecher's Plymouth Church, and were not much edified at his discourse, which was old and commonplace. The building was crowded, and we had the greatest difficulty to effect an entrance and escape being trampled to death. There is nothing new or original about Mr. Beecher, and he is an absurdly overrated genius. Few Americans have the power of a good delivery, and he fails altogether in this respect. One of the greatest living elocutionists I heard in New York, and I knew him personally, was an Englishman, Mr. Bellew. He died lamented in the four quarters of the globe. It seemed strange that a man of such undoubted abilities, who gave all his wealth away to the poor, who never acted or thought unkindly towards any one, should die in poverty, deserted by those whom he made and brought to light in the world of knowledge. Ah! such is life!

What an excellent arrangement the planning and numbering of the streets of New York appears to an

Englishman! With the exception of Broadway, Madison Avenue, and a few others, this noble city is mathematically laid down. The principal thoroughfares are called and numbered "avenues," and the streets at directly right angles are numbered from one upwards. The beauty of this simple arrangement is the facility it affords to new-comers. Instead of prying about, asking stray policemen the way to Fulham Road, Stanley Crescent, or Kensington Gardens Square, you perceive the number of the street on each lamp and corner wall, and, of course, Thirty-three Street is two beyond Thirty-one Street. This is a most admirable arrangement, though I doubt if it would answer for London, as in our metropolis scarcely two streets run parallel; but in the suburbs, where everything is laid down previously, in new towns, as Brighton, and growing watering-places, it would succeed beyond a doubt. When the magnificent bridge is completed over that mighty expanse of water connecting New York and Brooklyn, the whole will be included in one metropolis, and New York will rank amongst the first cities of importance in the world. Instead of an underground railway, the Yankees have a light railway, supported by T iron uprights, some thirty feet in the air, along the Ninth Avenue. A novel way of travelling!

The Americans are very callous to the loss of life. Their enormous steamers, and ferry boats of gigantic proportions, are constantly blowing up, sending hundreds in a moment out of the world. Their light and wooden bridges, of stupendous dimensions, are frequently falling, sometimes when a train is well in the middle. I have passed over some of these doubtful structures when the more particular American passengers, who have set some value on their lives, have exclaimed, quietly, " Thank God! safe over the gulf once more!" as if they were quite prepared to see the whole thing, or, as they call it, " infernal arrangement," come tottering down, killing everybody in its fall. They have, as a nation, distinguished themselves for their steamer collisions, fires, and balloon ascents. I was in New York when some lunatics started off in a balloon to cross the Atlantic. The aëronauts were greatly lionized before starting on their voyage. The ascent was a success, but they descended at a much more rapid rate than they had any intention of doing, and they have been in hospital ever since, hideous spectacles to behold. " Bound to come!" is one of their favourite expressions. It originated from the fact of a gentleman who went up a long way in the air in a balloon, when the whole thing collapsed, and the unfortunate man pursued his travelling in quite the opposite direction. The spectators, who were watching him from *terra firma*, on beholding the mishap, remarked, " He's not here yet, but he is bound to come!" His funeral was largely attended. It is characteristic of certain of our race that we look on the bright side of everything, even to " *Up* in a balloon, boys!" It would, perhaps, be more in harmony with the views of the Americans if they started a pathetic opposition song, " *Down* in a balloon, boys!"

We left one afternoon, at four, in the "Bristol" from Twenty-eight Pier, North End, for Fall River and Newport. This steamer is, I believe, the largest of its kind in the world. It has tier upon tier of saloons, and suites of rooms piled one on the top of the other, fitted up superbly, regardless of expense. But from outside it is an ungainly looking spectacle, and a sort of monster that would appear to you in your dreams if you were troubled with "rats." It has extraordinary accommodation for galleries of loiterers, refreshment stalls, bars, shops; and as there is no motion whatever, you can hardly realize you are shooting through the water at railway speed. Miss Bella Wynter, an actress of some note, distinguished herself by giving a concert in the evening for the benefit of "reformed characters." The donations were munificent. The progress of certain reformatory institutions was read out, and appeared most satisfactory to those who took a keen interest in promoting the welfare of fallen angels. I could not help thinking it was a great encouragement to go to the bad, in order to fully appreciate the evil of it, and to ultimately reform, and be praised and lauded for being like ordinary people once more.

The weather became so boisterous we were compelled to steer clear of points and promontories; but, although there was a tremendous sea on, and the wind blew a gale, it made not the smallest impression on our floating city. I took cabin 92 with Hanton, but, he having to make other arrangements for a berth in an adjoining cabin, the key of my door, which was left on the outside, was turned by some Yankee cad, and, as it was missing, it was presumed it was thrown overboard. I kicked at the door, shouted, and rung the bell off its electric wires, when I disturbed, at last, a person in the next cabin. Luckily there was a door leading into this cabin, and he could, if he was so disposed, let me out. I heard him call out, when he was wide enough awake, " I guess I shall be glad when you have accomplished your exit in that quarter. What has happened to you ? " he angrily inquired.—" I want to get out," I said.—" Well, *get out*, you lunatic asylum," he shrieked, " or else I will d—d soon show you the way out."—" Which I only wish you would do, stranger, for I am locked in, and without your assistance I shall be a prisoner here till the steamer has passed Fall River." He came to the door, and I found my friend quite one of the right sort, and he was greatly amused at the trick that had been played on me. The weather was too rough for us to put in at Newport, so we came on to the railway terminus at Fall River, and caught the morning train for Boston, and reached Tremorne House with a tremendous appetite for a ten o'clock breakfast.

The town of Boston is a bustling, noisy place. The society, as I have already remarked, is of a fastidious turn, and the would-be "Upper Ten" love sentiment and romance. I freely admit that in some cases it is only proper and just to adventurers to be particular. I will speak of them as I found them,—kind, good-natured, intelligent, with an overwhelming opinion, in some instances, of their mighty importance, and their exalted state of perfection in morals, science, and civilization. The most noble and truly charitable people I met with in America are the Unitarian Bostonians. They are very far removed from mean, unmannerly actions, and have the greatest contempt and scorn for those whose lives are one continued course of error and superstition.

I was most kindly shown over the principal places of interest, Bunker's Hill included, where an American observed,—" There is the tallest pillar in the States to commemorate the occasion of our having whipped you Britishers, and kicked your proud army out of America with half their number of rough, untrained Yankees,—as your history will tell you," he added.—I said, " English history only alludes to the great achievements of our forces, and where our troops have proved victorious. We love to dwell on successful battles, and picture our enemy in his worst light, and our brave army slaughtering thousands anyhow as they encounter them. We give several pages up to Agincourt, Assaye, Waterloo, but pass over in a few words the defeats on our side, such as Bunker's Hill. I have heard our version, please tell me yours." And he did so, much to my amusement and Hanton's horror and astonishment, who repeatedly contradicted the American, and told him, in rather strong terms, he was not adhering to facts.

Later on we visited the Naval Dockyard, and were accompanied by an officer of the United States Navy, who most kindly took us over the ironclads, turret-boats, and monitors, the workshops where the "Pennsylvania" is being constructed, the "Vandeleur" dismantled, and several others of huge proportions, of terrible power, are being vigorously pushed on. I questioned a great many of the best mechanics and foremen, and found they were principally Scotch and English, taught and trained, many of them, at Woolwich, Sheffield, and at Sir William Armstrong's factory at Newcastle. The American Government pay them nearly three times as much as they can get in England, hence it is that so many of our best and most valuable hands have left us to construct the most deadly weapons and ships, which one day may be used against us. And is this all our art and science go for in times of peace and plenty—to annihilate and destroy man's ingenuity, when ministers' and rulers' spleens or digestive organs are affected, or their wishes and ambitious ends crossed and thwarted by toadies and under-strappers ?

We received very great kindness and consideration on the part of the naval officers of the United States; and I should class them, in point of knowledge, bearing, and discipline, second to none in the world.

England and America are both much too strong to go to war, and I hope, for all our sakes, it may never come about. It would turn the world upside down for these two powers to decide which was the stronger, and bring ruin and desolation to millions of homes in every quarter of the globe.

Harvard University is a fine building, and turns out some splendid men. Perhaps the greatest wit of the day is to be found in the person of Professor Oliver Wendell Holmes of this College—a man universally beloved and respected for his literary talents on both sides of the Atlantic. Few men of Professor Holmes's high mental calibre have fewer enemies; they can bring nothing home to a mind so pure and lofty. He is a man the Americans may well be proud of. In the evening, we dined with some naval officers; afterwards visited Booth's Theatre, and heard the familiar tragedy, 'East Lynne.' The Bostonians were in raptures with it; just their " size."

The principal fault I found with the American services was allowing too much freedom to exist between officers and men. The greatest kindness they could show their men would be to keep them in their proper place, to allow no undue familiarity, and to insist on more respect off duty. Subordination and discipline are thought cold, cruel, and hard expressions with our cousins. Some are learning it by slow degrees, to their cost. I refer to one of their recent military trials.

We left Boston at 8 A.M. by rail, and travelled in great luxury in Pullman's drawing-room palace cars to Portland, thence by cab to the Grand Trunk Railroad terminus, where we lunched, and proceeded to Richmond in sleeping carriages, in which were arrangeable rows of upper and lower beds when the time came to turn in. We engaged a compartment of the sleeping car to ourselves, as we had not the face to go to bed promiscuously with Yankee ladies and gentlemen. I should be very sorry to see a lady relation of mine travelling in this way. I don't dispute the comfort, the civility of the conductors in charge, nor the orderly behaviour of the passengers, which is beyond question; but, for modesty's sake, I recoil at the very idea of seeing my countrywomen in their midst at such a time. Ladies, married and unmarried, undress before one, and in their night-dresses jump into bed, the gentlemen doing the same, and getting into the upper berths. Of course, if they are married, travelling with their wives, they sleep in the lower berths together, which are large and commodious.

At one we made Richmond; the weather was

bleak and killing when we changed trains; and, the down express having been detained somewhere up country, our train this journey was certainly not "on time," as they choose to call it. In pacing the platform, waiting for the train, we became acquainted with a whole family of New Brunswick people. Two of the girls of the party were remark- ably stylish, handsome, and accomplished. On inquiry, we found they were bound for Quebec and the Falls, and purposed taking much the same route as ourselves. All this was very nice, and the mamma and aunt put the most implicit confidence in us when we told them about ourselves; and we were allowed to escort the young ladies into their compartments, and see they were properly provided for a long journey.

After an early breakfast at Richmond, we took the train, and, passing through somewhat monotonous tracts of the same sort of country as from Boston, we reached Quebec at midday. The hills *en route* to this are of no elevation, and have a wild and deserted appearance. The brushwood and thick undergrowth in places is stunted, and the trees are of no height. The railroad runs through towns and villages with no protection of side railings, fence, or hedge, as is so common elsewhere than in America; no gates at level crossings; and cattle pass to and fro regardless of the danger they incur. The locomotives are of great power and size, provided with cow-catchers, and it is very seldom an engine is thrown off the line when they charge a herd of cattle; it is generally much more "awkward for the cows." The engines are more civilized in the backwoods of America than they are with us. An engine here never forgets itself by whistling you deaf, or shrieking and shouting like a mad thing, on entering a railway station. In fact, they never blow a whistle, but the driver rings a bell on approaching a terminus or passage. Drivers and guards ignore signals during the day, but at night, if they don't attend to "danger" and "caution" signals, they are fined if an accident takes place. The permanent way is simple; no chairs or fish-plates, but the rail nailed down to the sleeper. The ordinary broad gauge is universal. The speed of trains averages (stoppages included) eighteen miles an hour. The jolting and jerking of the train are beyond joking, and, apart from the discomfort, the wonder is that trains do not frequently leave the line. The safety of the enormous cars, sixty and eighty feet in length, is, therefore, established beyond question. Our heavy, bulky, ill-shaped, clumsily built railway carriages would never answer here.

We stopped at St. Louis Hotel in Quebec, but there are really no good hotels worth mentioning out of the United States, with the exception, perhaps, of Toronto, Ottawa, and Montreal. Quebec is an old-fashioned looking town, situated on rising ground. It has one or two good streets, the others are small, pokey, dirty byways. I don't know why, but

Quebec always reminds me of Falmouth, so I suppose there must be a similarity. The heat during the day was intense, reaching 90° in the shade, and at night it was very cold. The town has a population of 80,000, of which nearly 60,000 are French. The suburbs are exceedingly pretty, boasting of fine country-seats of the most important timber-merchants. The drive to the Montmorency Falls is varied and interesting. Neat little cottages of French settlers line the road, and pretty, well-behaved, clean children greet you with flowers for sale at every turn. The settlers in the neighbourhood of Quebec are industrious, steady, orderly people,—different in this respect to the city folk, who are inclined to be noisy and rebellious, particularly at election times.

We had the honour of escorting our New Brunswickians to the Montmorency Falls, which are well worth a visit. I am informed these Falls are considerably the highest in America, although the discharge of water is insignificant compared with many. The scenery is wild and beautiful, and Quebec looks at its best from this point of view. The noble St. Lawrence, alive with boats, steamers, and ships of every nation, appears like a sea. The suspension-bridge overhanging the edge of the Falls was swept away some time back, carrying with it a vehicle and pair of horses, and a man, woman, and child, which were in the act of crossing at the time. Not a vestige was ever seen of anything again. This

Fall, like many others, gets frozen over in the winter, and the icicles formed by the dropping water reach the top, resembling a sugar-loaf. The effect is very beautiful.

On the following day we attended the races; this was but a scratch meet, and the show of horses poor. The betting was confined principally to about a score of men who belonged to the local services. A fair trotting-match followed, the owner being a leading lumber-merchant, who, the driver of our carriage told us, was one of "the blood of the land,"—meaning, I presume, one of the Quebec *élite*. The buggies of this part of Canada are similar to those so common in India, and are called "calâshes."

A magnificent view meets the eye on reaching the citadel: it embraces a tremendous sweep of the surrounding country. One of our party, an Oxonian, thinking we were making such slow progress in our journey, lost all patience with Hanton, and on our return to the hotel we found he had left, with a note to the effect that he had seen quite enough of the United States and Canada, and was off there and then, *viâ* San Francisco, to China, India, and Australia. I heard afterwards they "went" for him out West. Hearing he was troubled with an over-abundance of "stamps," they considered him "mighty elegant game," no doubt. It was his first trip out of England, and probably his last. Poor Taylior! The roads out of Quebec are made of logs of wood, being the cheapest and best for the country. There are some very pretty drives in the neighbourhood, and kind, hospitable people living a short distance from the town.

The Governor-General, Lord Dufferin, was at Quebec on a tour of inspection, and, knowing an officer on his Lordship's staff, we came in for a capital ball, which was given at the Fort, and other amusements which followed in his honour at the citadel. The athletics of Canada, judging from the display I saw at Quebec, were very contemptible in comparison with English sports. Lord Dufferin gave away the prizes. In the afternoon Lady Dufferin opened a bazaar in aid of poor Catholics. The only way we managed to escape the fair sellers was by speaking Hindustani. We were beset by lovely creatures on all sides. I should be sorry to say the amount of money poor Hanton expended on baby's socks and absurdities of a like nature. His handsome face was the general attraction, and resulted in the loss of his purse; but Hindustani quite " stumped " the charmers finally. They produced French, German, Italian, and Spanish linguists; but the strange foreigners, in passing the different passages out, defied them all at last.

In the evening we went to Cool Burgess's theatrical entertainment, which was of a seedy nature; but some of the *troupe* followed up the proceedings the next day by attempting, or threatening, to carry out practically the tragedy part of

'Running A-muck.' This little performance was about to be enacted at our very hotel; but, fortunately in some respects, for the strong arms of Hanton and others, no bloodshed was the result, and peace ensued for the benefit of all parties. Charlie was not so sure it was not a Yankee way of advertising and creating a talk on their behalf. If so, they acted better off the stage than they did on.

The cathedrals and churches of both denominations are well worth seeing, and some fairish oil paintings decorate the walls; one, in particular, at a Roman Catholic place of worship, of an old man with a long white beard resting on a broken cloud, with a garment thrown loosely about it, represented the Creator. I never, in all my travels, saw such a thing. The idea was so strange that I could not refrain from showing how deeply I was affected. The Catholics are very tenacious. You should not gaze too long on some of their best pictures, nor intrude near the altar. They are not so particular anywhere else, and, not knowing the local peculiarities of these people, Hanton and I were ordered away from before a superb representation of the Prodigal Son; but we were quite prepared, and pretended we were deaf and could not understand the warder. The rage the little man got into was most amusing; he beckoned, hissed, and tried to frighten us by looking like a savage tiger. All we did was to stand where we were, and, with a *sans-souci* air, pretend we should like to know the meaning of his gestures and uncalled-for looks.   It was as good as a play to watch Hanton, who in turn beckoned to him to approach us, and then pointed to the picture, as if he was unconscious of its presence. The poor man evidently took us for deranged people; and, when his assistant was brought forward, who addressed us in English, we answered him in Hindustani.   Nothing short of physical force would have removed us; but the whole thing was delicious. I know it afforded us many a good laugh afterwards.

The heat of Canada brought on one or two sharp attacks of my old complaint, jungle malarious fever, and I was cured by doses of quinine, arsenic, and iron.   There are few even of the most learned of the faculty who rightly understand the deadly effects of the poisonous medicine on the whole system.   It is almost sure to seriously affect one or other of the senses, if not some of the organs.

A trip, when I was convalescent, to St. John, New Brunswick, and back by way of Prince Edward's Island, set me up, and we left Quebec, after a round of gaiety, by steamer for Montreal.   The night before starting we were invited to dine at the citadel with some of the officers of the local artillery.   A Bengal gunner commands, and is fully appreciated by his subordinates.   The Canadian Dominion no longer entertains regular troops from England, but finds it cheaper to support and protect itself. We visited the battle-field of Abraham, and Wolfe's

Monument, erected on the spot where the gallant chief fell in the hour of triumph.

When Lord Dalhousie was Governor-General of Canada, he caused a second monument to be put up near Durham Terrace, to commemorate this important and bloody encounter between the French and English; but it is to perpetuate the memory of both Generals, Montcalm and Wolfe, friend and foe, that this magnificent piece of workmanship is erected. Verily a noble act, worthy of such an honourable and gifted man as Lord Dalhousie!

The jail of Quebec is one of its proudest buildings. It has a very respectable air, and must afford a great inducement for some to go there. The fort of Quebec is antique, and is only for show. It gives the place an important look, which is the main desideratum, but it would not stand much. The guns are of the Armstrong pattern. A plentiful supply of ammunition is in store, provided by the Woolwich Arsenal. Lord Dufferin has quarters in the fort. His Lordship is popular with all classes, and a general favourite with the officers. Her Ladyship is equally esteemed amongst the Canadians. It so happened they left Quebec by the same steamer as ourselves, and we had a most pleasant run up the noble St. Lawrence to Montreal.

The river steamers are unusually large and commodious, and fitted up with every requisite and comfort. One admirable arrangement I noticed in these steamers is the convenience of large plate windows instead of small port-holes, which are so common in the usual run of vessels and steamers classed as A1. The scenery is very beautiful along this route, and I found but little time for reading or stopping in the saloon. On account of the Governor-General being on board, we were beset with processions, guards of honour, and royal salutes. All this was rather amusing to the Yankees, whom we met in great numbers travelling to see Canada and its inhabitants. It amounts almost to a part of the American education that you should at least know every town of importance between Quebec and New Orleans, and from their boasted capital to the Pacific in the West. How many of the middle classes of England have travelled out of their own country ?

Montreal, of all towns in America, is the most English in all its ways ; but the people come short of the indomitable perseverance and energy displayed by the go-ahead Southerners. The population consists of 180,000, the majority, unlike Quebec, being mongrel Englishmen. There are some stately edifices and handsome buildings to be met with in and around this magnificent city. The cathedrals, and Catholic and English churches, are rich in frescoes, mosaics, and paintings, the finest being that of the Jesuits. This building is of greater dimensions, and is in better proportion, perhaps, than the cluster of churches which surround it. Some very pretty houses stud the hill and principal drive. Sherbroke

Terrace commands an extensive view of the city, river, and country for many miles round. Montreal we found warm during the day, but very chilly at night. It has a growing commercial business, second to none in Canada. We paid M'Gill's University a visit, and were much enlightened as to its internal arrangements. Some of the departments were not, in my opinion, judiciously managed, but the whole system was entirely new to me, and, in many respects, at variance with our plans and method of doing things. They had some very excellent men as professors, and many a good man they have turned out to shine in the world of fame.

We received the greatest kindness and hospitality from our friends at Montreal, and participated in some very pleasant parties. The ladies of Montreal are most delightful creatures—winning, captivating, lovely to behold. I am told few bachelors visit Montreal without coming away engaged men; and no wonder! They did much to endear their adopted country upon our memories with very lively feelings of ecstasy and festival. This being the height of the Montreal season, we were fortunate in coming in for many good things.

Taking the 5 A.M. train on the Grand Trunk Railroad, we reached Lachine, to come down the celebrated Rapids by the nine o'clock steamer. While at Lachine I got on board the wrong boat, and did not find out my mistake till we were off.

Fortunately, or unfortunately, for me, the steamer had to pass very near the wharf, and, acting on the spur of the moment, I made a run along the deck, and jumped. Of course the impetus of the boat had much to do with the extraordinary leap I took, which Hanton (who was watching me) said was at least thirty feet. One thing is certain. I had no idea, when I took the jump, the wharf was such a distance off, or I should never have attempted it; and the only wonder is I did not break my leg. I landed well on my feet, to the astonishment of those looking on.

Getting on board the right steamer at last, we were soon off, and experienced the most delightful sensation, "shooting the Rapids." The steamer is quite at the mercy of the rollicking torrent, and it is only by putting on full steam that they can go faster than the current, and so keep the head of the boat straight. In being hurled along in this novel style we passed within a yard or two of the wreck of a steamer which touched a rock, and was immediately swamped. The occurrence took place some short time before. In places the water is quite shallow, in others unfathomable. Standing at the bow of the boat, and looking back, the stern is up in the air, and looks curious enough. This mode of travelling is not unlike the way I have come down the Ranee, in India, on " mussucks," or inflated skins of bullocks fastened together, from near Dalhousie to the foot of the Himalayas. It is only safe when the river is in flood. You then, descend six thousand feet in about twenty-five miles, and accomplish the journey in three hours.

The rapids of Montreal are much more dangerous navigation, for the slightest false move and the steamer is lost. The Victoria Bridge comes in sight as you descend the last rush of roaring water. It is a noble structure, with twenty-five openings. The twenty-four piers are very massive, with bulky-looking buttresses, to protect the bridge from fields of ice which pass down during the winter months. The bridge is of great elevation, and ordinary steamers and river vessels pass under any of the openings. The bridge is only for a single line of rails, and is of the tubular pattern. It does not bear close inspection, and looks better at a distance. In the afternoon we rode out round the country, and the following day rode in to Ottawa, and had a week of delightful weather.

Ottawa is not nearly so important a city as Montreal, and yet many of the chief offices of Government are here. The Canadians who have been any time in the country without going to England become narrow-minded and prejudiced in their views. They look down with contempt on the Yankees; and I think, in some things, the latter are infinitely preferable to men who express sourness and childishness in all their whims and fancies. Some Canadians go so far as to suppose they have all the talent and industry of the mother country,

and are a long way advanced in civilization before
London. What does this betray—jealousy or
ignorance? It is very extraordinary how the English language can be idiomized by off-shoots of the
old branch. Australians, or " Cornstalks," have
their peculiar way of speaking English. Half-
castes of India have theirs—a sort of quick accent
to the end of words, commonly called " che che ";
and Yankees and Canadians have much the same
singing, nasal way of talking, which, I must say, is
not elegant, but exceedingly catching. Instead of
saying, " I beg your pardon, will you oblige me by
repeating that question?" a Yankee would curtail
it by asking you " Haow?" or a Canadian by
" What-say?" They pronounce marry, " murree";
and very, " vurree." They are fond of shortening
long words. Instead of " I intend to send a tele-
gram,"—" I 'll wire," or " I 'll 'gram." If they
shorten sentences, they add words which are quite
unnecessary. A Canadian or Yankee will tell you
he " guesses," or " reckons," or " calculates," while
he is certain and sure of what he is stating all the
time, and when there is no occasion to " guess." I
met some splendid specimens of honest John Bull
in Canada; but all things being equal, the Canadians, as a whole, are not superior to the Yankees,
who are absurdly cried down because we fail to see
their good and noble qualities. And talk about
bribery and corruption, what can beat certain
worthies of renown in Canada? It is considered

by some a necessity, for those seeking office, to
adopt.

The Lieutenant-Governors, judges, members of
the local board, and other officials, are returned by
the majority of votes. At Quebec, where the French
Canadians predominate, great disturbances at times
take place at elections, and the appearance of
Dominion troops and volunteers is required to
quell a riot. An instance of this sort happened
recently, when fifty mounted volunteers put to
flight thousands of an armed mob bent on mischief.
I was informed the whole system of voting is one
of bribery and corruption. Sometimes the candi-
dates for office are unaware of what is being done
in their names to secure the votes for their return.
" Do you want to sell your cat ?" is a common
saying when a vote depends on it; and the "pup" or
"pussy-cat" is sold at from ten to fifteen dollars, and
the vote taken down by the purchaser, who is no
other than a professional vote-gatherer. The "cat"
or "puppy dog," of course, is left till called for.

We returned to Montreal, and left for Lachine a
second time, where we embarked on board the
Royal Mail Line steamer, " Corsican," of the Canadian West Company. We found everything clean,
comfortable, and absurdly moderate in price, cabins
large and commodious, fitted up with every want.
This line of steamers is infinitely superior to the
ordinary run of British passenger boats. The fare
and berth are included in the charge, and these do

not exceed the railway charge. Of course, opposition tends to comfort and to diminish the cost of travelling, which in some places is preposterous, and quite beyond the reach of many people inclined to run over a few thousand miles of country. The only hindrance to progress is the number of locks along this route, which become fewer after leaving Cornwall, when most of the heavy rapids are passed over. It was in one of these places we came into collision with a bulky steamer, which did not answer her helm, and immediately afterwards ran into the " York," on entering the St. Lawrence, without doing any harm. We were fortunate in having a piano on board; the New Brunswickians and Miss Bella Wynter added greatly to our pleasant evenings. Mr. Norman and Mr. R. House, passengers per " Prussian," formed our party; the former, a philosopher of novel ideas, afforded us immense fun.

The magnificent scenery along the noble St. Lawrence is grand beyond description. At times you might almost fancy yourself transported to Fairyland, everything appears so very beautiful and engrossing. Nowhere did I see anything equal in point of beauty to the varied and lovely scenery of the Thousand Islands. Autumn is just the ripe time to see all this to perfection; the countless shades of diversified, rich foliage, clustering one with another in gorgeous tints, puzzle the eye to decipher. The small islands, generally destitute of life, with a wild, romantic look, are overgrown with mighty trees and wild, beautiful flowers born to blush unseen. The hamlets are few and far between, situated, generally, in enchanting little spots, and they remind one of Robinson Crusoe and the dreary, solitary life these people pass. Here, indeed, *is* freedom—no taxes, no laws, and no society. You travel over stony heights, impenetrable jungle, gigantic forests, and much wilderness, before you see anything of civilization, even in the form of a homestead, where some hardy son of England has settled down, for a lifetime, far away from his beloved country and his dear belongings. The poor wood-gatherers, hewers of timber, and light-house-keepers, have, indeed, a lonely life of it. The weather we found changeable. At times the heat during the day was almost unbearable, quite tropical, and at night bitterly cold.

Navigation is very difficult and dangerous in many places up the Thousand Islands. The rapids are terribly severe, and only the most powerful boats can face the strong current. Ours had some difficulty. The most extraordinary thing I noticed here was that the water, contrary to custom and the laws of nature, did not always find its own level. It is quite perceptible, no optical delusion, and it was before dinner, too. Of course we know water will find its own level, and the water here is not different to water elsewhere; so the only way I can account for this apparent paradox is, that the eddies and whirlpools have under, cross, and submarine currents, differing from the main channel and discharge, causing long valleys in places, hollows, gorges, ravines, and low tracts, with a surface perfectly still. I pointed it out to Hanton, who said, "That's nothing." No one appeared struck with it, but I never witnessed anything so strange before. I can find no mention made of this in any of the guide-books of Canada, which is as remarkable almost as the phenomenon itself.

On nearing Kingston, a high wind suddenly sprung up, and very shortly the sky was overcast, and the weather looked so threatening, that we were compelled to put in at Kingston, and wait till the impending storm was over. Even after the gale, the lake was as a sea, and big, rolling swells came one after the other, and sent the steamer pitching and tossing about as if we were far out on the Atlantic.

What a contrast the towns on the American side are to those on the Canadian! Take Prescott, one of our border towns, and, on the opposite side, Ogdensburg. Both have had the same commercial advantages; and yet, one is pinched and crammed with an over abundance of poor, showing clearly a social evil somewhere, whereas the other town is alive with factories and great public concerns, displaying energy and perseverance on all sides, and the true sources of what goes to make up a nation's strength and welfare. For every dollar spent at

Prescott, a hundred changes hands at Ogdensburg. This will show the relative wealth of the two towns under different administrations and Governments.

Kingston has some advantages over other neighbouring towns, but its belongings are too consequential, and lamentably backward in encouraging science and general improvements. They refuse to be dictated to by their official leaders, and show selfish, stuck-up provincial prejudices, which are highly amusing to an outsider. It was, from all accounts, a capital place to be quartered at in days gone by, when Queen's troops garrisoned the town, and the people showed their usual national hospitality and good fellowship; but things have changed, and number one is now the first consideration of the majority.

Leaving Kingston, we entered the smallest of these enormous lakes, which is nothing short of an inland sea. Vessels of the first class ride on its waters, and have to battle with terrific tempests common to lakes. Lake Ontario takes a steamer two days to traverse its entire length, and land is quite lost to view, which will give some idea of its mighty expanse. Coburg and Port Hope, on the edge of the lake, look very pretty from the water, with clusters of thick belts of jungle in the background rising to the ethereal sky; and trees of varied shade, in their rich autumnal foliage, fill in this picturesque landscape. This sort of exquisite scenery is the same in various parts of the lake.

We landed for good at Toronto, and bade good-bye to the civil and obliging skipper of the " Corsican " and a goodly company of passengers, Major Temple included. We put up at a clean, comfortable hotel, styled " The Queen's," and had the pleasure of meeting Mr. Oswald, a Montreal gentleman, who was here on a professional tour. After dinner at Roossan, we visited the local theatre, and witnessed a strange German slang performance, which greatly " fetched " the natives. I experienced much kindness from the clergyman and other gentlemen of Toronto, and regretted I was not able to prolong my visit to this growing, important town. I was agreeably surprised to find Toronto so far ahead in public institutions, and fully appreciated the liberality of the age—working for one purpose, the advancement of mankind. There are good broad roads and streets in the town, pleasant public walks and gardens, fine rows of comfortably, richly-furnished houses, and decent blocks of buildings here and there. It has a few good churches, libraries, clubs, and institutions. My first taste of snow in Canada was here, and it came down in earnest. In the suburbs there are some splendid houses, and the officials and gentlemen entertain freely enough. But alongside of mansions you find primitive wooden houses and queer hovels, which reminded me of Australian villages. Wood is in great request in Toronto. I saw big buildings constructed entirely of timber. Churches, roads, houses, railway stations, even to the rails; and it is used as a substitute for iron and stone wherever possible.

The hotels of Canada are on the same principle as the general run of such things in the States. The most objectionable part of hotel life is the fare. Everything you order is served up at once on small plates, which are placed in a semicircle round you. Yankees and Canadians love to eat a little bit out of each in turn—sweet and sour, solid and soup, it matters not a jot; hot or cold, raw or burnt, they appear quite contented with what is put before them, and don't take ten minutes to bolt the most awful amount of oily, tasteless food ever set before a civilized, rational being. It quite sickened me at times. This, of course, only refers to hotel life; and if the fare is bad, the wines and spirits are still worse.

As I have already observed, Canadians, as a rule, are more narrow-minded than the Yankees; for we see in the latter race what liberality and enterprise can do, what practical science has achieved for a practical people. The Yankee is an expensive, extravagant fellow; he spends his money freely, and appears, at times, to value it but little. If he loses it all, nothing daunted, he will start vigorously to work as if nothing had happened, with as much spirit and heart as ever. A Canadian, if he fails, gives it up, goes off, and tries something else. They are jealous of the Americans; and well they may be, for in some things they are a long way behind.

Canada would do better by itself; she wants independence, I think, to raise her dormant power. England, I fancy, would be glad enough to let them have the country, too, whenever the hulking child can manage for herself, but at present the authorities don't pull together; there is a vast amount of little party feeling, small conceit, pride, and vainglory, in too many of those high and mighty in power. But Lord Dufferin has done an immense amount of good, even in his short reign, by his manly, vigorous, straightforward government.

CHAPTER XIV.

IT became very rough on Lake Ontario before we left Toronto, and boats from all directions came rushing in for shelter. Two half-pay lieutenants of the Royal Navy joined our party on to Hamilton and the Falls. We stopped two hours at the junction station, which gave us time to see all that was worth seeing at Hamilton; then went on to Niagara, and put up at the International Hotel, on the American side, kept by a civil and obliging Canadian, Mr. J. Fulton. Our luggage was somewhat roughly handled by Republican custom-house officers, who opened and pulled about our portmanteaus, suspecting us, I suppose, of smuggling contraband goods over the frontier. Nowhere in all my travels did I come across such a rough, rude lot as these thief-catchers of Niagara. I cannot think they can be any ornament to their Government, nor is it with the sanction of Congress they can act and behave in the way they do, under the authority of the stars and stripes of their free and independent country.

Rising early, we were informed the proper thing was to engage a carriage and pair for the day to drive about and see the Falls from different points of view; but having done so, and passed through the ordeal of experience, I should advise visitors to Niagara not to be hampered with guides and a carriage, which are thrust upon them as a necessary consequence by a most courteous proprietor on the premises of every hotel. We visited in our rounds Luna and Goat Islands, Cave of the Winds, the shoot or vertical railway, suspension bridges, and Three Sisters' Island—in fact, everything of importance in the neighbourhood, drives included.

It was drizzling during the morning, but at noon it cleared up, and we had most delightful weather, which continued until we left some days afterwards. Niagara is pronounced by affected Canadians Nccargarrah, which is the Indian pronunciation. Yankees call it Niâgra, with an accent on the i and a, as in French. I was anxious enough to get out and gaze on the great Falls, the roar of which had greatly disturbed my night's rest. How shall I find words to describe this mighty torrent, falling over 160 feet in a direct drop! The Three Sisters' Island separates the Canadian from the American Fall. The former is grander and larger than the latter, but you turn your eyes from one to the other in wonder and awe, each time seeing something new in this glorious rolling volume of water, unequalled by anything of the kind in the world. The rainbow formed by the spray at the Horse-shoe or Canadian Fall is one of the most remarkable phenomena of Niagara, and should be witnessed at various times of the day. The lighthouse which

is generally seen in all the photographs and pictures
of the Falls has been removed, on account of the
dilapidated and ruined state of the main supports
and foundations.

The scenery below the Falls and beyond to the
lake is magnificently bold.   There is a wild, un-
earthly look about the panorama to the left and
right, as you descend the various turns in the river,
gazing back from time to time to view the Falls in
entirely a new aspect, which presents one of the
most remarkable sights I ever saw.   Our boatman
pointed to an abrupt part of the cliff as we passed,
and said a dog had fallen down the cavern some
time ago.   Everything had been done to try and
extricate him from his perilous position, but without
avail, and to keep the poor animal alive they lower
food to him daily.   Of course, when the winter
comes on the unfortunate dog can't escape being
frozen to death.   The rope where Blondin crossed
was still fixed from the American to the Canadian
side.   It is not situated *over* the Falls, but a considerable distance *below*.   This is contrary to what
I read in some Indian papers.   Another Blondin
used to walk from one side to the other every morning before breakfast as a gentle exercise, to prepare
himself for greater accomplishments afterwards.   He
would, on getting half-way across, purposely fall
into the rushing foam below, a height of over 150
feet.   A Yankee told me the hotels were thronged
during the performances of this duplicate Blondin,

and it was the making of the Niagara season. "But," he went on to tell me, "the thing was chiefly a hoax; the fellow had an invisible wire rope, which he would slide down. 'Cute, he was." Certain hotel-keepers remunerated the man, and it paid them remarkably well.

We returned to view the Rapids from the Three Sisters' Island. Our guide told us a very melancholy story connected with the dashing cataract above the Falls. The current even here is so strong that nothing can go against it. It appeared some friends of his, lately married, spent their honeymoon in one of the pretty villas on the river, some miles above the Niagara Falls, and amused themselves by pulling about on these romantic waters, till one day, not long ago, paying more attention to their courting than their navigation, they drifted with the stream into the yawning current, and were hurled on and on, and down and down, over the cataract. The boat was now upset, and they were separated; the unfortunate girl sunk, rose, and was carried on with the rushing waters; seizing hold of a passing log, she made a violent struggle to escape the inevitable death of falling over the Niagara Falls. All was to no purpose, and she threw herself from the log of wood as her lover passed, and, clinging to each other, they met their awful deaths together! They were never seen again.

Not very far up is the notorious whirlpool, boiling, bubbling, and dragging down everything which comes within its circuit. No living thing can possibly ever get out of that alive. Gigantic rafts, trees, and logs are sucked under, to disappear for minutes, and then shot up with great violence and force, to be whizzed round and round until they are drawn down; and this is repeated any number of times.

The grandeur, sublimity, and fascinating charm of these ever-rolling waters grow upon you the more you see them, and fill you with many beautiful thoughts, and you find yourself getting poetical and sentimental. I lounged on the long, sweet-smelling grass, and indulged in a delicious smoke, and then, with half-closed eyes, I dreamt of all sorts of pleasant things, the roar of ever-rolling, monotonous, dinning waters in my ears, until I began to get quite used to it. At first sight one is almost disappointed with the overrated account previously heard of the Falls; but view them the following day,—at sunrise, at noon, at sunset, at moonlight, when all around is calm and serene save the rolling masses of water, —and each time you will detect something more beautiful, more splendid and powerful, until you are lost in thought in contemplating that mighty volume of water, which roars like thunder and ends in vapour!

Nowhere has Nature concentrated such supreme grandeur in any one view as is to be seen at Niagara. In the rolling torrents are depicted every feature of might, force, and anger peculiar to the various actions of that element. The bald, wild, romantic scenery which surrounds all this, and the lofty peaks of cliff, covered with rich foliage, gigantic forests beyond, encompassed with broken bluffs and thickly-wooded heights, form the most powerful picture the mind of man can grasp.

My cigar had gone out, and Charlie was amusing himself by tickling my neck with a straw. " Dreaming, old boy? Get up, and let's be off. I'm peckish, and it's long past tiffin hour." All sentiment and romance vanished on hearing this practical announcement, and mechanically I got on my legs and walked back to the hotel, and met the remainder of our party—two of the fair sex, two naval officers, a nobleman of renown engaged in writing a book, Sir S. Hoote, Mr. Clarke, Charlie, and myself. It was agreed we had done Niagara right well; and much was still before us; so, giving instructions for our boxes to be packed and the bills produced, we set forth for London and Paris in Canada. We passed over some river or lake (St. Clair, probably) by boat, without moving from the car. The whole train went over in this way. The cars are run on to steam ferries, which cross over and meet the rails on the other side, and away the train goes,—no delay, no fuss, no accident, —and the arrangements are perfect and complete. We rested at Detroit, and found it very much the same as Lansing and Collingwood in population and commercial interests. The people are industrious and contented, thriving, and well-to-do colonists. Lake Erie hardly comes up to Ontario in varied scenery, although it is larger and has a much more important trade on its waters. The people in these localities are more orderly and quiet than in any other part of Canada, and set to work in greater earnestness, good-will, and spirit. English, Scotch, a few Irish, and fewer Germans make up the population.

We have now reached the most extraordinary town on earth—Chicago. This city was burnt to the ground about two years ago, the inhabitants homeless, reduced to the most abject poverty and ruin, displaying misery and death on all sides to the survivors. Spontaneously the whole civilized world came forward to help them with their charity. Never were people more in want of it. But such charity was not thrown away on them. It has afforded the world one of the great lessons of this age. In less than twenty months they had rebuilt their city on a grander scale than ever. What indomitable energy, perseverance, untiring industry, pluck, and manliness of character is shown in these Chicago people! The population has increased twofold, its trade encouraged and enlarged in all directions by a hard-working, prosperous· people, who deserve the world's praise for what they have done for themselves, and for maintaining the credit of their enlightened country.

We inspected some of their enormous elevators.

Trains full of wheat are run into sheds, immediately emptied, and the grain shot up into lifts, where it is cleaned; and, the process gone through, it is passed down into shoots, where vessels are ready to receive the rich produce of their land, to be borne across Michigan and other lakes, through canals, to the St. Lawrence, and thence over the Atlantic to feed starving Europeans. The machinery of these elevators is very perfect. Everybody is at work, and the amount of grain cleaned, stored, shot, passed, and laden is ten thousand tons per day. A vessel is drawn into the docks, placed, receives her cargo, and is off under weigh in less than twenty minutes. No one is asleep here but during proper hours. All are up and abroad by five or six o'clock in the morning. Early rising is undoubtedly a sign of the industry of races. In Ireland the lazy shopkeepers, who don't make it pay so well, rise and open their establishments at nine or ten o'clock. In London, eight seems the general time. In Scotland, it is much the same hour as London. On the Continent they keep the Dublin hours; but in America all the world is astir at seven, and shops were opened and streets filled in all the important towns throughout the Great Republic at that early hour.

Vast improvements have been made at Chicago in laying out the principal streets, thoroughfares, squares, parks, &c., since the fire. The streets are wider, and more ample for traffic; noble rows of new buildings have taken the place of the primitive, ugly-looking blocks burnt down; novel and original architecture greets the eye at every turn; hotels, banks, shops, offices, public institutions, halls, lecture-rooms, and exhibitions, form the chief buildings of Chicago. The suburbs are poor, but the streets are broad, and trees line the pathways. All were busy, and in a fever of excitement on their several duties; no loafers or stragglers to be seen save ourselves. We went all over the place, and saw some of the remains of burnt blocks of the ancient Chicago still standing. But what a fire it must have been to have made the very stones melt!

The gardens and parks are in their infancy, and at present don't show anything very grand in picturesque and landscape gardening, but they promise well. Some of the drives out of Chicago are rather fine. The lake looked very pretty, and fleets of boats were departing, carrying with them the produce of their rich country for distant lands. We stopped at the Grand Pacific Hotel, which is well managed, and considered the best house on this side of New York.

In the afternoon we paid the "Grand Chicago Exposition" a visit. This is truly a marvellous undertaking, and worthy of such energetic citizens. A very fair show of things. I saw some of the most modern agricultural implements here. Great taste and ingenuity were displayed in many of the inventions, and it was satisfactory to see such encouragement given by the local and administrative authorities to the inventors and others in the machinery line. The substantial cotton and woollen goods, rich carpetings, elegant furniture, and novel inventions of all sorts and descriptions, showed what stuff the people were made of. And this Exposition is the result of a ruinous fire, which brought desolation on all, and laid waste a whole city !

Before leaving, we went to hear Mrs. Victoria Woodhull's lecture. The hall was well filled—if not altogether with the *élite* of the city, at least with the most respectable and orderly members of good society. The majority of the audience were of the fair sex ; and they took the keenest interest in the descriptive and powerful language of the lady lecturer. As she advanced in her views of "Woman and Her Work," she became warm and excited, and she occasionally used the strongest and most unguarded terms in speaking of women. Forgetting where I was, I could stand it no longer, and—a thing I never did to any of her sex before—I hissed her down, Hanton and a dozen Englishmen present joining in, and stopping her from insulting her sex any longer. She gave utterance to the most abominable language and coarse sentiments in crying down—or, as she imagined, speaking up for—women. Mrs. Victoria Woodhull is a talented woman, without any proper modesty, and of very unrefined, low tastes. She contemplates lecturing in England ; but if she does so, I sincerely hope no English lady will honour her by her presence.

Leaving Chicago, we took the Great Pacific Railroad to San Francisco, and we had three days and nights without a break. We passed over a barren country, devoid of trees, shrubs, and vegetation, which gives one a taste of the Prairies; but it is a rich wheat country. Then we entered broken and raviny lands, and passed through wooden villages and primitive townships. More dead-level wastes, the only sign of civilization being the railway. The carriages and cars are most comfortably arranged along this route. All being joined together, you can pass from one to the other, and so travel the entire length of the train, a distance of several hundred feet; drawing-room, palace, sleeping and hotel cars, in addition to the ordinary cars, form the train. In the hotel cars (which are generally about the middle of the train) small dining-tables are set up, similar in style to what you see in saloons and cafés. The length of the carriage being 60 feet, will give one an idea of the extent of these moving hotels. Wines are iced, and dishes served up piping hot, strange to say for America. A smoking-saloon is at the end of each compartment, and when the time comes round you turn into your state bed-room, where everything is provided for you most comfortably, and you enjoy as good a night's rest as if you were at your hotel. During the day the paper-boys pass through the train at different intervals, offering books and daily or weekly papers for sale. Hawkers, pedlars, and fruit-girls bring their stock round for inspection. I say inspection, as I don't remember any one buying a thing from any of these people.

Across the vast plains, you enter a beautiful country stocked with splendid trees, and watered by crystal streams from the adjacent hills, with a lovely sky overhead; magnificent birds of various kinds, sizes, and beauty, are warbling on nearly every tree, and wild fruit and lovely flowers are in all directions. This will prepare one for the Rocky Mountains, and the bold wild scenery along these mighty heights, covered with the most gigantic trees in the world—a hundred feet round, and four hundred in height.

Salt Lake City is at last reached, and one is prepared for anything from this extraordinary mongrel type of humanity; but I was agreeably surprised to find the Mormons were not very different in their ways and language to other people " out West." I think, as a rule, they are more honest and superstitious, perhaps; but with the exception of having several women in their houses of various ages and looks, whom they designate as their wives, the Mormon is, in all other respects, as similar in his tastes and habits, and as industrious, hard-working, steady, and orderly a colonist as is to be found hereabouts. It grieved me not to have the honour of shaking hands with Mr. Brigham Young; but that worthy sent us a message expressing the disappointment he felt in not being well enough to receive us. A visit to the Tabernacle is not thrown away.

There are a few good houses, but most of them are wooden. The streets are broad, and the city, on the whole, viewed from a distance or height, has the appearance of an Eastern town. It has a certain Oriental stamp about it. The women are happy enough with their lot, and get on admirably together, all things considered, and I doubt if they fight and quarrel more in Salt Lake City than they do in any city of England or elsewhere. The men like it well enough, I fancy, for, if a wife gets noisy and quarrelsome with her husband, a second Amazon will surely rise to settle matters for him.

We were going about asking so many questions, that we were at last asked if we intended coming there to settle. Hanton said he would not mind trying it for a time out of curiosity; but the Destroying Angel did not approve of our making so light of such a sacred subject, and intimated if we came there once, we would have to settle down for life, which did not suit either of our books. Mormonism, I feel convinced, is on its last legs, and, on the death of Young, if the United States Government don't suppress it, the Mormons themselves will let it die out, as they get more enlightened and mix with other people. The railroad across the American continent has done more damage to Mormonism than anything else. We must not be too hard on them for the wretched state they are in, seeing how far removed they have been from civilization and the means of improving themselves in arts and science and all the elegance and refinement of polished society. The disadvantages they have had to encounter have been very great, and it is only a .wonder they are as good and moral as they are.

Crossing ranges of mountains, and back by rail to Lincoln, we branched off into New Mexico, where some big game shooting was promised us; and, after many days of hard travel by rude carts and on horseback, we reached El Paso. The country very much resembles the same monotonous features as the Missouri tracts, here and there broken by colonies of settlers, who live and work for their daily bread much as they do in Australia. We were obliged to rough it at times, and put up with many inconveniences far away in the backwoods and wilds of New Mexico, but fully appreciated soft, comfortable spring-beds after a shake-down on straw with nothing but the saddle for a pillow. We met some very queer customers " out West,"—men who set no value on your life or their own, and have no compunction in drawing their revolver on the slightest provocation.

We started, comfortably enough, with a roomy conveyance, but which we had to give up, with all appurtenances, to pursue our journey across pathless tracts by the shortest cuts. At times we encountered as disreputable a set of men as ever walked this earth. I have invariably found the surest and safest way to meet wild men or wild animals is to trust them as friends.   It will unnerve a bushranger as it will a Bengal tiger to appear *sans souci*.   You can't offer a tiger your hand to shake or your flask to drink from, but you can stop where you are or approach him, and eye him as unconcernedly as you would an ordinary animal, as if you were in the habit of meeting tigers and bush-rangers every day of your life.   If one of these backwoodsmen greets you with "Well, b—— stranger!" return the compliment with a sweet smile, for compliment he means it, poor man!   If they stop you and ask for "bacca," you must, in ordinary language, d—— him, and tell him you are short, that is, if he looks mischief.   One of these beauties catching hold of Hanton's overcoat, which he had taken a great fancy to, said he felt inclined to "trade" him a "six-shooter" for "that over-boy," producing his "six-shooter" as he said so, and with the other hand he was busily engaged in examining the texture of the material, to see whether it was quite worth the Colt's revolver. Hanton coolly replied he was not on the "sell" that day, but on the "buy."   Which answer was thoroughly understood by the man, who walked off sulkily, and, when some eighty yards off, he took "a quiet pot" at Hanton, fortunately without effect, and then he was lost in the bush and jungle. To go after him or return the salute would have been of no use to us.

In Nebraska, on our return, we met some Red Indians—dirty, savage-looking fellows. The chiefs were introduced to us by Mr. F. M. Barnes, belonging to the United States Agency, a gentleman who is a perfect master of their language, and has large possessions in the Indian State. The so-called Red men of the Ottoe tribe we also encountered, who refused spirits, but gladly partook of tobacco and some other things which we offered them. One chief accidentally struck me a severe blow with a tomahawk after he had finished smoking, which caused me to start; and the poor man's sign of submission and sorrow was most ludicrous. I patted him on the back and grasped him by the hand to show him I knew it was an accident, and we parted the best of friends. The performances and feats on horseback of some of these fellows are skilful, and display a thorough knowledge of horsemanship. They are biggish men, but not equal in strength to Englishmen. We beat them at throwing and lifting weights. I never saw a Red Indian lose his temper, but I am told they become very savage and brutal when in a rage. One old man was pointed out to us who had admitted having "scalped" and cruelly put to the most excruciating deaths over a hundred of his enemies. Of course this was long ago, before he and his tribe became domesticated and acknowledged allegiance to the Great Republic.

In Kansas, Missouri, and Texas States I found

much the same sort of ill feeling prevailing amongst certain classes of the lower colonists and settlers to the Washington authority. They openly spoke of the time that would come for them to oppose and resist the present mis-government of their States. They maintain that they have no power or word in what is being done at head-quarters, and their grievances are not looked into, and in some cases spurned. Of course I cannot say how much of this is true, but it is certain that this prejudice is spreading, and should be met by competent hands, who ought to see for themselves that the rights of all parties are preserved, order maintained, and good government encouraged by local powers. Is the Republican authority insufficiently strong to hold sway over these distant parts of America; and must the United States Government lose many of its richest provinces because they are inadequate to rule so vast a continent? Time will show.

The State of Missouri presents the same characteristic features as the dried-up flat fields of certain tracts of Australia. Much of the great wastes of the dead-level portions of land bordering the river might with advantage be brought under cultivation if irrigation was adopted, and this without much cost, as the soil is rich and prolific, and would yield a fair return for a little labour. Picture these boundless, barren wastes a few hundred years hence, when populated with striving, industrious colonists, with all the advantages which science and art by that time have achieved in the agricultural line! The prairies are utterly devoid of vegetation and growth of any kind, and consequently give but little trouble to settlers commencing operations, as there are no stumps of trees, rocks, and stones to remove. How such rich fertile land can be so barren is a mystery which has never been solved.

Arrived at St. Louis, we were most comfortably housed after so many hardships, and thoroughly enjoyed the advantages of civilized life again. The town of St. Louis stands on the Missouri River, and not far from the junction of the two streams, Mississippi and Missouri. This latter river is like the dirty Ganges, and is, on the whole, just about as interesting. Higher up, nearer its source, during the dry season, you might fancy yourself in South Australia, the Missouri as Lake Torrens, and the distant heights Gawler and other ranges. The air is close and misty, with light clouds, weather hot and dry, but not unhealthy. A trip down the river when in flood is highly interesting, and the scenery as you descend becomes less wild, and with dotted farms and plantations here and there, and you might imagine you were back in civilized Europe. At St. Louis we visited, in company with a distinguished officer of Engineers, the enormous bridge which is being thrown across the Missouri River. The works are ponderous, and everything is done on a gigantic scale. The centre arch is 510 feet in the clear. The arch is of iron girders, circular hollow tubes, and tapering towards the crown. The rise of arch is one-sixth the span. The centering is con. structed from supports thrown out from piers and abutments of the bridge, in order that no obstruction should be given to the important navigation on the river. Large steamers will be able to pass under the centre span when the bridge is completed. Each link (forming the iron arch) screws on, and is 12 feet in length. Lateral and vertical tie-rods hold the circular hollow tubes together, so that the whole is connected, and steadies the bulky but light-looking structure.

The masonry here, as at Chicago, is of a very superior kind, and it is not to be wondered at that such good work is executed, considering how cheese-like, huge, massive Ashlar blocks are cut and dressed. The coursed rubble masonry of some of the larger engineering works of these cities amounts almost to perfection,—not a blade of a knife could be passed between the joints, and the lines are true and regular. Their designs are bold, full of invention and novelty, and many valuable and useful lessons are to be picked up from the skill evinced in their great engineering works throughout their vast dominions. The courts of law are fairly managed, and, on the whole, general satisfaction is given. The banks, railway offices, and other large buildings are important-looking edifices, and are after the style, class, and order of our own. We experienced great kindness from the officials in charge of the several departments of Government, and had only to declare ourselves Englishmen on a tour of pleasure to meet with the utmost civility and condescension from these obliging gentlemen, who went out of their way in some cases to help us in seeing everything that was to be seen, and granted us unlimited information in all matters lying within their knowledge and province.

We accompanied some Red Indian chiefs to the St. Louis Museum, and were much amused at the intense delight the " Chamber of Horrors " and " Infernal Regions " gave them.   I need hardly say it was as novel to them as it was to ourselves.   We travelled by way of Cairo through the Kentucky State.   The country is very monotonous, and presents the same sort of flat and unbroken tracts, which are, however, brought under cultivation, and are very productive of wheat, Indian corn, and tobacco, and, lower down in the Southern States, cotton and other rich products, which are steadily on the increase. The people are very quiet and contented.

It is curious to note the marked difference between the classes in and about Lincoln and those in the Alabama State; where they are many miles from any large town they are quite half a century behind the age.   It is most to be noticed in the old-fashioned way they dress themselves.   I never came across such primitive people anywhere in the States as here.   Nothing seems to interest them beyond the local news of their wooden villages.   They know very little of Europe, and are not sure whether Queen Victoria is still sovereign of Great Britain. Some had heard that a war was going on between France and Prussia, but did not know whether it was settled yet. The men dress with longish coats, tight-fitting trousers like our grandfathers wore, and the women wear oddities of bonnets which entirely hide the face, unless you view the physiognomy from the full front. They appear very pious and orderly on the Sabbath, and attend some place of worship regularly. The men don't swear quite so much on Sundays, but congregate together; they chew, smoke, talk, and spit more. Very few had heard about the notorious Alabama claims, and those few had but vague ideas of the matter. They don't bother about newspapers or politics, and live entirely for themselves.

The country hereabouts reminds one of 'Uncle Tom's Cabin' stories. All classes I spoke to on the subject of the negro emancipation considered it very injudicious on the part of Congress to give the blacks so much power and freedom. It was foolish to trust them, as they only abused the kindness and gratitude shown them by their over-zealous liberators. These very primitive settlers, of the old Puritan stock, had in some cases never taken the trouble to go beyond their own plantations, and had not for a score of years visited their nearest township. They had some idea that St. Louis, Lincoln, Charleston, &c., were the biggest cities in the world, because, simple beings! they had heard of no others. A great deal of ignorance and superstition prevails among these colonists in out-of-the-way places, but, as a whole, they are honest, good-natured, and industrious, and mean very well. We became quite objects of curiosity when we told them of our nationality, and it puzzled them greatly to understand our travelling such a distance to see their country—"a country like theirs!" They were constantly asking us where we were going to settle, and if we were well stocked with "stamps" (*i. e.*, money). Races of whites along the Mississippi River have a peculiar way of singing and drawling out their words when talking, not unlike the country folk of Cornwall and Devonshire. If these good people possess any pedigree of their ancestors, I feel sure they would be able to trace their origin back to the West of England yeomen, for they are like them in all their peculiarities, manners, and customs, of the same stamp, without any exalted ideas of progression and general advancement of mankind.

We were prevented going on to Jamaica and the West Indies on account of the yellow fever, which was creating terrible havoc amongst the people of the Southern States, and great fears were entertained that it would spread North. Most stringent orders were circulated to the New Orleans embarkation officers to keep the strictest watch over the harbour, and enforce all quarantine regulations, in order to prevent this fearful malady getting beyond their power of dealing with it. We were not at all anxious to be under quarantine orders for a month, so gave up all idea of visiting the West Indies, and retraced our steps. Besides, the Cuba insurrection had stopped all communication between the ports for the time being, so we had no alternative. It was a great disappointment to me, as I particularly wished to see Jamaica. A whole family of my people were out there—a favourite aunt, countless fair cousins, and their father, who was in chief command of the troops.

We then travelled North, and halted for a time at that no Elysium for pigs, Cincinnati. There is not much difference in the style and order of the towns. When you have seen Cincinnati, you have seen Parkersburg, Washington, Baltimore, and Philadelphia. The " White-house," or " Capitol," at Washington, is a stately-looking pile, together with other public buildings, and which marks this town as important from the fact of its being the head-quarters of Congress. We were anxious to pay our tribute of respect to the representative of the great Republican Government, but President Grant was "out of town." Some English gentlemen we met here spoke in the highest terms of General Grant's reception of our countrymen, and the pleasure they experienced on being presented, and discussing all the chief topics of the day with a man of his liberal and practical views.

Leaving Washington, the scenery was very monotonous and flat until we approached the Potomac. The railway clings closely to the river for a considerable distance, twisting in and out of low hills, crossing rushing torrents and strange-looking aqueducts of doubtful structure, coming upon views, here and there, of an arm of the sea, which look very picturesque, and are, in places, undoubtedly beautiful. The Yankees, though, misapply terms when they call this sort of scenery " elegant " and " handsome "! nor do I agree with them that it is even " superb " and " grand"! Coming along in the cars we had immense fun with some American ladies, who are never at a loss for an introduction, and freely enter into conversation without much ado. " There, Britishers, look at that! Isn't that view *elegant* ?" asked one of these ladies, of very bewitching manners.—" I regret not being able to see it *quite* in that light," said Hanton. " We don't apply such expressions to scenery, but only to your fascinating sex," added Charlie.—" Good again, old hoss !" remarked the American belle. " What think you of our country ?" inquired she.—" I am well pleased with it ; it is a large country—a great country !"—" Guess you are not far out there. When I was over in your little England, I was afraid to go outside at night in case I stepped over into the water. I reckon we could stow away you and your boasted land in a corner of Texas, and the old boss would work on without being any the wiser. Did you ever hear, stranger, a story of the elephant being troubled with a flea on coming out of the ark?"   Such was the turn our conversation took with the ordinary class of lady travellers.

Americans, from the highest downwards, all " *Sir* " each other.   They dearly love rank and title of some sort.   On " interviewing " you they will promiscuously address you as " General," or " Colonel," or " Judge," and then drop it as suddenly for " Mister."   Common servants prefer being called " helps," or " assistants."   A lady friend of mine at Philadelphia, engaging a domestic, had to make stipulations beforehand that she would give up her drawing-room and parlour twice a month to the " help," in order that she might be able to entertain her friends.   And where was the mistress of the house to go?   Why, arrange to " visit " that evening; or, if that were not feasible, the servant would give up a side parlour to her mistress!   The servants of Philadelphia are certainly most independent and overbearing at times.

It is very absurd to notice how intensely jealous these Americans are of their towns and cities, particularly of New York, Chicago, Washington, Philadelphia, and Boston.   A story is told of the Chicago people, that when they heard of the recent Boston fire it quite alarmed them until they heard that the terrible flames had been entirely subdued.   Telegrams came pouring into Boston, " Is your darned fire out yet?"   They were very uneasy for a long time for fear Boston should boast of a bigger fire than theirs !

Philadelphia is a large, straggling place, but the inhabitants are extremely proud of themselves, and their display of superiority over other cities is most absurd. The Independence Hall, where the Old Congress party held its sittings, is worth a visit. They are also building and adding largely to their University. Whilst at Philadelphia I visited some of the public schools, and it is greatly to be regretted that a branch of study so important as natural science should be so generally neglected. The imperfect system of universal education adopted for the masses in all countries is, in proportion, much the same as our national standard. In some instances, this little knowledge has been very detrimental, and the means of producing very pernicious results in people who would have been happier and more contented if left in their profound ignorance. Cheap, exciting literature of a sensational character is brought within the reach of half-educated, gluttonous people, who would prefer a life of ease and idleness to honest labour and improvement, which advocates ideas foreign to themselves and their calling in life. There is a vast difference between the man whom you inform that he *has* a grievance and the man who finds out for himself, on inquiry, the demoralizing influence he brings upon himself by being in a state of utter ignorance. The main thing in promoting good government and the advancement of all civil and social rights is to substitute a higher standard of education than that usually adopted. To encourage this most beneficial object for the chief good of all, is to award tempting prizes, open to all classes of citizens. Our present limited knowledge of things would put natural science as the first and foremost of all studies, worked and built up on the surest order of truth and logic. I would suggest the higher branches of education only when classics, mathematics, logic, and a sound knowledge of physics were acquired—studies which would be of material good in their practical calling in whatsoever station of life they may choose to adopt. Our great desire should be to instruct and to be instructed. Half the rulers of the world, placed to govern their fellow-men, show themselves to be either fools or fanatics in dealing with mankind. Their pride blinds them to plain facts, and, in their zeal for popularity, they display gross ignorance and profound contempt for mental culture.

The long, trying journeys by rail through the States, for days and days at a time, fairly exhausted our nerves and patience, and we were not sorry when our tour by rail was at an end. The great convenience of Pullman's cars diminishes the discomfort of long journeys. The sleeping-cars are undoubtedly a great boon, and from the drawing-room-palace-carriages you can see the country to advantage ; but still, with all the luxury of American railway travelling, it is more dirty than at home. The conductors of cars are civil enough in their replies, but to an Englishman they are cool and impudent in their general behaviour when travelling on duty. They will come and sit alongside of you, as if they were quite as good as the passengers, and had rather more right there than any one else. The black porters bother you for money and cigars, and imagine they have certain claims upon your generosity.

A poor Yankee, called McDermott, we met "out West," finding we were English, introduced himself, and told us his adventures, and how terribly reduced he was. Although a Northerner, he was away in the South when the Civil War broke out; and, as enlisting and fighting were the order of the day, he went in for it too; but, not wishing to go all the way back, he stopped where he was, and joined the Federals, and fought against his own side. He was several times slightly wounded, and taken prisoner, released, deserted; he re-enlisted, was victorious one day, and defeated the next, until General Lee's army was finally starved, repulsed, and captured. Many strange stories he related, which I have been able since to verify as to their correctness.

The officers subordinate to the colonel commanding, were, in his battalion, returned by the wishes of the regiment. Some of these officers, on being elected, were proved (according to the men) unfit for their position; and, when such was the case, they would hold secret meetings to try their officers whom they deemed unworthy. McDermott assured us if the officer declined to give up his appointment in the regiment, they would "go" for him the next time he went into action. He said he never actually, to the best of his knowledge, " shot a man in the back," but he had witnessed several cases. This rough, coarse man, who had seen so much, had a very tender heart withal, and was moved to tears when he told me the fate of the good doctor, of his regiment, who was a true friend to the men. After a bloody encounter near Richmond, when both sides withdrew, neither gaining the day, the doctor, with several others, was attending to the wounded, when a dying Northerner cried out for something to drink. Immediately the doctor produced his flask, saying a kind word as he passed on to others who were in such need of assistance. The dying Yankee soldier had fallen before discharging his rifle, and, taking it up, he took deadly aim at the unconscious doctor, who was administering to the wants of a wounded man a few yards off. The poor doctor fell over, gave one look at the wretched man whom he had been so good to; and he, who was in the vigour and prime of life a second before, was dead before the dying murderer! It would appear McDermott was of no strong patriotic feeling; for, while this promiscuous fighting was going on, he was just as willing to join the

Northerners as he was the Southerners, and any extra rations or pay would have induced him to do so. And so this bloody warfare was carried on, generally by men who took really no interest whatever in the movements of Senators and vexed questions of Congress politicians. In fact, those of the Northerners who were posted up with what they were fighting about, thought the negro emancipation premature and misdirected.

McDermott's career had been varied, and not without interest. Starting in life as a sailor, he roamed about the world, and was shipwrecked several times. The narrowest shave he ever had was when the Royal Charter was wrecked within sight of England's shore. After this he sailed with a bullying captain, who ill-treated him, had him placed in irons, until his life became a burden to him; and, when the ship touched at Bombay, he deserted, and took service with the East India Company, in a regiment just off to engage in quelling a disturbance in Central India. He behaved so well, that when the campaign was over he received his discharge, and a letter of approval from his colonel. He once more sought the sea, but got tired of it on reaching New York, and became a porter and check-collector at Stewart's warehouse, Broadway. He threw this up for a better appointment in the Southern States. When the civil strife took place he commenced soldiering again. This over, he has since been variously

employed as porter, stoker, and messenger. In this
latter capacity we found him homeless and destitute—a manly, devil-may-care, rough individual,
but honest and good-natured with it all, and one
who would stick to you through thick and thin in
a row. He is truly a wonderful specimen of
humanity, and if he ever returns me the money I
lent him (to take him back to his brother, where he
can get work), I shall not be mistaken in my estimate
of the man's character.

We stopped this time at the Grand Central Hotel,
which is not the largest in New York, but more
central, and I changed about in order to see every
phase of American hotel life. The excitement which
prevailed throughout the city was very alarming on
hearing that the eminent banking firm of Messrs.
Gay, Cooke & Co. had stopped payment. It was
denied at first; but when the bankers announced
officially their bankruptcy, several houses of the
highest repute, linked in some business transactions
with Gay's, were compelled to stop payment. These,
in turn, found themselves connected with minor
houses, and had distant agencies scattered throughout the States, who, by themselves, were unable to
carry on business, and, consequently, were ruined.
The panic in New York now became general, and
bank after bank fell, the largest establishments shut
up shop, and ruin spread everywhere. All important
commercial concerns in the city felt it. I walked
down Wall Street, and it was terrible to observe the

look of wildness on every countenance. Rage, vengeance, remorse, anguish, misery, and madness were depicted in the faces of the passers-by. This general smash has shaken the town brokers and financial men more than the late war. The most eminent, honourable, and wealthy of yesterday are paupers to-day; thousands and thousands, living from hand to mouth, were thrown out of work, without the prospect of being employed for the year; the papers alluded to countless suicides of people of every rank in life; the railways and other public companies, which are bound to carry on their business, reduced their establishments, and the *employés* were cut down twenty per cent. in their wages. The men dismissed will be sure to meet their doom as criminals in Sing-Sing (*i. e.*, their gaol), and the fate of the poor women will be worse.

With Beresford I went to the Club, and heard all the London news and of further smashes in the city. At the Club I was the object of a good deal of curiosity. My friends approached me with awe and dismay. I demanded to know the reason of their strange behaviour. " Why, old fellow," cried a dozen voices, " we had no idea we should ever see you again. A story is told in the papers of your untimely death, and we have just recovered from mourning your loss ! Are you really yourself, and have you been in the flesh since last we saw you ?"

A paper was produced, and sure enough a certain individual answering to myself was killed in New Mexico at the hands of wild Indians; but, the name not being quite the same, they thought it all the more truthful on that account! I was greatly amused, and considered so good a joke should not be lost on some of my English acquaintances. So, without adding anything, I sent the paper home, and if they were so disposed to misconstrue names, of course they could do so. Unfortunately for some, it turned out a very serious joke, and on my return to London my people thought I was dead and gone, and when I arrived were actually lamenting my loss! It did not stop here, for others had taken it up, and I had to identify myself to my agents, so it was not unlike a second Tichborne affair on a juvenile scale.

At New York I formed the acquaintance of the Spanish Consul, at whose house I met some Mexican celebrities, a distinguished Russian, and an Englishman, who had been across the American continent, and the latter was about to write a sketch of Mexican life. It was very remarkable to find, in this queer conglomeration of mixed people, how universally any gentleman coming from California was distrusted in his accounts of travels and anecdotes. Much as you may laugh at wit in a good story, it loses its truthfulness at once if it is connected in any way with California. The Yankees themselves place no faith in their countrymen hailing from that quarter. Is it because the very worst characters have made it their home, and in all their actions and ways are coarse and ill bred? The low, blasphemous language usually adopted by those "out West," as it is mysteriously called, show them to be people of no proper feeling for others. The names of the Creator, Jesus, and saints are introduced into all their sentences, as if it were absolutely necessary for them to figure, and impossible to be expressive and to the point unless a string of unmeaning words are brought in.

To an Englishman of refined feeling, this sort of thing is met with scorn and indignation, which turns at last to horror and disgust. We remonstrated with many of them for using such terrible language, but all to no good, and on inquiry we found they meant nothing by it. They spoke of everything we hold in such reverence and awe, and cling to as sacred and dear, in a manner quite unconscious of the true meaning of those holy names. I saw many of my countrymen run away from these roughs—their language was so truly awful, and hatred towards them ensues as a matter of course; but, after all, we should not be so ready to cry out, like the Pharisee of old, "Thank God I am not as this man!" If they had had the advantages we have had, I dare say they would be very much better men than we are, who are inclined to think ourselves immaculate and right in all good works.

The "check system" for luggage is certainly one

of the greatest boons imaginable travelling in the States. In fact, I don't know what would be done without it. The plan is so simple: you hand your luggage over to the porter on leaving for a long journey, and he presents you with brass tickets, on which are numbers stamped. You have no further trouble. On arrival at Quebec, Chicago, or New Orleans, you hand over the "checks" to the hotel porter, who claims your luggage, and starts off there and then, shoots it up the lift or vertical railway of the hotel, and you find your boxes have reached your rooms before you. Unfortunately, I lost the check tickets of certain boxes I left at New York in my journey round by the Pacific, and, on arrival at the Fifth Avenue Hotel, I informed the proprietor, who kindly said it would be all right if I could satisfy the head-porter. This official, with one or two others, asked me if I could for certain tell him what was inside one of the boxes. At that instant I really could not enumerate the articles from memory, but said that in the writing division of a travelling portmanteau he would find several letters addressed to me. Could I mention any particular one? Yes, I could; an official document from the Secretary of State for India, with the Duke of Argyll's own signature in the corner, was to be found between the cross-bars—I was certain of that. So it was agreed I should claim my own property, provided the description I gave of the said letter was satisfactory. On opening the box, and producing the document, it was most ridiculous to observe with what curiosity the writing was scrutinised. "*This* a Duke's signature?" cried one; "but he has forgotten his titles and his full name." Some one now appeared on the scene who explained it was all right, as it was the custom for an English noble merely to sign the name of the property he was lord of. This being deemed satisfactory, I was permitted to lay claim to the portmanteaus.

Yankee porters and messengers, unlike my own countrymen, consider themselves insulted if a gratuity is offered them. This is an immense boon, and I should be delighted to find our plagues of porters take the hint. I know nothing so trying to the temper as to be bothered by an army of these fellows who line the staircase to your carriage-door on your leaving an hotel or public place of resort. It is not the few shillings you think of, but that *men* who are paid servants can lower themselves by thus cringing before you as beggars for the sake of a paltry coin or two.

I recommend Cook's tourist-tickets as most convenient when travelling in a country you know little about. I tried them once in a longish tour in the States of several thousands of miles, and nothing could have been more admirably arranged, even to the hotel coupons. Wherever I used Cook's tickets they were treated with the utmost respect, from the far-off shores of the Pacific and the Gulf of Mexico

to the City of New York, where they have their
head office, presided over by one of the partners,
Mr. Jenkins, a most civil and obliging American
gentleman.   It is optional whether you take the
steamer or railway, and a period of six months is
granted you to run over a pre-arranged course of
travels.   And the coupons are for any of the first
hotels.   On leaving, you tear off as many strips as
you have been days at the place, and this meets all
incidental expenses.   The great beauty of this is
there is no fuss and bother at the last moment
calling for and settling long bills.   Much valuable
time is often taken up by preposterous charges of
swindling landlords.   Cook's   tickets   obviate
all this, and, to a novice travelling in a strange
country, I can with great confidence recommend
them.

With our Russian, Spanish, and Mexican acquaintances we strolled down Broadway, to inspect
the money market, the state and growth of the
panic, which had now reached its height.   The everlasting dollar was on every Yankee's tongue.   A
certain class can talk of nothing else; they are at
it all day long, and, in their Babel of dreams, build up
imaginary towers of the almighty coin spreading
aloft even to the gates of Elysium.   At my hotel
the terrible tragedy in real life of the Stokes-Fisk
affair was enacted.   Almost opposite my door Colonel
Fisk fell dead, shot by that fiend and cur Stokes.
For so diabolical an act he has gained not only the

sympathy of the Yankees, but is a perfect hero amongst the lower herd. There is no denying Fisk was a very shameful character, but that did not justify his being murdered. We knew some of the judges, and were admitted to see the trial. The court was densely crowded, and Stokes's day had at last arrived. Great bets were made for and against him, and the excitement of the Americans was at boiling point. There sat Stokes in the prisoner's cell waiting his condemnation. He is a handsome-looking man, of about thirty-five, and has a cool, *sans souci* air. He awaited to hear whether he would be hanged or not this time, for he had so often been condemned to death. His beautiful sister, with a worn and anxious look, was keenly taking in every word which fell from the prosecution. The parents and other relations of Fisk, the deceased, sat eyeing each other mournfully. In a comparatively short time it was very clear how one-sided the trial was, and that Stokes would be let off. The interest was getting burdensome, and the sentence was proclaimed to an eager mob of excitable roughs, who hailed Stokes as the lion of the day. He was ordered to confinement in "The Tombs" (New York Prison) for three years for killing Colonel Fisk. Vulgar, low, and poor men are usually hanged for murdering people; but Stokes, being born a gentleman, an extravagant dandy, personally of a beautiful appearance, with great means at his bankers', no doubt will soon be out of jail, fresh and ready to share a glorious career amidst the fast and gay of New York.

As I have remarked, Englishmen are treated with the greatest consideration by the upper classes of American gentlemen.   And are not Britishers trusted? Go and ask the Wall Street speculators what they think of London banking-houses and our foremost men of business. " Englishmen," they say openly, " we can trust. You are honest. John Bull's word is not to be doubted. We knew we were dealing with a nation of gentlemen in that Alabama affair. John Bull pays his debts like a man!" An American clergyman (Irving) told me it must have been greater pleasure for John Bull to have paid that 15,000,000 dollars than it was for Jonathan to have received it. That it was mag-nanimous on the part of England, and a precedent for future ages, when arbitration will take the place of force of arms, cannot be gainsaid.

Yankees have, as a rule, great respect and re-verence for England and her beloved Queen. It is to be regretted they do not adopt many of our national sports and games, and do not take after some of our fine old country squires more in this line. But the time is coming when they will not so neglect useful, healthy, and manly sports; and as we get to know more of each other, we shall see each other's noble traits, and love all that is beau-tiful and good for the advancement of each other, and be shining lights of the most brilliant achieve-

R

monts in civilization. And now I bid America a fond good-bye, with many longings and hopes of a future visit to its ever-increasing and prosperous shores.

We were followed by a great company of delightful acquaintances to Cunard's Pier; and after some little difficulty in getting out of the mud on account of the low state of the tide, we steamed out of the harbour in the "Abyssinia," watching as long as we could the distant glimpses of New York and its magnificent waters, as the sun sank below the horizon, and left us out on the wide Atlantic, to "*sneak over*" under the most favourable circumstances. A most lovely moonlight night followed this evening, and everything was calm and delightful. We sat up till all hours smoking and pegging. My friend of Dawlish, Mr. Wykeham, I met at New York, and found him amongst those on board. I experienced the greatest pleasure from his agreeable and enlightened conversation, and our meeting thus was one of the most extraordinary circumstances I met with in my American travels. Our passengers were a very queer, mixed set—a few of the so-called *élite* of Yankee society,—amongst whom might be classed Mr. Jerome, of turf notoriety, a gay and festive individual (his beautiful daughter has since married young Lord Churchill); a very fascinating, clever widow, Mrs. Le Roy, with grown-up sons who might be taken for her brothers; a Mrs. and Miss Yznagha, Messrs. Post, Rigg, and others. A

Mr. Smith, of Philadelphia, was an exceedingly gentlemanly, polished man, who preferred Continental life to anything else. The remainder of the noisy element were of the " bagmen " tribe, or better known as " dry-goods'-men,"—in other words, dealers in shop goods.

We had a very pleasant time of it for a day or so, when we encountered a vessel full rigged, with sails put about, and the lower ones torn to shreds; her helm was hard a-port, and the American gonfalon was flying upside down, as a sign of distress. We bore down upon her, and found she was a powerful and magnificently fitted-up vessel, of near 2,000 tons, laden with a cargo of some 1,400 tons of tobacco, wheat, and cotton, her name " Robinson"; but not a living soul was found on board! Every nook and corner were searched, but to no purpose,—not even a corpse or remains of a human being was left behind to inform us of the meaning of this phantom ship, abandoned, with a splendid cargo, for no apparent reason, on the high seas! Had the crew mutinied, killed their captain, and taken to their boats? No, for the boats were intact, and no displacement of anything was palpable. Had the ship left some of the fever-stricken ports with the germs of poison on board, and one by one had they died of the pestilence? No, for bodies would be lying about. Neither had they starved, for water and provisions were largely stowed away for a long voyage. It was hopeless to speculate what was the cause, until the whole thing was brought to light by finding that some attempt had been made to sink the unfortunate craft, in order (so the captain and others supposed) that they might claim the full insurance money, and had, before she had been scuttled, got her crew off in a passing vessel. This was the only way to account for it, as it was found water had penetrated the lower chambers; but the wheat and other cargo had most effectually stopped the leakage, and kept the vessel afloat up to this time. The donkey-engines were in perfect working order, and were set in motion. The water being cleared, the ship examined and tried, our captain, in spite of the inquisitiveness of the " City of Montreal," one of Inman's line, hauled down the American stripes and stars, and ran up the British ensign, to the horror and cries of sentimental ladies of Madison Avenue fame, who begged to be allowed to have a strip of that flag which they so dearly loved and prized !

By this time the " City of Montreal " had come up to us, and, eyeing us very suspiciously, she went on her way. The captain claimed the vessel, put an officer and twenty-two men on board of her, and told them to make for Halifax, which was then quite close. We had lost a whole day pottering about, testing the vessel, and seeing she was not water-logged and unseaworthy before so many lives were entrusted to her keeping. Such a prize of £50,000 is not picked up on land or water every day, and it was well worth a little trouble. A high wind sprang up, and a heavy swell made it difficult, at last, for the boats to go and come. Night came on before one of these had reached the vessel, the wind increased, and the poor little boat, without any light, was cast off on a wild, dangerous night. It was pitch dark, the waves rose, fell, and broke with a roar, which showed the perilous position of the boat. Our hearts sank within us. The vessel heeded not our signs, and, in fact, was not aware of the missing boat. This small craft had had such dangers that day. She was nearly crushed by getting under our stern when the steamer pitched, and on another occasion, when in front of the vessel, she was nearly stove in by the martingale point when the ship gave an extra lurch. We steamed about very cautiously, and at last picked up the boat. Three cheers for the large-hearted and plucky men, who had yet to gain the other vessel, which feat was safely accomplished. A blue light from either ship showed all was right, and we parted, she for Halifax, we on our course. We came across no more Robinsons, Smiths, or Joneses, and by the following evening we had run 350 miles.

On entering the Gulf-Stream we experienced singularly warm weather, quite summer over again, although this was towards the close of the year. The wind increased during the day; the barometer showed that a gale was imminent, and preparations were made for some dirty weather. The next day strong winds worked the ocean up into billows mountains in height. The enormous vessel was dashed about like a cork on the angry waters; the roar of the wind was awful. The passengers were battened down,—in fact, no one would have ventured on deck; but I, being a good sailor, and knowing the officers, watched the storm with great interest. I glory in a storm. The noble vessel behaved admirably, and was in right good hands. Never did a captain do his duty more thoroughly. The gale changed into a hurricane. The storm abated for a time only to increase in fury, and mighty waves swept the deck, going clean over the ship. We hove to, and were completely at the mercy of the winds and waves. At midnight a terrific cyclone came upon us. We were being driven along due east, when instantly the wind changed from north-west to south-east, and caught the sails, which had just been set. We were very nearly over. The sails were torn to shreds, and went with a tremendous blast; our maintopgallant-mast and other minor masts and supports were snapped and lashing the air; the wind howled and hissed through the wreck most piteously. I never witnessed such a grand storm! Again we hove to, and allowed the elements to do their worst. A short time after this, a poor sailor, called Vincent Jarvis (but on account of his jovial, light disposition, was surnamed " *Merry* " by the crew), weary and worn from hard work and exposure, went aloft, and during the gale was blown overboard. This happened in the morning, and I shall never forget the consternation it caused at the time.

The cry of " Man overboard ! " is an awful sound. It was unusually terrible on the present occasion. The order to reverse the engines and lower the biggest boat was instantly carried out, and ropes and life-buoys thrown to the wretched man, who was vigorously striking out for his life. He was of powerful frame and a strong swimmer, and all were in hopes the unfortunate man's life would be spared. At one time he was thrown up on the crest of a mighty wave almost within our grasp ; the next second he was drawn down into an awful gulf, and the huge billows dashed over him, and for a time he was quite lost to view. But poor Jarvis struck out manfully. The pitying, longing, imploring look he gave will never be forgotten by those who were so near and ready to save him. One more look, as another wave sweeps over him, and the poor sailor is gone for evermore to his long, long rest ! The boat which had been lowered in hopes of rescuing poor Jarvis for a long time was in a most perilous position, and was with the greatest difficulty saved. I, with some others, ran forward, and pulled the ropes and hauled the boat with its crew on board.

A gloom came on all as we steamed on, leaving one behind us who was alive and well but a quarter of an hour before, now with his God ! The life-buoy was left where it had been thrown to mark the place, and was being tossed about on an angry billow, covered with gulls and other sea-birds to shriek to the roaring winds and waves. A subscription was immediately set on foot on hearing Jarvis had only been married six weeks, and a sum of £60 was subscribed by the passengers for his wife before the day was over.

After this Atlantic gale, we were fortunate in having very delightful weather for the remainder of the voyage. The wind had exhausted itself, and the angry billows were once more tranquil and at peace. After a storm comes a calm, which is highly satisfactory, all things considered. My friend, Mr. Wykeham, had had a very serious attack of gout, and I was glad to be able to be of service to him during our recent perils, when everything was in such a state of tumult and disorder. We sent up rockets, and showed blue-light signals to the mighty "Cuba," outward-bound, as she passed us on our port tack. Our American passengers were greatly amused at the fears entertained by some of the nervous elderly ladies, or, as they called them when together in solemn conclave gabbling, the " hen party," and their husbands " the roosters," many of whom were parsons and spiritual advisers, the Yankee phrases for these worthies being " sky pilots." It is very noticeable with what disdain cultured gentlemen look on priestcraft in this age. Here was an instance of it,—they were regarded as a parcel of old women, and their mild and pretty sayings as arguments unworthy of a sensible child of ten years of age. Their worn-out sentiments and exploded doctrines are inadequate for the mind of man of the present day, and are only regarded as true and infallible by the weak and ignorant who have never read and thought for themselves. All the priests in the world cannot limit the lofty aspirations which are gradually dawning on mankind by slow degrees in various stages of growth and development by the pioneers of truth and science. Priests are playing a useless and unworthy game when they attempt to silence knowledge. If they love a perfectly wise and true God, they cannot do their Creator a worse service and insult Him more than by harping on the same unmeaning stories and fables of gone-by ages. They are too ready to denounce the noblest and most glorious truths corroborated by logical and high-minded philosophers, who work for no other object than that of promoting truth and progress for the good of their fellow-men, and who, far removed from mercenary, selfish motives (peculiar to the low and vulgar herd), possess in the highest form the faculties of reason and conscience—the greatest gifts a wise and loving Father has given His creatures, granting unto man that power of rightly directing the human understanding, and properly appreciating the beauties of the glorious works of nature. I have no objection to priests believing any nonsense they choose, but I strongly object to those persons who waylay you, force their beliefs down your throat, and attempt to stifle your conscience by imaginary fears, utterly regardless of your feelings, by dishonouring what every true scholar should prize above all things—intellectual development of man. Such was the impudence we had to meet with from these ignoramuses, who sheltered their wits behind folds of robes which did not permit of their being regarded in any other light by our sex but as women. A man is power·less when attacked and insulted by priests and fishwomen. The surest and safest way to steer clear of violence and a breach of the peace is not to attempt to argue theological vexed questions with one who cannot keep his temper.

The weather continued unusually warm, due, no doubt, to the influence of the Gulf-Stream, which affects even the climate of England. The advantage we derive from this course is a very serious matter of jealousy with some Yankee patriots, who contemplate cutting off the Gulf-Stream, dam it, and divert it through some of their waste icy regions. There is no saying when the American of the period will reach the moon, if he progresses in thought and action as he has done the last fifty years!

Rising at daybreak the morning of our coming in sight of land, we were well rewarded by witnessing a most magnificent sunrise. The sun rose like a ball of fire, encircled in folds of dazzling golden orbs, which, with radiating tinted beams of various hues, lit up the whole heavens in splendour unsurpassable. I never saw a sunrise equal to it before. The land of "ould Ireland" now came in view, and the small round towers on the blank, barren coast of Kern, the scenery of which is wild and beautiful. We approached very near the bold, treacherous rocks of the "Cow and Calf." A large vessel, under full sail, passed very adjacent to the most dangerous point. We then kept close under the cliffs, and passed between the mainland and the lighthouse. What a place to live in! The cold suddenly became intense, and fell some 15°. Our light American clothing had to be changed for English apparel and Ulster coats.

We touched at Queenstown, and the captain's first care was about our prize, the abandoned vessel, which we had picked up on the high seas, and run into Halifax. His joy was beyond control when he heard of her safe arrival; and, with tears in his eyes, he came out with a "Thank God!" and, rushing up to two of the most beautiful women on board, he gallantly bestowed a kiss on the cheek of each lovely face, as three cheers went up from the whole crew and the passengers collected round to congratulate the captain on his good fortune; and with a request from all that he would be the bearer of an address signed by every passenger, and accompanied by a purse, for the acceptance of the gallant officer and brave men, who, at great peril to their own lives, launched a boat, and pulled out in a terribly heavy sea to try to rescue the poor sailor who fell overboard. Also a second address from the unanimous votes of those on board to the noble captain and his trusty officers, expressing the entire confidence we had placed in them on the occasion of one of the most eventful and perilous voyages on record by a Cunarder crossing the Atlantic.

The majority of the passengers (of the sterner sex) were so elated and. overjoyed at reaching England safely, that I regret to say the quantity of liquor imbibed that night was more than they could carry without showing it, and some serious escapades resulted.

We did not see the beautiful coast of England to advantage, owing to foggy weather, on rounding Anglesea and the green bold heads of Caernarvon, Denbigh, and Flint, as we steamed into Liverpool. We stopped at one of the most comfortable hotels in this part of England, the Adelphi. Mr. Jerome, who is generally ripe for any excitement, racy songs, and revelry, amused the company by occasional outbursts of genuine frolic and genial mirth. He remained at the hotel with Mrs. Yznaga, who fully appreciated his lively humour and funny ways. Mrs. Yznaga was accompanied by her daughter, a lovely young woman, of surpassing charms.

We visited, in our rounds of Liverpool, the docks, and other important hydraulic works of such renown, and were much pleased with this most magnificent city. We were well treated at the Club, and met many agreeable acquaintances. The Adelphi Hotel appeared very different in size and grandeur to the New York hotels; but then you have not the bustle, noise, and the discomfort of these monster palaces. A great number of foreigners reside in Liverpool, and you must leave the place before you can get clear of the " bagmen" and " shoddy class " of Columbians (and the eternal dollar-talk extends even to here),—men of no great intelligence beyond being cunning and sly in their own way of buying and selling " dry goods," whose jokes are vulgar and of a low, depraved order,—and of the great number who glory in dealing with " cottons up," " tobacco steady," " shirting down "; to which might be added, that their love and lust of gain from the weak, unitiated, and needy was " firm," their charitable propensities at " par," selfishness " steady," and covetousness ever on the " increase." There is very little to be learnt from these men. The worst class of our snobs and cads are of this type, and they disgust the more refined and polished Englishmen, who only hear of the doings of these individuals, and imagine the American gentleman, who quietly passes unknown through the land, to be of the swaggering, bragging, boisterous class of Yankees.

Once out of Liverpool, we are rid of the smoke and fog of this densely-populated, important city, and enjoy the dear old country of glorious England. To fully appreciate our beloved country one should go abroad for a time. Oh, how I love everything English! Even the cows, horses, and sheep in the fields look so big and fat, happy, contented, and English! Truly a country worth living for, and dying for, too. "Dulce et," &c. What millions have fallen to save you from the invader, plunderer, and to preserve your prestige, which is still the first and foremost in the civilized world!

CHAPTER XV.

ARRIVED in London, I made for my pet Club, and heard, to my horror, news had been received of my sad death out in Mexico. I started for Kensington, and acquainted my people of my existence in the flesh. I went straight to the familiar door, and learnt that the household were in sad grief at the bitter intelligence just received from abroad of the death of a member of the family. The servant did not recognize me at first, but, discovering who I was, prevented me from rushing into the drawing-room, as I was told I was "dead in there, sir!" The cries and lamentations issuing from the said room were heartrending, and it made me sad to think I was the cause of all this anxiety. I was at my wit's end to know how I could adjust matters and settle everything, when a bright idea struck the servant that I was to wait in the dining-room, and one by one should be sent for. Servant entered. "A gentleman is very anxious to see you, madam, and is waiting in the dining-room."—"I can see no one!" amidst tears and sobs, was the reply.—"But he has come from abroad, and wishes to see you, please, at once."—"From abroad! Who can it be? Some one, no doubt, who can throw some light on this horrid murder!" I stood under a dim light, and the mater, bowing, eyed me suspiciously as she demanded my pleasure. Throwing off my Canadian overcoat, I approached her with,—"And is this the cool welcome you give me?"—"Good God!" shouted the excitable mater, "Fettey's ghost!"—and she fell into my arms fainting. Others followed, and my hands were soon full. Two unusually tall, fine women fainting off in one's arms simultaneously was more than any ghost could stand, and I stoutly remonstrated, "One at a time, if you please." My beloved relative muttered out, "It is *not* Fettey nor his ghost, but some vile impostor, who has been sent here to mock me in my grief! This is worse than death!"—and, before fainting off again, the servants were ordered to remove me. "It *is* poor Fettey's ghost, I feel assured!" cried many voices.—"No, I am not a ghost; but I am ready to eat *some*" ("ghost" is the Hindustani for *meat*), I said, for I was indeed dreadfully hungry, and completely worn out and exhausted ; so, ordering food and wine to be brought me, I astonished them by eating a tremendous meal, and laughed heartily at their unnecessary fears for my safety.

I had hurried back on purpose to use all the influence I could bring to bear at the War Office to be appointed on the staff of the Ashanti Expedition. I knew several at head-quarters, and my application as a volunteer had already met with great support by the officer in command of the organization, and I was expecting to hear of my getting orders to join the second batch, which was being then equipped, and on the eve of starting. Although I was strongly recommended, and my name placed on the scroll of the next detachment going out, my services were never required, as, having applied somewhat late, I was not fortunate enough to go with the first of the expedition; and the authorities having made up the full complement of officers, I should not be sent out unless those already there were to die of yellow fever or be killed in action. It was a bitter disappointment to me not being nominated earlier. The war was easy and the burden light. The fortunate few returned overwhelmed with honours, and a run of promotion unparalleled, for a few days' sport in the wilds of Ashanti during the healthiest part of the year.

The Christmas season in London has its charms, and we expected to be particularly gay and lively. Town was fast filling, and people were coming in from all directions from the country and abroad. It was about this time I heard definitely from the Horse Guards that my application, which had been backed so strongly, for active service with the Ashanti expedition was noted, but it was now too late, and they could hold out no hopes of an appointment, unless— But, bad luck to it, I did not accompany the force! This will make the third expedition for which I have volunteered,—Házári, Abyssinia, and Ashanti,—but have been fruitless each time in my endeavours to get an appointment as field engineer. Hanton applied for the first two, but was fortunate in getting away with the latter. He was on leave at Murree when the Black Mountain War broke out in 1867, and, thinking he was sure of an appointment, started off before receiving orders, and reported his arrival at Abbotabad. He was over-zealous to distinguish himself, and was immediately ordered back to his regiment, with a tremendous official wigging.

Shortly after this, applying for a staff appointment, he had to fill in the necessary form before the application could be entertained by those in authority. In the column " State whether you have ever volunteered for active service, and been mentioned in despatches," Hanton wrote underneath, " Yes; volunteered lately for the Házári campaign, but was not mentioned in despatches; on the contrary, received the strongest censure, and was severely reprimanded for acting without orders, and sent back forthwith from Abbotabad at the instance of the commanding officer."

For the novelty of the thing, I accepted the kind invitation of a fair cousin (known to the literary world as a strong-minded woman, an authoress, and an editress of a monthly magazine) to meet her at the Ladies' Club, in Berners Street, of which she is a member. The whole thing amused me greatly,

—the expostulating ladies and their unusual conversation. They have a secretary, who is of the
masculine sex, and the only male to be seen at the
establishment. I understand he is a confirmed
bachelor, with mild, moderate tastes, but has a
care-worn, mournful look. Their debates and com-
mittee meetings are of an extraordinary character.
The President, of course, is a lady, whose duty it
is to bring forward and represent the rights 'and
wrongs of the lady members. One of these charmers,
on an occasion of a general meeting, rose to introduce the discussion of the day, a grievance which
influenced most of them; but, as it so happened,
several of their strongest members took quite an
opposite view, and the debate soon became hot and
powerful. More than one rose at the same time
and addressed the President, who, being fairly
puzzled, implored the ladies to control themselves,
and not all talk at once. I believe nothing was
definitely settled, although the agenda of business
is constantly being brought forward. Altogether,
matters are not quite so satisfactory as they might
be at the Ladies' Club.

I educated a very pretty girl (the daughter of
an artillery officer, deceased) for the stage, and it
was about this time she made her *début* at one of
the theatres. The piece had taken considerably,
and she was greatly praised 'by some of the papers.
Her voice was full and rich, if it was not powerful.
She had acted before in private assemblies, and had

sung at mixed concerts; so when my dark-eyed *débutante* made her appearance in this well-known piece she was not altogether a novice. Her love for the stage amounted almost to madness, and, much against the wishes of her family, she broke away from home-ties and restraint. It was highly satisfactory to watch her progress, and to speculate on the success that would attend her future career. She was so overjoyed on gaining her first triumph, that when it was all over the poor girl fainted away. She smiled when she was brought round, and said to Hanton, " This is my first weakness, and it shall be my last."   .

In company with a few fellows from St. James's Square, we were, with great difficulty, admitted to the Geographical Society when Sir Samuel Baker gave an account of his African exploration. The Prince of Wales and other people of note were present. I never remembered to have seen the room so crowded. We were glad to make our escape before it was quite over, and, having nothing to do, we strolled off to hear a political-satirical song at one of the music halls, which was causing considerable discussion, entitled, " The Damn Scamp." New verses of all the chief events of the day were introduced every evening; also a song called " The Blues." We went to see the tone of the Oxford, Pavilion, Evans's, and other places of pretended doubtful character; but I find that, as a rule, these haunts are generally the most proper and orderly of assemblies in London, and yet elderly gentlemen get horrified when they hear of any one going there. The " Judge and Jury," perhaps, is not one of. the most highly instructive places of amusement in town; but I think one may learn very useful lessons by attending, once in a way, second and third-rate houses. It is interesting to observe how such places prosper and advance year by year, and how the class of people who patronize them improve even in their own idea of amusement.   Apart from the morality of the thing, I would not waste more than a few nights in the year, on special occasions, at the Alhambra, Argyle, Cremorne, and other like places.   A man must have a very low taste to attend these amusements regularly; but, when properly managed, I can quite believe it is just as well to collect people of certain vitiated tastes in one place as to have them spread over many quarters.   And if healthy amusement is offered, with a view to improve the tone of their morals, so much the better for themselves and society at large.   I visited some very queer resorts in London, not to satisfy any idle fancy, but in order to study the kind of life which exists and is practised by the majority.   I can be a bystander without being a participator,—watch events and study mankind without being contaminated with depraved characters.

I went out of town about this time for a week to enjoy some good runs in Sussex.   The sport was fair, and Hanton, who was with me, was invariably first in at the death of the best runs with the Colonel's hounds. We had some shooting, too, but I fail to appreciate this kind of English sport. It is too difficult, and not worth the bother, as the game are so domesticated, that no man with any true feelings of a sportsman would stoop to fire at tame birds. It does away with the whole thing as sport, and brings the noble art of the gun into gross ridicule. It would not be so paltry if one's party were not made up of men who scarcely know which end of the gun to place to their shoulder, and are dangerous companions to have by you when they take to discharging their fowling-pieces.

There is a vast amount of humbug about this affectation in pretending you are a keen sportsman and love to shoot tame pheasants; it being considered a manly and fine thing to talk about to women and non-sportsmen. Several men I know have given large sums of money for purchasing preserves, and care but little for shooting; but it is the fashion at present to kill time and money in this way when the season in London is at an end. And witness the absurdity of some M.F.H., who attempts to lead the way across country, and never has had courage to go out of a smart canter, and would think just as much of jumping a hedge as he would of committing suicide. Of course, there are many M.F.H.s in England I challenge to ride anybody or anything, and, after a few Irishmen of my acquaintance, I class Englishmen as the best riders in the world. The firmest seats, and with a thorough knowledge of horsemanship. Scotchmen, as a rule, are about the worst riders in the world. There is a great deal attributed to the Scotchman which he does not deserve, and is wholly without foundation. I doubt if a Highlander ever distinguished himself in the prize-ring, for instance. They fight well enough when subject to strict discipline, but any men will do that. Scotchmen are too cautious to risk anything. I don't know what they might have been; I know what they are.

During the Christmas week I amused myself by taking my younger cousins, and semi-cousins, and a host of others to the various pantomimes, much to their delight. I think I took nearly as much pleasure in seeing 'Puss in Boots,' at Drury Lane, as they did. The next best pantomimes of the season were at the Crystal Palace and Hengler's Circus. Payne's Toy Depôt in Oxford Street is well worth a visit. Some of the ingenious toys on exhibition are perfect marvels in themselves, and I was more interested than the children in witnessing their extraordinary mechanism and working powers. The toys at this establishment are most reasonable, and stronger than any others. Amusing the young being the order of the week, the Zoo., on a quiet day, and Madame Tussaud's wax-works were in turn gone over, and I experienced the greatest delight in making them happy and joyous.

The fog during this season was considered the very worst London had seen for a score of years; but I am told Londoners say the same thing every year, that this fog is even worse than the preceding one. The cold was very intense while it lasted, but, with this exception, I did not mind the winter of England. I have felt it even colder abroad in the Punjab plains during this season of the year.

We were in the habit of occasionally attending the sacred musical rehearsals at the Albert Hall of a Sunday afternoon; and, if not so engaged, would meet at a certain fashionable house in the West-End, where the leading actresses, best singers of known repute, *savants*, and first *artistes* of the London world generally assembled. We were enabled to have the *entrée* into this society, which some, not acquainted with the culture, knowledge, and refinement of these fascinating mortals, are apt to denounce in unnecessary and harsh language. More highly - enlightened and profitable acquaintances than these gifted ones it has never been my lot to meet with. Their manners are polished and natural. Charitably disposed towards all, their moral life is beyond question, and they delight in brilliant wit and high intellectual conversation. Your *artiste* is, as a rule, most cruelly wronged by Mrs. Grundy and her old women associates, or silly people, who pretend a great deal, but know very little.

I was present on the occasion of Dr. Kenealy giving his last and final address in the celebrated

Tichborne trial. The court was densely crowded. I took my seat as one of the barristers, so had a good view of the proceedings and the several important personages, from the Chief Justice to the extraordinary Claimant. The betting was one hundred to one before the address was over, and the excitement throughout Westminster was at fever-point. All who had watched the case impartially were of one opinion as to the final issue.

Poor Sir Edwin Landseer's complete collection of paintings were on view at the Royal Academy, and filled most of the galleries. Every picture, drawing, and caricature executed by that skilful artist was exhibited, and had been collected with the greatest difficulty from every part of the kingdom. Tens of thousands inspected the unique collection, for such an opportunity would never again occur.

I dined at an old-established club, where there were present all the officers of one of the first scientific volunteer corps of the land. It was given by the colonel commanding; and never had I been present at so *recherché* a regimental banquet. I have dined at the Albion, St. James's, and Willis's Rooms often enough, but no dinner was equal to this one. The viands, wines, decorations, and speeches were unequalled in taste and order. This regiment stands first in line of precedent, and well it may, for a finer body of well-trained, smart, intelligent mechanics you would not find anywhere. Every man is an artisan of some order. They belong principally to one great firm. Particular attention is paid to their education, position, and physical attainments. For some years past they have distinguished themselves at Wimbledon, Aldershot, and the Dartmoor manœuvres, and also in their high standard of proficiency in examinations and inspections. The officers are all scientific men of considerable note, who have made a name for themselves which is known at head-quarters. With such a regiment in active service there is no question as to how well they would perform their duty. If all volunteer corps were equal to this one, a more splendid and effective service for the purpose they are intended could not be possible. It is a pity greater stimulus to promote good fellowship and *esprit de corps* with the regulars is not adopted. When scientific and titled men engage themselves as officers to volunteer corps,—men of wealth an d position, who have the means and can take an interest in advancing and improving this strong arm of our national defence,—we shall find the volunteers thought more of than our regulars, and one will take the place of the other. It ought to be the pride of every Englishman that he belongs to so noble a service. When this change takes place, we may expect to see the volunteer system on its legitimate footing with the nation. At present half the volunteers are ashamed of saying they belong to so laughable and contemptible a body, mainly because they have not gentlemen as officers.

CHAPTER XVI.

AFTER a few more rounds of dinner-parties, broken by attending lectures on scientific and professional subjects and duty at Chatham, I left for Devonshire, and spent most of my time at the Plymouth Club—the only public establishment approaching civilized life in these parts. There are some nice places round and about Plymouth and Plympton; at which latter place I resided for some short period. I amused myself in my leisure hours reading the latest books and writing short articles for the papers. I attempted to show the waste of time and money it was in sending half-educated Scripture-readers to India with a view to convert the heathen. Really very little practical good has been done by missionaries. We have held that great country, India, for upwards of one hundred years, and, after many valuable lives have been sacrificed, and millions squandered to keep up appearances for the support of missions, the result has been *nil*. I don't suppose a score of converts of an intelligent order will be found throughout the land. The class of people who pretend to embrace Christianity are the most degraded of the country. They are the lowest of low, the most ignorant and degenerated of outcasts, and are spurned and loathed by their own people as much as they are by the whites. No European would think of employing a native Christian, as they are known to be the greatest rascals, unfit for anything. Educate your shrewd Hindoo up to our standard of mental culture, and he will see the folly of believing in his own superstitious doctrines, but he won't accept our faith; he will tell you he can see nearly as much silliness in our creeds as in the one he had just forsaken. The consequence is, these men join the new and growing faith of the Bramo-Somaj, which is nothing more or less than pure Theism, of which Baboo Keshub Chunder Sen is at the head. This gentleman visited England some few years ago, and made some considerable stir in the London world at Exeter Hall meetings.

But you ask, how about these elaborate returns and forms, which are all so satisfactory, submitted by the legion of missionaries scattered over the Indian continent? Surely they are doing good, and securing happiness to millions of benighted homes, and bringing the different creeds over to our way of thinking? The circulars which are read at the various mission meetings in England of the work done by those good and holy men are highly satisfactory; but I think it only right and proper to state that these missionaries are prejudiced, and that the reports and circulars originate from *them*, and are not at all in accordance with facts which have come under my notice and what I know to exist. It must have

taken thousands of pounds to convert every intelligent, well-educated man in the Bengal Presidency during the past ten years. A great many
take to Christianity as a very paying affair. They
have nothing to lose and everything to gain, and
can easily gull the soft, half-learned missionary by
saying "Yes" to anything he may say. They are not
at all particular as to the truth, and, as a rule, speak
only what is truth by accident. Lord Macaulay gave
a very just estimate of the ordinary Bengali's worth
in this respect. I should advise missionaries to stop
at home, and take to some more honourable calling,
not ruin our *prestige* by propounding worn-out
legends and old ladies' stories, in bad Hindustani, on
barrel-tops, in bazaars, to a crowd of ignorant, nude
Hindoos, who cannot possibly believe in the truth of
Christianity unless by a great stretch of conscience,
and leave them alone in their glory, to enjoy
a religion which suits them down to the ground.
Educate them if you like, but waste no more lives,
valuable time, and millions of money, left by old
maids on their death-beds, on such a thankless and
unprofitable task. If missionaries are so constituted
as to only care and live for this sort of thing, then
there is no occasion for them to go abroad, but start
at home, where charity first commences, and they
will find a grand field for their missionary enterprise in all the back slums of our great cities, starting
with Plymouth.

It was about this time that the subject of cremation was renewed, and lengthy discussions appeared in most of the papers in answer to a well-written article by Sir Henry Thompson. No ordinary mortal with but a glimmer of the knowledge of physics would, on mature thoughts, allow himself to be weighed down by prejudice, and insult common-sense as to what should be done with our beloved dead. If the corpse were kept six weeks, say, in a proper place before it was cremated, all sentiment by that time would have exploded from the minds of the survivors, and they would only be too ready to have it disposed of in this way. If the relative was a mother-in-law, for instance, the time for cremation might be shortened. As regards all sentiment, and from a sanitary point of view, there can be no question which is the best and only way, and that our present system is undoubtedly wrong and improper, in spite of what some learned Bishop said recently, that such a mode of disposing of the dead would greatly interfere with the general re-surrection. But the Bishop was a very funny fellow, and if he was not poking a joke at his congregation, he might, if he so preferred it, be buried instead of cremated.

The 'Autobiography of John Stuart Mill' was creating considerable stir amongst all classes of thinkers, and I read it with much gusto. Truly an extraordinary man, with profound knowledge of certain things. He allowed petty trifles to annoy his great genius, which showed that even he was a narrow-minded man on more than one point. He was a forced man, with a miserable opinion of our race at best, and thought life not worth living for after the freshness of youth had flown. I honour him as a philosopher, for his candour, and his liberal, honest, outspoken views. The most tangible of them will live for many a century. I have heard bigoted fanatics and silly men, who had not the brains to follow him in his mighty plans for re-modelling society, nor read half-a-dozen lines of any of his standard works, speak of this great genius as " a wretched, insignificant materialist, of no mind or soul for anything beyond himself." A man who lived less for self, and of so unassuming a nature, I suppose the world never saw. I can picture the conceited, insincere, and uncharitable bigot giving utterance to such unwarrantable sentiments as these, utterly without foundation, unless in his own mean mind. All that can be said of Mill is, that he lived in advance of his time, and his great, pure soul was lost on the imperfect hosts of this age, who only cavilled and made light of the best and wisest of his mighty aims to induce mankind to work and think for themselves, instead of being, as they are, abject slaves of error and superstition. People who have always looked through green spectacles imagine everything in nature green.

The dissolution of Parliament and an appeal to the people came upon all like a thunderbolt. Although Mr. Gladstone's gigantic notions of change and reform were well devised, and in some cases successfully carried out, all could not follow him in what he deemed most expedient for governing mixed and varied classes of Englishmen. The people appeared dissatisfied with his rule, and brought in Mr. Disraeli's party in great triumph. It is just as well, perhaps, that there should be an opposite party, to overhaul the mistakes and blunders which must necessarily follow from the actions of one class of thinkers, never mind how advanced they may be in their own ideas; but an unprejudiced man must see it matters little which Government is in power. The conduct of one is very similar to the other, after all. Provided intelligent men are unfettered by religious prejudices, the laws and regulations for the masses are identically the same in the end. It was a good thing for India, perhaps, that the Duke of Argyll was no longer to pass inconsistent orders from his office at Whitehall for a country he only knew of from hearsay, ten thousand miles off, and that a more liberal-minded man should take his place, who would be guided a little by the opinions of tried veterans of the Crown, who had spent half a century in discharging their duties in the service of the Indian Government. The time will come when more power will be given to the representative of the Sovereign ruling two hundred millions of people, and less red-tape formulæ gloried in by the India Office authorities.

It was my good fortune to escort one of my numerous fair cousins out with the hounds and harriers. The jumping and " banking" in this part of England is rather severe in some places. But my cousin, who is acknowledged the fastest and best rider in the county, and quite accustomed to leading the hounds, was in her element; and I will admit she excelled every lady rider I ever met with in England, and gave me enough to do to accompany her in her " straight going." At our first meet, her groom unfortunately checked the horse he was riding in taking him over a high stone wall; the result was, that the poor animal, with terrible force, struck his leg against a sharp-edged stone, which inflicted a gash several inches in length, tearing the knee-pan open. We were so eager in getting away, that we heeded no one, and did not hear of the mishap till after a splendid run of over a score of miles, across a very rough bit of country. I was immediately summoned to give a helping-hand, and with a coarse darning sail-needle as well as I could sewed up this terrible wound. The poor horse then walked into Plymouth, which was some miles off. With this exception, we were fortunate in all our various meetings, and the bright, joyous days spent in her company I shall never forget. We ran together evenly, as we always shall, I hope, to the end of the chapter.

One lady, jealous, I suppose, of my relation's

perfection as a horsewoman, was once bold enough to try to vie with her in taking an unusual jump. The pluck of this lady is not to be gainsaid, but she failed, and was thrown, much to her concern, in a most undignified manner, before the eyes of the whole field, and had to wait until her horse was caught for her.

I shall never forget rather a bumptious young fellow, called Scrap, who invited himself to show her the way over an ugly jump. She bowed, and smiled her consent to his proposal. So away went Captain Scrap at the jump, higher than himself. But either he or the horse (or may be it was mutual) suddenly altered their mind when it came to the point. After repeated attempted runs to clear it, my cousin asked if she might be allowed to show *him* over; and, to his amazement, the jump was cleared most beautifully, to the intense amusement of numerous equestrians who had collected round to watch the proceedings, at the instance of the said little Scrap. If it had been played on purpose, it could not possibly have been acted better.

I spent some time after this in the neighbourhood of Falmouth, at an aunt's, who was a few years back considered the belle of Cornwall. If she is no longer a great beauty, she has still her charms, which are unequalled, and I very much enjoyed my short visit to her house, and the many nice houses on the pretty river Helford.

It struck me as a puzzle quite beyond my comprehension why farmers should make enormous banks and earth ramparts on some of the richest and most valuable of their lands, and thereby waste so much area. I was curious to measure some of the hedges which divide the fields, and found them actually twelve and eighteen feet at the base. This unnecessary waste of good land is common to Devon and Cornwall. If landed proprietors would substitute light walling, railing, or wire fencing in the place of these monster mounds, straggling in all directions, they might reclaim thousands of acres in both counties. The roads, too, are disgracefully laid out, and twist about where there is no necessity, thus lengthening the distance, and taking up more ground than they otherwise would do. The good people of these counties evidently don't study or appreciate the beauty of utility in all and everything, even to their district roads and hedges.

After leaving Cornwall, I made Southampton my head-quarters for a time, and entered into all the gaieties which were going on from Portsmouth and Ryde to Weymouth and Torquay. On hearing the intelligence that my nearest and dearest relatives were coming home from India, I put off in the mail-tug when I heard that the "Venetia" had been signalled. I boarded that ship far out at sea, when I discovered, to my disappointment, they had not changed at Suez, but were coming on slowly by the "Cathay," so returned to Southampton rather crestfallen. With my cousin I spent some delightful days on the water, and visited Cowes and Ryde for some very rare fun. We were fortunate in seeing the warriors from Ashanti arrive at Portsmouth, and afterwards visited the sick and wounded at that palace of hospitals, Netley. On my second excursion in the mail-tug I was more fortunate, and met my dear ones all safe and well on the deck of the trusty ship "Cathay," and escorted them (after a day's rest at Southampton, where they were welcomed by a legion of belongings) on to Plymouth. Returning, I had occasion to halt at Plympton, and I shall never forget the disgraceful conduct of the drunken herd of Plymouth which came out in thousands to revel in a day of debauchery and drink on Good Friday. They like Plympton, so I understand, from the fact of its being without any police to keep them in check and order. It is an extraordinary thing why this is permitted year after year, and the authorities so apathetic and sleepy in not maintaining the peace.

A friend of mine at this period expressed a great wish to see me, and invited me to dine with him on a certain day, where I should meet some very noted turf men. The day arrived, when my friend, who I had always thought "wanting," informed me after dinner that he had by bitter experience bought dearly his complete knowledge of horse-racing, but he had, for his wife's sake, vowed he would never bet again. He had now invited me down to put me "up to a thing or two," and clear "a haul" on the coming Derby. This was certainly very kind and good of him, and I firmly believed him at the time. His favourite was "George Frederick," and he was able at that time to get 22 to 1.

I wrote off to London and made my book, when who should I come across but an old club bird of greater experience, and his advice was all for "Atlantic"; and vast were the little bits of news he quoted in support of his hobby. He had for half a century made horse-racing a study. I in a weak moment hedged, and I shall always regret the step I took in not laying on the original sum and sticking to George Frederick, who proved the best horse after all.

I was in time to share in the gaieties of the carnival at Torquay, and the perpetual festivities of this Naples of England. I met my dear old chum Hanton at the Royal Hotel. The tone of Torquay society is more refined and polished than anywhere out of London, and enjoys advantages unspeakable over Brighton and Scarborough, preventing a mixed class from participating in vulgar prejudices of an odious character. In this respect it boasts of being very un-English in its tastes. This *naïve* and bewitching trait, so essential an element in society, recommends Torquay as the first and foremost watering-place for prudes and flirts, people seeking recreation, and those who are inclined for fast and gay life. You can freely enter into the particular set you have always so much desired to your heart's content, and leave it without being known or thought of again by people who forget the past and bury what is unpleasant.

I remained for a few days at Exeter, or rather in the pretty suburbs at Alphington, and recruited late hours by falling in with some very methodical relatives, who adhered to what they thought was only right and proper. They were exceedingly kind to me, and I enjoyed my visit very much, in spite of a little severe discipline. The noted cathedral was being restored, and great commotion was caused among the so-called "Low Church" party by a reredos having been erected at the altar. It was referred to that large-minded, practical Christian, the Bishop, who, taking the advice of the law, ordered it to be removed. I was present when his Lordship gave his judgment, which was clear, lucid, and quite to the point. It met with general approval by the various denominations who thronged the Chapter-house to hear the verdict. Some thought that as a work of art the reredos might remain, and, on the case being appealed from and referred to a higher court, the Bishop of Exeter's decision, which was thought so just and right, was eventually revoked.

Some talk was caused by a clergyman of the High Church party who, by clandestine measures, forced a beautiful maiden to confess her manifold sins to him. The parents, who were greatly enraged at the whole proceedings, reported the clergyman, who maintained he only did his duty, and got his back up about it, when an estrangement between daughter and parents took place, and the house was divided against itself.

I heard rather a good story at Exeter of the irregularities of the late Wimbledon rifle shooting practised by the innocent and mild volunteers. A certain crack shot who was firing hit the wrong target, and made a bull's-eye for another man who had not yet shot. Instantly coming up, he begged he would say nothing about it, as it would only disqualify the crack shot from further shooting, and prevent his participating in the winning score. The man who had not fired therefore reaped the benefit of a bull's-eye shot.

Poor Livingstone's bones were landed at Southampton amidst great excitement; but the admirable arrangements for preserving order and checking the noisy crowds, showed how the authorities were prepared for an unprecedented emergency. A great fuss was made by the nation on his remains being interred in Westminster Abbey, but they failed in doing anything practical for the family. A paltry sum was voted them, and there it ended. After such a life as poor Livingstone's! To me it seemed so inconsistent with what was done for Sir Garnet Wolseley after a few weeks of Ashanti sport on the Gold Coast. What were the dangers the one man underwent compared to the other? Which of them did the most good and perpetuated England's honour—the brave, unassuming missionary, or the gallant general, at the head of picked, skilled troops, shooting unprovoking savages?

I spent many delightful days at the Isle of Wight about this time, and was present at a few merry gatherings, where I met old, true, tried friends. While on a visit at Corfe Hill, we inspected all places of interest in the neighbourhood, and the fleet lying in the Portland water—the "Northumberland," "Triumph," "Agincourt," "Sultan," ironclads, and "Devastation," a turret-boat. These are about the best and the pride of our Navy. They are mighty to behold, ponderous and massive for defence, capable of discharging thunderbolts and projectiles from monster cannon which nothing can resist. It might well be asked when Engineers were trying to vie with the Artillery, what would be the result of an irresistible force coming against an immovable body? Our Navy was never better than it is at this day, with all that has been done by the red-tape authorities for and against this gallant service. It is still replete with brave, clever officers, who love their noble calling, and with intelligent, well-disciplined men, who have a thorough knowledge of their duties. They are more than a match for all the combined foreign navies. If other powers could arm and equip temporary fleets for active service, so could

England. Our experiments, with a few exceptions, have proved successful. Who would then doubt the proficiency of our grand old Navy, which has undergone such re-modelling and changes? When the time comes for them to do their worst with shipping, towns accessible to the sea, and coast fortifications of England's enemies, it will be interesting to watch their deadly mission and work of destruction, and see whether our speculations of what they are worth are true or not.

I was much amused at being taken for a man who was then monopolizing all the big people of the land, and had created a name for himself in history, but the only thing which could possibly remind them of this noted celebrity was his worst feature. It was a little annoying to be taken for a great man, because so much is expected of you, and the laugh is sure to be turned against you on their finding out their mistake. It is very curious how taking a foolish notion of this sort becomes. In the man I unknowingly represented they saw one who was young enough to be his son, of a bigger frame, taller by some inches, and different in every respect, the strong resemblance being my weather-beaten and sun-burnt countenance.

Weymouth is all very well at a certain season of the year, if you are living far enough away from the bridge and the swamp. It is a disgrace to the authorities that they do not pay more attention to the sewage arrangements. Sad blunders have been carried out here at a loss to every one concerned. Portland is a terrible hole to reside in—hot, dusty, and God-forsaken. I pity those quartered there—even to the convicts. The queer, pebbly beach and breakwater can be seen in a few hours, and done for for ever. Returning, our party visited Messrs. Debenham's brewery, and tasted some very delicious, light, wholesome beer, admirably suited for India.

I visited my kind relations in Weymouth, and spent many pleasant evenings in their society, and made some nice friends.

After a week or two at Southampton and in the neighbourhood, I went up to London, and commenced to take an active part in the gaieties of the season, when I was fairly knocked down with jungle fever and ague, which compelled my leaving town, and residing for a time in Brighton, where I had often gone for convalescence, and recruiting my wasted energies. The chief amusement was skating on rollers at the rink; and many severe tumbles I got before I became an efficient. Some of the young ladies glided most gracefully, and displayed considerable art in performing extraordinary fancy curves.

Although this was not the Brighton season, we had very good fun on the whole. The pier was generally the place for appointments, where the charmers were never tired of hearing 'Madame Angot' played by the pier band, and echoed by sundry others in various parts of this juvenile

London. 'Madame Angot' was played early in the mornings by organ-grinders; all day long, and up to the last hours of the night, the band played it, even on Sundays, only a little slower. The air was hummed by servant girls cleaning the rooms, dashed off on the pianos by ladies, and whistled by boys in the streets. Never did a people get 'Madame Angot' on the brain as the Brightonians did; young and old, rich and poor, wicked and bad, fools and geniuses—all were affected with the complaint.

I met Hanton at his club on my return to London, and we went that evening to the *fête* given by the President of the Institution of Civil Engineers, at the west galleries of the International Exhibition. It was a brilliant affair, and one of the most successful on record. Strolling from one gallery to another, Charlie had much to tell me of all his doings of the past, and what was in store for him. He begged me to join his party going in a drag from Chester Square for the Derby; but I was obliged to decline, as I had made another arrangement, which was a sad disappointment.

I accompanied the Hantons to the Opera, Drury Lane, to hear Madame Nilsson on her first appearance for the season from America. It was her favourite piece, 'Faust,' and she never acted Margherita better. Her voice I thought even more beautiful than last year. Our box was splendidly situated, so we were able to see and hear her to advantage. She brought down the house over and over again, which was crowded in every part to suffocation. The heat during the evening was intolerable, which rather marred the great pleasure. Madame Nilsson was repeatedly encored, and the Grand March was performed so magnificently that house was not satisfied until it had been played three times.

The arrival of the Czar of Russia in London afforded John Bull an opportunity of feasting his eyes once more on royalty, and tens of thousands thronged to see His Imperial Majesty, who was magnificently received wherever he went. I saw the procession on the occasion of the visit to the Guildhall, and had a good view of all the notables, the Czar included, from an upper window in Charing Cross. It was a very grand sight, and His Majesty afterwards said how impressed he was with the crowds and magnificent buildings along this important part of London. I saw the procession from a window in Whitehall on its return from the Lord Mayor's banquet, and the excitement of the living mass of human beings which filled the streets was beyond the power of the police authorities. The only wonder was how so much order was maintained, and the throng kept back from deluging the cavalcade. In the midst of all this appeared the inevitable hearse, which was forced by degrees back into Trafalgar Square, and there remained until the crowd dispersed. The Czar was altogether delighted with his visit, and, all things considered, he was better worth cultivating than the Shah.   I have a great contempt for the latter sovereign, but am charmed at the noble bearing, dignity, and manly character of the Emperor of Russia.   I was present on His Majesty's visit to Woolwich, the review given in his honour, &c.   He left England better pleased with us than when he came, and was fully appreciated by the English nation.   The Duchess is young, and, being an only daughter, has been somewhat spoilt.   It was but natural she did not understand the position she should take, and it was to be regretted that a slight misunderstanding as to precedence should have occurred.   Her Royal Highness is likely to be very popular with all classes.

The Derby Day of '74 proved that "George Frederick" was the best horse, and many were again terribly sold.   The Prince of Wales was, perhaps, the largest winner.   It was a race which told more on professional book-makers and turf gamblers than any others, and "outsiders" and "non-professionals" reaped the benefit.   Tens of thousands of Englishmen who love a little excitement stake a "fiver" or "tenner" on some horse they know nothing about, without the ghost of a chance of ever getting any return for their money. It was just such an instance as this; and for once in their lives they were fortunate. The day passed with the usual excitement going down, on the ground, and returning; the same sort of ordinary betting expressions and turf remarks; the arrangements and general conduct of the crowd; the same class of people; same sort of luncheon—ham, chicken, and champagne, with repeated doses of this latter at intervals during a dry, hot, dusty day. I wonder if the Derby race fifty years ago was any different to what goes on now-a-days?

Miss Thompson's celebrated picture of the 'Roll Call' was creating unusual sensation at the Royal Academy. I had read and heard a good deal about it before I went there with some noted artists, and it was highly interesting to listen to their severe criticisms on the first pictures of the season. A more instructive collection had not been exhibited for some years, and altogether I was well pleased and charmed by seeing the handiwork of a friend so greatly admired and universally appreciated by all classes of painters.

At the Opéra Comique, 'Giroflé-Girofla' had been introduced, and duly noticed for what it is worth. It is light, pretty music, after the style of 'Madame Angot,' but I doubt if it will ever take with the English public as this latter piece does. We went the round of the theatres, and were delighted with the new opera at Drury Lane, 'Il Talismano,' in which Madame Nilsson took a prominent and leading part. The magnificent way it was put on the stage in so short a time was perfectly marvellous. It is likely to become very popular if Madame Nilsson, the best voice of the day, takes to it as

she has begun.   Hanton and I whiled away an hour
or two one evening at the Alhambra, to see ' Flick
and Flock,' the acting of which was slow, but
the scenery very imposing and grand.

It is absurd to close your ears and eyes to what
is being said and going on under your very eyes
in London. People pretend to think such is not
the case.   Too awful for a tried cabinet minister
or head of a noble and distinguished family to lower
their honoured names by debauchery and immoral
practices.   But that does not alter the facts existing;
and however one may spurn such notions as being
impossible, it cannot lessen what actually goes on
sub rosâ amongst the majority of the wealthy and
great of the land. Far too much. is gravely put
down to women, and not enough to men. The
tables should be turned if Mrs. Grundy values what
is truth. But I doubt very much whether fashionable ladies are aware how one-sided the story of
life is as told them, and how their trusted husbands
behave when out of their sight. Is it right to keep
them in ignorance, and give them but a distorted
account of daily life which occurs within their own
atmosphere, or tell them the bare-faced truths, and
so give them an idea how they should act with
regard to re-modelling the characters of the real
life their husbands lead when they are free from
petticoat government? A few remarkable divorce
cases of late will show how necessary it is that
this subject should be considered by wives who

may suspect their husbands of broken vows. Women have more power over our sex than they choose always to admit; but by proper, judicious means they might reclaim many a weak-minded man from ruin and crime. Few women care to exercise their authority, and tremble under the threats of brutal husbands. But the matter is more theirs than ours.

Rather an amusing occurrence took place at the Underground Railway Station, South Kensington, at the time when King Koffee's umbrella from Ashanti was being exhibited. An old lady, in terrible distress, came up with a long story to the busily-engaged ticket-collector that she had lost her " gingham," and searched everywhere for it but found it not. What was she to do ? whom could she go to for information? she feared it had been stolen ; when the wag of a collector replied she might possibly get some information touching its removal from Sir Garnet! The joke was fully appreciated by the bystanders.

I spent one or two very delightful days with some new cousins and friends near Marlow, in Bucks, and was well pleased with the pretty scenery, grounds, and fine houses in this part of the county. A most remarkable feature I noticed in the vulgar rich of England. Their fathers or grandfathers, honest, good men, starting in life to accumulate wealth for their ripe old age, commence their career by holding broad Liberal views, that is, if they are capable of seeing beyond the surface of things.

They make their money when they have all their wits about them, and on retiring to a fine seat in the country suddenly change their Liberal ideas as they get older, become doggedly obstinate, and cling to old worn-out sentiments, which are dished up afresh and ready for the hungry youngster in these go-a-head days.

It is hard on those who have been liberally educated and have travelled to be forced to say against their convictions that thinking is an unpardonable crime. " Papa is an old-fashioned Tory, you know, and pretends to think he is right, and everybody differing from him not only wrong, but a fool !"

On analyzing this state of things, it can be generally traced to people who ape what they consider the aristocracy, hence so much narrow-mindedness, weakness, and gross ignorance is tolerated and adored by the powerful and wealthy of Old England.

We made up a party on one occasion for a trip up the Thames, employing a horse to drag our boat. All went well for a time, when the boy driver had to get down and open a gate for the horse to pass through. The tow-path ran close to the edge of the river, but beyond the gate two paths diverged, and, before the boy could come up, off went the horse by himself, at a smart pace, dragging us across the river, and with considerable force shot us into the bank. Luckily no harm was done, but the fright of some of the young ladies was highly amusing. After some pleasant rides in the country, and delightful meetings, with charming spins at croquet and badminton, I returned to town, and accompanied my fair Carry to the concert at St. George's Hall,, under the patronage of the Duchess of Edinburgh, for some charitable purposes. Carry's performance was greatly applauded, and took extremely with an admiring audience. The next evening she was the belle of one of the best balls I was at for the season.

At a bachelor's dinner-party at Hornsey Rise, I was telling my friend of an extraordinary circumstance which was causing no little talk in certain fashionable circles, and of the proposed compromise made by the gentleman who had jilted an old love when he was in the "Blues." Poor fellow! he had taken it very much to heart when he found he could not well get rid of her, and had met some one else he fell in love with straight off. So he was once more in the "*blues*," and was sorely puzzled how to act. I saw my host colour up, and look at me in a very ferocious manner, as he said, in a firm voice,—"I will show you his photograph," and he produced it. "So this is the gallant guardsman!" said I, eyeing the gorgeously dressed warrior, looking as if he were ready to annihilate anybody or anything. "I am afraid you do not understand," said he, "that this gentleman is my future brother-in-law." There are certain times in our life when we feel ourselves very small; I experienced this at that moment. I had to say something by way of apology, after my unfortunate remarks, appeared very indifferent, and immediately introduced another more suitable subject.   Like a sensible man, he did not take offence at what I had so inappropriately alluded to, and we were very good friends in spite of what had been said.

I met Major M——, and dined with him at the Criterion, after a drive in the Park, where, as usual, the Princess and Duchess were exhibiting themselves to a sea of human heads.   The Princess looked as beautiful as ever, and still kept up her popularity amongst all classes.   The Duchess, although very well liked, will never be the favourite the Princess is.   The Prince is universally beloved.   He is a fine, manly, practical specimen of John Bull, and will make a sensible, matter-of-fact king, in spite of what has been said against him.   He is not possessed with an over-abundance of brains, but, what is better, perhaps, for a man of his exalted rank, he is thoroughly good-hearted, and incapable of anything mean and unmanly.

In the evening we attended the Royal Geographical Society, Sir H. Rawlinson in the chair, to hear lectures on Central Asia, by an American, who had penetrated to Kokan, and into the heart of hitherto, to Europeans, unbeaten tracts.   Afterwards Sir D. Forsyth's Mission to Yarkand was elaborately discussed. Sir George Campbell, lately returned from the Lieutenant-Governorship of Bengal, was introduced, and upheld the Indian policy in respect to the explorations undertaken at the instance of Lord Northbrook's Government, in carrying out the schemes of former rulers for opening up the rich provinces beyond our Himalayan frontier into Central Asia.

It was announced at this meeting that some of our party encountered a troop of Russian horse in these parts, under very different circumstances to what was predicted. This time they met as mutual friends of a Mussulman chieftain, who did all in his power to help them in obtaining information for their Governments. A few thousand pounds of British money have well been laid out in encouraging the Yarkandees to trade with us. But of all things the most likely to stimulate these sleepy people to acts of commercial speculation and civilization, would be a railroad. The much-talked-of Euphrates Valley Railway would be a step in the right direction, if carried out, for opening up many countries, and enriching Europe with increased wealth of mighty empires lying dormant behind the scenes in Central Asia. This great work at present devolves on England and Russia. Many hard struggles and severe battles will have to be undergone before we can bring these people over to our way of thinking, and show them the advantages of

European civilization. God grant we may never fall out with Russia, but together co-operate in advancing the interests of these nations which we are attempting, slowly but surely, to subjugate by legitimate and peaceful means! British gold will work wonders if judiciously dispersed to greedy Mahomedans, but there can be no doubt money will not always tempt fanatics and savages, and that, sooner or later, we shall have bloody war with these people. Our only hope is that Russia may not, for her own lust and love of territory, fall out with us over the division of spoil.

After Ascot, and attending a few more pleasant evenings in company with Hanton, broken by dinners and balls at Willis's Rooms, lectures, conversazioni, at-homes, garden parties, scientific gatherings, delightful days at the clubs, and merry meetings, such as his cousin's wedding at St. George's, Hanover Square, our programme for the London season of 1874 came to an end, and we left town for the north of England, with an intention of going first of all to Norway and Sweden, and, ultimately, having a little fun with the Spaniards; but our plans broke through, and we found ourselves, after many days of travelling and various excursions by land and sea, settled at the Alexandra Palace Hotel, Edinburgh.

CHAPTER XVII.

WE reached the modern Athens at a glorious time of the year, when everything was looking its best, and the holidays just beginning. What an extraordinary fellow John Bull is for his holidays! Does he not enjoy them? The Highlands are, after the London season, generally overrun with Cockneys and Yankees. Fortunately for us, we had started just before the influx of the usual class of tourists had commenced their peregrinations in this direction, so we had hitherto escaped the bulk of the objectionable element.

Much has been said about the beauty of Edinburgh by impartial Englishmen, and rather more by Scotchmen. I had deducted the fine colouring of the description they had given of their noble city, and I was not disappointed; on the contrary, allowing for all *pros* and *cons*, I was agreeably surprised; but I should have appreciated their show-capital more if they had not ranted and dinned me sick with what I could see and hear for myself. The Scotchman would be a much better fellow if he had never been blessed with a Scott and a Burns. Their love of speaking of these men becomes loathing after a time. We

all know and value the works of these talented
Scotchmen; but to have the same never-ending
panegyric stuff dished up by high and low, rich
and poor, in hours and out of hours, is calculated
to disgust one with the very name of Scott
and the whole of his countrymen. What Englishman endowed with ordinary common sense would
think of introducing a Shakespeare or a Newton
into every conversation, and take a certain
amount of praise and credit to himself for being
of the same nationality as these worthies? The
42nd Highlanders, or Black Watch, who were
engaged in the late raid on the Ashanti coast,
have been eulogized, fêted, and raved about by the
whole nation of Scotchmen because as soldiers they
only did their duty; but the 23rd and Rifle
Brigade, who were also there, have been quite
forgotten. Fancy if Sir Garnet Wolseley had
been a Scotchman! Could anything more dreadful
have happened? We must thank Heaven that he
was spared being a Highlander! The world would
never have heard the last of it, that is certain!

It is a generally accepted fact that Scotchmen are
exceedingly "clannish," intelligent, money-making,
industrious, straightforward, honest, staunch men
of business. Some of this I will admit; but I
decline to believe they are more so than their
equals in England; and what I am sure of is, that
they are not half so brilliant and clever as the
English and Irish. They are, as a rule, slow in

arriving mentally at most things. They are much more suspicious, and imagine most Englishmen have an eye to take them in, and are dogged and obstinate whenever they get hold of an idea.

A Scotchman is more adhesive when he has discovered you are not a rogue; but he invariably starts with the assumption that every man not of his country he meets with is dishonest and bad principled. It takes him a long time to find out whether he is right in his first impressions. Sometimes he is too dull to understand the Englishman, and, in that case, avoids him. Scotchmen refuse to trust men generally, but take a one-sided (and the very worst possible side) view of human beings. It is no wonder, then, as they are plodding, clanny, and suspicious, they should make commerce so profitable a calling. A Scotchman is everlastingly comparing his profit and loss account, and takes good care never to hazard anything which does not show a fair return for his trouble and outlay. I am speaking of them as a nation, and as a nation they are very contemptible in my eyes. I have many personal friends Scotchmen, and truer, nobler men are not to be found in the world; but they are totally different from the ordinary class of their countrymen, and owe their education, training, and teaching to England and those they have met abroad in Europe and elsewhere.

Another practice they glory in is their imaginary line of ancestors, and what wonderful men their forefathers were, as if it mattered to any one what their fathers might have been, or how their ancient race of Macs and others fought each other over a coloured print, or hacked themselves to pieces about a clan or a herd of cattle. Englishmen of common sense now-a-days take no interest in anything of this sort, and we treat a Scotchman, if he is a gentleman, for what he is worth, not because some pseudo Campbell or Duncan finds it difficult to trace his family back as far as our friend thinks he can his. There can be no doubt he must have had people *then*, and consequently his family is no older or younger than the meanest beggar or the most mighty sovereign ruling the greatest nation on earth.

We all know how bad even some of the most powerful of rulers and noblest of lords were in gone-by ages—corrupt, base, savage, and ignorant in all their ways, and of no credit to the races of to-day. I have no objection to a man being proud of the great achievements of his fathers, but I think there is no occasion for him to be continually harping and annoying his friends by reiterating the same a score of times. A Scotchman is a perfect pest when he commences talking of his pedigree, because you never know how long he will be at it, and how far he will take you back into the dark past ages of ignorance and superstition to find a father !

Edinburgh is a wonderfully picturesque city, and is naturally the most beautiful of any town in Great

Britain. The views are varied and comprehensive from the castle and monuments, and embrace the principal portions of this wealthy and important capital. We went on a short visit to some of Hanton's friends at Salisbury Green, as we had previously arranged not to separate unless compelled. We came in for a good ball, which comprised the *élite* of the Scotch; but I must say I do not approve of Scotch manners, unless they are toned down considerably by the more refined and graceful bearing of purely English ways. I have met some charming acquaintances in Scotland, but they have not been genuine Scotch. The shrill, inelegant accent and general countrified style of the pure Scotch young lady is not taking, nor is it an advantage over her polished sisters of good society in England. I defy any country to produce such combined specimens of purity, grace, elegance, taste, and culture as are found in English girls common to London society. If there are Scotch girls possessing all these attributes, then they have learnt them from the English girl of the period.

Scotch women are very high-principled, amiable, and thoroughly good-natured, quite as much so as the English. They are, as a nation, more sedate, reserved, and better educated than the corresponding classes in Ireland or England. But in the higher branches of knowledge they are deficient, and backward in seizing at all the recent superior wisdom of this enlightened age. In this sense they are slow to learn, and display weakness and fear in meeting the glorious truths which have lately dawned on us. The Scotch being naturally a primitive nation, prefer believing in worn-out ideas to keeping pace with the march of intellect of the day. They pay such devotion and homage to the god of this age—filthy lucre—that they are naturally the most thrifty, economical, provident, and niggardly people alive. In many instances their miserly, greedy propensities have been the making of them and winning the money of their less-gifted fellows. It is an open question whether this is a trait worthy of a great civilized nation, the ignorant and easily duped being victims of the grasping money catchers, who get fat and rich by plundering the helpless and poor. They accomplish their ends by legitimate means, I admit, as they are not so foolish as to come within the pale of the law in matters of this sort; and so they become wealthy and powerful, admired and sought after, eulogized and pampered by the world at large.

We spent many pleasant days at Edinburgh, and having seen everything of importance, we visited the suburbs, drives, and towns for many miles round, Leith and Granton included. A very philanthropic nobleman is carrying out extensive improvements to the piers and harbour works at Granton solely at his own cost, and has greatly astonished the Scotch by his purely unselfish and benevolent acts.

We now proceeded northwards, and were well

pleased with some of the very pretty scenery which broke upon us near Linlithgow, about Bannockburn, and Stirling, where we broke the journey, and made some excursions in various directions. Our visit was brought to a triumph by a picnic at the Bridge of Allan, at which we were honoured by a few pretty Scotch girls, who added greatly to the day's enjoyment by their lively behaviour and provincial address. The scenery at the Bridge of Allan was some of the most beautiful we had seen in Scotland. The thickly wooded groves, broken heights, and running streamlets of this part were quite romantic enough for the occasion, and more than one engagement was the result of that day's commemoration, and will give certain parties ample scope for gossip for many a season yet to come. The Castle, like every other similar place or thing in Scotland, is of great historic renown, and one is deluged with guide-books and guides, facts and legends, until one is mystified with puzzling, rambling, flowery anecdotes of imperfect narration of what happened in ages long back. It is a great pity Scotch history is not more condensed. A great deal might with advantage be left out; and other matter of later years, of much more importance, could be substituted. If every little trivial event is to be noted in the doomsday book as it has been in the form of Scotch history, my sympathies are all for the youth of the fiftieth century. Stirling is a quiet town, and has a society which is cordial, sociable, and more refined than most Scotch towns in that part.

The country round and about Crieff, Drumlithie, and Inveramsay is barren and wild in places, utterly bereft of vegetation, with no trees or green, and is only broken by stony waste plains. This sort of thing makes one appreciate all the more the beautiful views as you come upon them along this route. But there is a singular monotony in some of the most pleasing scenery about Huntley, Forres, Elgin, and Nairn. It is totally different to the more bold and varied type of mountain grandeur which is to be met with along the other line, *viâ* Killiecrankie, to the Highlands.

We stopped at Perth, Montrose, and Aberdeen on the way to Inverness; but there is nothing very much to be picked up from the people who inhabit these towns. I was amazed to find that they take no interest in what is going on in London. I don't think I noticed in more than half-a-dozen gentlemen's houses any of the leading papers and reviews. They are content with a local paper, which contains borrowed stale news, generally of little moment to the community. Although the artisans are primitive and moderate in their tastes, they are most useful, hardworking, and industrious citizens. We went the rounds of the factories and mechanical shops, which abound in these towns, and visited all works of an interesting nature, and were much pleased and edified at all we saw. They deserve great credit for having made such progress in many of the departments of mechanical contrivances, and much useful information is to be learnt from this steady, energetic class of Scotchmen. I paid particular attention to the working-men's clubs, reading-rooms, and institutes; and found they were well kept up and patronized by more than the labouring classes. These men are sober, persevering, contented fellows, and are not so noisy and boisterous as our English workmen of a like class.

The Scotch are a queer conglomeration of mixed people—some affable and amusing, others sulky, cross-grained, and unsociable. You find the most kind and generous, canny and selfish people mixed up in one family. The man who has never been out of Scotland will hold to his primitive ideas with the most dogged obstinacy, while his- brother, perhaps, who has travelled, read, and seen things for himself, will be liberally disposed towards the great promoters of the age for advancing the welfare and happiness of mankind. They are, as a nation, honestly inclined, and make true friends. But you must bear with them in many of their absurdities, otherwise they will show they can be very uncharitable when they like,—indulge in cant, and rant one sick with sleepy, stupid ideas one has heard from many of our venerable grand-dames,—and all this with an air and grace that the most despicably proud noble might envy. They attend all the services of their beloved national Kirk, and wind up their Sabbath with imbibing more whisky than any other civilized mortals could stand. It is astonishing how much of this spirit is consumed by the Scotch after their Sunday devotions. I have seen a very fair quantity of drinking in many parts of the world, but no nation can vie with the good Scotch in this respect. One thing is certain, that their sacred drink is pure and genuine; and, after getting very drunk on it, they are not much worse for hard work on the following morning. If this were not the case, such a state of things would seriously contribute to the degeneration of the whole nation in time. As it is, they are a hardy, strong race, thanks to their glorious, bracing mountain breezes. I doubt, though, very much, their being physically stronger and more powerful than their smaller brothers, the English. My countrymen are tougher and more wiry, have greater powers of endurance, and bull-dog pluck, and *can stand punishment better* than the Scotch. It may tell on a Highlander being knocked down, but an Englishman is a much more dangerous opponent to encounter after he has met with a slight disadvantage at starting. This is my experience abroad of the two races in the four quarters of the globe.

Arrived at Inverness, we stopped at one of the best hotels the place could sport, and met Sir S. Hoote and others, so were able to enjoy a quiet rubber of an evening. This is a game the Scotch don't understand or appreciate, and class it with cribbage, and amusements at cards of a like nature. One old gentleman—a swarthy Highlander—once "cut in," and sat down to play a very extraordinary game of his own, and said we were wrong in marking anything but the score of ten for the game. He had never heard of short whist! Billiards and other such amusements are not frantically indulged in by Scotchmen, and they are not very keen at hunting or shooting. Fishing is much more to their mild taste; and, whenever you dine at a country-house, the good host is sure to tell you of very extraordinary draughts of fishes and monster salmon he has caught in his day; and this sort of talk he will glory in for many hours together, commencing from some loch far north with an unpronounceable name, and ending with some place to the south, which makes you turn black in the face trying to give it utterance. We made up a few delightful walking-matches from Inverness, and slept in out-of-the-way places and small roadside farm-houses and inns; and went fishing and shooting in localities where we had opportunities of doing very severe havoc amongst the birds of the air and trout and salmon of Scotch waters. Returning, we came round over the hills by Dulsie, and walked in under a very powerful sun to Inverness.

Inverness boasts a cathedral, an Established Church, and many minor devotional institutions of various sects and denominations. There is a good view from the Castle, which is used as a courthouse and residence of the circuit judges and other dignitaries, upholders of the majesty of law. It is, like the whole town, well kept, and is scrupulously clean and orderly.

Inverness is considered the capital of the Highlands, but has only a local trade of small magnitude, and is not half as important a town as Truro or Hereford, for instance, with all the fuss that is made about it. There are pretty walks along the river and across the small island, where occasionally a little fishing can be had. But the most comprehensive and one of the most magnificent views in the Highlands is to be had from the sugar-loaf hill on the left of the river Ness, now tastefully laid out as a cemetery. The scenery from this point is varied, and possesses many charming sights. The pretty winding river, thickly wooded belts on either side, rising hillocks studded with rich foliage of every conceivable tint, Inverness lying below, the fort on the other side of the river, show off the whole town with prominent effect. The line at this juncture is broken by a broad expanse of the sea, until the snowy peak of Ben Wyvis is intercepted against a heavenly sky, and the transcendently gorgeous shades of the lesser mountains vary the perspective, and complete one of the most beautiful sights I saw in the Highlands.

Our friend, Sir S. Hoote, who had been waiting to join Captain Fitzmore in his yacht on a cruise round the northern coast, was overjoyed to hear of the arrival of the tight little craft, as she put in at Inverness, after experiencing rather roughish weather in the North Sea. He brought with him a full crew of men, and a party of pleasant club-birds and ladies from town. We dined on board the first evening, and the following day most of them landed and left for some stag-hunting with Lord ——, who joined them at Inverness. We ran out to sea, and up the coast to the Orkney and Shetland Isles, returning to Inverness. The most lively of our party was the charming Carry, known in town under the *sobriquet* of "Still Waters," who shone in all her brilliancy on a trip of this sort. Free to act as she pleased, and away from stern parents, she gave vent to her natural exuberance of spirits, and was the life and soul of our party. I shall never forget her captivating powers, her genial wit, her bewitching ways, her pleasant, agreeable conversation, and lively anecdotes of all the courts of Europe.

We now proceeded, *viâ* Dingwall, to Straithpeffer, where we stopped to indulge in drinking the mineral springs, which are supposed to do one good; but they are just as nasty as any of the fashionable German waters, and never did any good for me, but, on the contrary, invariably made me very sick. I don't mind bathing in them, but drinking the horrid stuff is quite another thing. On one occasion, I remember going off to sleep in a bath heated to 120°. The result of this was a return of my old complaint, jungle fever, for a time.

A very remarkable incident occurred whilst here. Lying in bed rather late one morning, I heard a disturbance outside, and voices squabbling about a missing pair of slippers, which " boots" was supposed to have mislaid. On inquiry, I discovered that the slippers in question were the property of a friend of mine, the Scottish chief of a royal line, who had been here but a few days previously, and had now telegraphed from Archanacheen for his slippers! He was in company with Professor Overdone, who was making a tour in this part of the Highlands. I was sorry I had not the pleasure of meeting them, for, on arrival at Archanacheen on a visit to that charming Loch Maree, and across to Skye, I just missed my Punjabee friend. Before two days had passed at Straithpeffer we got to know every visitor of any consequence in the place. Being the only Englishmen, we were marked men; and, by the aid of a few nice people who were there for the season, we got up a dance at the Spa, and indulged in rural native amusements to our hearts' content. We made one or two rather long walks from this place, the greatest being to Ben Wyvis, which was almost clear of snow at the time. The natives firmly believe that if the ruling sovereign ever hears Ben Wyvis is bereft of snow, the mighty estates of the Duke of Sutherland will be confiscated by the Crown.

x 2

Our next walk was to the top of Knock Farrel, Cat's-Back, and round by the mountains. There are curious vitrified remains of an old fort at Knock Farrel. Our geologist was sorely puzzled to explain its formation and extraordinary shape. Not many miles from this elevated point, where there is a very extensive view of the surrounding country, lies an ancient cemetery, some of the graves being of great antiquity, the most recent ones being officers of both armies, which fell at the battle of Culloden. One spacious vault in particular attracted our attention. It was fast falling into decay, and there were no signs of it having been attended to for many years. The surrounding masonry piers were in a very dilapidated state, overgrown with creepers and holly, and the mouth of the cavity had already fallen in. On approaching nearer we discovered it to be a family vault of a once noble line of powerful chiefs, who owned the country for miles round; but the race had died out, and the last resting-place of these worthies was neglected and in the state we saw it. Peering into the dark chamber, we observed fragments of cut stones, polished substances, and bones intermixed with a lot of rubbish. Curiosity prompted me to explore, and, throwing off my coat, &c., I was, by means of a belt, lowered down by Hanton into the chamber, and safely landed on an elevated ledge, which afforded me a hold, and I reached the bottom, going down the crumbled shelves. I had provided myself with a box of matches, and struck a light to see around the burial chamber. I shall not easily forget the hideous-looking spectacle. The once splendidly polished carved coffins were all but gone, and disclosed skeletons in various stages of decay. Some had already withered away, and but a small collection of dust was left to show what had once lain thère. Passing on, I scrambled as well as I could over bones and rubbish to a small enclosure off the vault, and there was laid, on a separate ledge, apparently the last scion of the noble house. The coffin was of stone, and the lid had been somewhat removed, either by some of the crumbling masonry having fallen against it or with intention. This was in a much better state of preservation, and I was anxious to examine the elaborate workmanship of the coffin and that part of the hidden chamber. I had been prowling about from place to place, lighting match after match, so that at this juncture of my peregrinations I found myself with only two matches, and I had much to see and a good way to get back over a difficult embrasure, which required steady piloting before I could effect an exit; so, striking a match, I peered into the coffin, and there beheld a most perfect skeleton, surrounded with decayed fragments of clothing, which had been decked out in gorgeous paraphernalia, with more substantial fastenings, the remains of which still glistened with a sort of laughing mockery at the different stages of decomposition and dilapidation it had seen. My match now exhausted itself, and I was left with only one. Striking this, and holding it well up above my head, I saw the whole distance before me; but I took a careful survey of my position before it went out, and I was left in the dark, with the grim, ghastly-looking skulls glaring at me and human bones lying in all directions still fresh in my mind's eye as I made my way over the remains, ever and anon stumbling and throwing out my hands to protect myself, grasping some uncomfortable-feeling thing, till I reached the light of heaven and breathed fresh air once more.

I had been so long absent, Hanton had almost begun to think I intended to stop there altogether. He could not go away, and was unable to follow me. I gave him a full description of my visit to the vault, and made him laugh heartily at my "interviewing" the skeleton in the stone coffin. The following day we proceeded through Sutherland-shire; but beyond His Grace's noble castle, which is unparalleled in this part of the kingdom, nothing seemed to interest us very much. The country, on the whole, is barren and bleak, although here and there intercepted with heavenly nooks and corners of surpassing grandeur and beauty. For miles and miles there are dead wastes and uncultivated tracts, which can hardly pay owning them. We used the coach into Hemsdale, and returned, *via* Golspie, to Straithpeffer by rail, and did the remainder of the way to Inverness by coach and waggonette. We were advised to take this route, as we should come· in for the best scenery, and we were certainly well repaid for our pains.

From Inverness we took the Caledonian Canal steamer, " Gondolier," superbly fitted up with every accommodation and comfort for passengers. The food was good and wholesome, but the wines they supply execrable, although I overheard some connoisseur (a Highlander) repeatedly pronounce the whisky as most excellent, and he liked it the more he drank it. He was a rough country parson, and would persist in talking to me on a subject he was ill-suited to discuss, and on which he appeared to be labouring under a very strange delusion, poor fellow! It is the principle which teaches, not the power or example of man. His was, I considered, a most hopeless case! I made some friends on my trip to the north, and had the pleasure of meeting them here again.

The scenery along Loch Ness is, undoubtedly, of the grandest and most magnificent to be found in any part of the Highlands. The steamer halted for a time at the Falls of Foyers, which gives time to see them; and the beautiful views which surround the vales, clothed at this season of the year in all their richest verdure, and the broken lines of elevated peaks below, above, around to the far distance, of varied hue and luxuriance; the calm, crystal waters of Loch Ness stretched out at the foot of thickly-wooded heights, a lovely sky over-

' head, and soft, gentle, mountain-breezes,—stirred one's soul to enjoy this delightful picture, speaking of peace and joy; and yet the Scotch see more beauty in Ben Nevis than in a panorama of this sort. Glenmoristan, with its amphitheatre of hills, Foyers nestling in its rich woods, Inverlarigaig, with its romantic pass and vitrified fort, Glen Urquhart and its hoary ruins of an old castle against a glorious background of hills,—fall into insignificance when they start in their raptures of Ben Nevis's charms. I certainly did not go off into ecstasies on beholding an unmeaning, wild, big mound, with a little snow on the top. There is nothing to break the monotony of this stony, barren height,—not the vestige of a tree or bush,—utterly destitute of any living thing. The altitude of Ben Nevis is about *half* the height of Simla, and is spoken of as a *mountain*, whereas the latter station is only called a *hill*. Scotchmen in India rave about the glories of their pet mountains, but they seldom see any beauty in Simla hills, of surpassing grandeur and mightiness, towering over twenty thousand feet into the heavens. We stopped at Ballahuish, and coached to Glencoe, back by way of Loch Leven, round by Lismore Island, into Oban, a pretty watering-place, if it can be called so, seeing that no one ever bathes in the sea, perhaps on account of its rocky coast.

We came by the "Gondolier" to Loch Lochy, coached a very short distance to Fort William, which stands on Lochs Eil and Linnme, and is on an arm of the sea.   Oban is celebrated for countless hotels, which live and prosper for the twelve months on a short season of principally English and Yankee tourists, who throng the place from June to September.   Of course, the hotel-keepers take good care to make hay while the sun shines, and charge enormously for everything.   Some are regular Jews, and these land-sharks annoy one at every turn, from the rising of the sun to the going down of the same.   Our foreign friend, the Austrian Count we met in our travels at Vienna, was here with his yacht.   He had come round from the Continent to see the Scotch coast, and enjoy some seal shooting in this neighbourhood of islands. I hardly knew him again, he was so sun-burnt; but it added to his appearance.   He had thrown off his court dignity, and appeared in his natural *sans souci* jovial manner, and was known here as plain Captain ——.

The day after our arrival at Oban, in company with Hanton, we noticed a family group of father and four daughters pass our hotel for a walk up the road to the neighbouring height, which com- mands a magnificent view of the pretty bay and surrounding hillocks.   We watched them until they were out of sight, and then, by means of our glasses, were able to see them on their arrival at the summit.   They returned after an hour or two, and again we were able to take stock of them as they passed quite close to us.   Such a group, at such a place, would, probably, be but little noticed if it were not that there was something unusual about one or more of the party. As it was, all eyes were fixed on them as they walked quietly along the promenade, which caused us to *feel* the presence of some one superior to us. What was that feeling? Have you never experienced it, when a great genius, for instance, enters a room, although there may be a score of others present, and without giving utterance to a syllable, or acting in any way different, you *feel* that there is a superior mind in your midst?

It was such a sensation that crept over me every time I encountered one of that party, and I was determined in my own mind to know that *one* person. Who was it—the father? No, but the eldest daughter. She was a tall and beautiful girl of twenty, graceful in her movements, modest in her demeanour, lovely in face; large dark eyes, set off with longish eyelashes. She kept her eyes fixed on the ground until one approached her, when she raised her lovely head and looked at you, her eyes penetrating one's very soul. "What a magnificent creature!" exclaimed Hanton.—"Superb figure!" chimed in the Count.—"A sweet face," added I.—"Beautiful colour, peculiar to the English woman," sang the Count.—"A remarkably handsome girl, that any country might be proud of. I must see that face again. Let us turn," said Charlie, as we rounded, in order, too, to avoid the strains of vile music from a German band which had taken up a position before the hotel. I think "dark eyes" was conscious of our noticing her, for she suddenly changed her course and made for a seat, the others of her party following her. In doing so, she caught her dress against a pointed railing, and, trying to extricate herself, let fall her parasol. Her companions unconsciously had preceded her, so, as I was nearest, I stepped forward and handed her the tiny parasol, which she took with a smile, blushing as she left me to rejoin her sisters.

The next day the Count and I arranged to go to Fingal's Cave. The wind having died away, we gave up all idea of going by his yacht, so took the ordinary steamer instead. Having reached the wharf a little too soon, we strolled about till it was time to start. Much to our astonishment, we saw "dark eyes" and party making for the steamer; and not thinking I was justified at that instant in taking advantage of our meeting on the previous day, I managed to be at the extreme end when she entered the boat. Ten minutes afterwards we were under steam. On our going down to break-fast, it so happened I found myself next to the father, and before getting up from the table we had entered into a friendly conversation—spoken a few nothings to each other. So far so good. It was a warm, bright day, and the bold, wild coast of Mull looked as well as it could. It was a great contrast to the more civilized green appearance of the Oban shores. The passengers, in groups of twos and threes, were discussing the merits and demerits of the peculiar scenery of these parts until we reached Iona, when we put off to see this island of such historic renown, where it is said Christianity was first introduced into Great Britain. An old monastery, the far-famed cross, graves of the Norwegian kings and bishops of ages back, which are mixed up together in happy motleys of various periods, the celebrated dismantled abbey cathedral, together with other ruins, were in turn seen, and more than once I found myself in company with " dark eyes " and her father, who was greatly interested in these antiquities. I found him a man full of general information, who had travelled and seen a great deal of life, and was a most pleasant, agreeable companion. By degrees I made friends with the daughter, and, after helping her from the boat, I took my seat by her, and entered into various discussions of the manners and customs of the people. Her father having sprained his ankle, would not risk rambling about Staffa, so was content with seeing Fingal's Cave from the boat; but we were anxious to see the view from the top, and again I was fortunate enough to be her escort up the queer-looking steps and over the slippery grass ramps.

The formation of Fingal's Cave, in places, is not unlike what is to be seen at the Giant's Causeway in Ireland, the shores of which isle are distinctly visible from Staffa.   From a geologist's point of view, this extraordinary phenomenon of nature presents one of the most interesting studies to be found in this part of Scotland.   Some ladies were quite sure it could not be natural, but that man, with the hammer and chisel, had been at work!   I nearly came to grief here, which would most probably have finished my earthly travelling had I fallen.   In looking over the edge from the top, the ground came away from under me, and it was with no little difficulty I managed to recover myself.   I could not help thinking that I lost a chance of being immortalized in guide-book fame. How well it would have read, in years to come, after this style:—"A sad catastrophe occurred at this spot, some time ago, when a tourist fell from the top into the yawning chasm below, and was never seen again!"

Leaving Staffa, we sighted the Hebrides, Skye, and other islands, which have all the same dreary, God-forsaken look; not the vestige of a living thing for miles and miles,—no beautiful green meadows covered with brushwood, no trees, not even a man, animal, or bird to be seen far or wide,—nothing but wild, barren rocks, which shoot up with something of boldness and grandeur.   A few cots and huts here and there indicate that the place is not quite deserted.   Tobermory shows visible signs of being inhabited, but by a class of people who can't understand English, and talk the most pure out-

and-out Gaelic. A Colonel Gardner, who owns considerable estates in these parts, spoke it, he assured us, as well as he did English, and certainly made friends with many very rough-looking, tawny wild men, more like savages than civilized Europeans.

Some capital deer-shooting, and fishing in holes and small lochs, are to be had all along these high grounds, which have been bought at fabulous prices by men who have more money than brains. It is considered quite the right thing to say you own a shooting-run in the Highlands for which you have given £10,000 or £20,000. Judging from the general uninteresting, bleak appearance of the Western Coast of Scotland, I should have imagined, if I had not been told differently, that it would have been utter ruination to own land of any considerable extent, so unprofitable and worthless does it appear to be.

Rounding the Island of Mull, and entering the Channel, the whole state of things has undergone quite a metamorphosis for the better. The land is rich and fertile, covered with vegetation, sheep and cattle abound, people are abroad, and villages scattered about in all directions, in cosy, out-of-the-way corners, safe from the cold blasts of wind which are so prevalent in this part of Scotland. These rough Highlanders resemble the Irish on the opposite shore, and great numbers of them are Roman Catholics. They are absurdly superstitious, and, in spite of being one of the most priest-ridden of people, are singularly honest and manly in all their actions.

On entering Loch Linnme, a small rock stands out not far from the bold, wild shore of Mull. This rock, called the Lady's Island, has an extraordinary legend, which the Scotch of these parts are fond of telling. A mighty chief, in days gone by, had a lovely wife he was very jealous of, and one day, being sorely tried by her, he placed her on the island to perish. Her shrieks and screams reached the mainland, and her brother, hearing her terrible situation, swam off and brought her back. He then revenged the wrong which had been done her by slaying her husband before her eyes. We will hope it was only a legend, although my informant was offended when I pointed out its improbability. That evening I dined at the Great Western Hotel in company with the Count and Hanton, before the latter left to make a visit at Inverary and other places in the neighbourhood; he was to meet me at the English Lake Windermere on a fixed date. The Count had given his yachtmen a holiday or two before starting off on a seal-shooting cruise, and only a couple of men were left to look after the tight little barque. Some rather officious gentleman present, overhearing our conversation, appeared astonished at such liberty being given sailors, and inquired whether the Count could trust them on shore without getting into mischief and drinking themselves foolish. The mild answer he received was that for their own sakes it was to be hoped they would not get into any mischief; but there was nothing he desired so much as their enjoying themselves, and sailors only had one way of doing that— by getting intoxicated. He hoped, therefore, they would get very drunk, but return to duty on board refreshed and sober after their day on shore.

We were well repaid by walking on Sunday to the top of an adjacent hill, and witnessing a glorious sunset. The colours of the waters, tints of the surrounding mountains, with a background of gorgeous and golden clouds, represented Oban and its neighbourhood as a perfect Paradise. The magnificent sunsets of the Highlands are proverbial, and are unequalled by anything to be seen in England. They are only surpassed by the grandeur and majesty of the Rocky Mountains and the mighty Himalayas. Vying with the beauty of Highland sunsets are the Alps in all their sublimity and magnificence, as the " shades of evening close o'er those heavenly peaks." For a great wonder, we had no rain for nearly a fortnight—a most unusual occurrence in these mountainous districts; we visited Skye from Straithpeffer, and made a long journey by waggonette and coach, and were assured by our Scotch friends, who accompanied us, that that was the only time in all their lives they had made such an excursion without meeting with rough, dirty weather. What appeared to me the most extraordinary phenomenon in these high latitudes, was that it was never dark. When far to the north of Scotland, at this season of the year, we found no occasion for using lights, because at 12 at night one can read distinctly. Of course, I knew it to be the case, but I never before experienced continual light for weeks together.

The glorious sunset we witnessed on Sunday, was prognostic of coming events, for on Monday morning, after saying good-bye for some time to Hanton and the Count, I found I was on board the same boat with "dark eyes," bound for Glasgow. Verily my star was in the ascendant! Papa, with "dark eyes" and her party, greeted me with a smile of recognition. My luck appeared so great, I could hardly realize a meeting so opportunely. "There is a tide in the affairs of men," &c., and I took advantage of it. I discovered in the father a lively companion, full of general knowledge, and we had many "hobbies" in common. The route from Oban is singularly interesting. We sighted Jura, Islay, Gorvillich, and Scarba Islands, which have the same characteristic features of a wild and deserted look. Leaving the Oban "Gondolier" at Crinan, we entered another steamer which was alongside the terminus in the canal. The arrangements of the steamers are most excellent, but there is an unnecessary delay at times in opening and shutting the lock-gates. The regulating of the hydraulic works are primitive, and the newer improvements might with advantage be adopted at all the locks along the "Royal Route."

The steamer which conveyed us up the Crinan Canal was very well fitted up, unusually long for its width, with a sort of double story deck. The pace was ten miles an hour. The canal is absurdly narrow, in some places not more than a foot or two to spare. Considering that it twists, winds, rounds in and out of low hills, it is a perfect marvel that such difficult navigation is attended with such success. The father of " dark eyes " and I had become great friends, and we found we knew some of each others' people who had been in the —th Dragoons together, which cemented our friendship. We exchanged cards, and then he asked me to dine with him that evening. His house was on the Clyde; I could get there in capital time; and he hoped I would stop the night, and not be in any hurry to run away. " Won't a ferret suck a rabbit ? " Of course I accepted, and was only too delighted at what was in store for me.

At this juncture, we reached a string of locks, and the young people proposed to walk to the end. I offered to escort them, which honour was granted me; so away we started. Miss M. ("dark eyes") and I paired off, and were together most of the time till we reached Ardrishaig, where we all embarked on board that most magnificent of boats, the " Iona," second to none of her kind in Great Britain. She is the fleetest steamer afloat, and can accomplish twenty-two miles an hour. She is of very light construction considering her enormous length and gigantic dimensions; she is flat-bottomed, and her tonnage is thereby greatly reduced. She is only intended for fine weather, and immediately runs into port if there is any chance of it blowing. She has proved a great success for the purpose for which she was intended, and has returned her owners enormous profits. She is capable of holding armies of excursionists; on the day in question 1,700 passengers were on board, and she was not at all crowded. She plies between Glasgow and Ardrishaig daily. The waters of Loch Fyne looked very beautiful, and were alive with yachts and fishing-smacks. The shades of colour of the hills far and near looked their best from the loch as we passed close to the main shore, sighting Cantyre and Arran in the distance. The "Iona" rounds the point, and, in her passage up the charming channel of Bute, calls at Tighnabruaich, Colintraive, and Rothesay, which is the Scotch Brighton. The scenery along this winding route is truly magnificent, and one of the sights of Scotland. Innellan, Dunoon, Kirn, and Gourock are pretty watering-places, fast growing into fashionable resorts for the great and wealthy tradespeople of Greenock and Glasgow. The heat of Gourock is notorious, and it has on that account, perhaps, become so important a place for invalids and those preferring a warm climate. There is a small colony of old Indian officers residing here, and it is appropriately known as "Asia Minor." One has a view of Lochs Coil and

Long at this point, and Loch Lomond, the finest of the Scotch lakes, is easily reached from Helensburgh. There are other routes more accessible from Glasgow, but the crowds which pass up and down do away with all pleasure of seeing that charming sheet of water, with its bewitching surroundings of hills, to advantage.

After spending a most delightful time at Mr. M——'s house on the Clyde, I returned to Greenock, and was very hospitably received by a Scotch gentleman I met in my travels, Mr. MacDonald, of large, extended views, and who had been half over the world. He most kindly showed me over all places of interest in Greenock. The important ship-building yards of Messrs. Craig, where a mighty steamer, of ponderous dimensions, the "City of Berlin," is being constructed; also other iron ships close by, where the never-ending din of hammering boilers and engines, smelting-furnaces, and volumes of smoke, greet one at every turn. Cutting and sawing, hoisting and lowering, iron coming in, and iron going out; the beating of small hammers and large ones here, there, and everywhere, with a good deal of order and precision existing amongst the hosts of workmen scattered about in various directions,—represents a ship-building yard in Greenock.

We next paid Messrs. Allunim's sugar manufactory a visit. I was very much interested in accompanying the head of the firm over the different departments, from the top to the bottom. The thermometer in some of the rooms stands as high as 140°. The workmen here undress, and wear but a slight covering over their loins. Many of them faint away, the heat being truly awful. Most of the firemen are Irish. The Scotch lower orders cannot be induced to take such office. The thermometers in the furnace and other rooms are removed, as it only made the men discontented. The bulk of the sugar at these mills is made from common beet-root. The coarse, filthy sugar imported from abroad undergoes a cleansing process, gets mixed up with the beet-root sugar, passes through towers of charcoal, manufactured from bones of animals, and is shot out pure, and white, and crystallized. The courtesy I received from these gentlemen in showing and explaining everything of note was very praiseworthy, and I met with the warmest kindness and civility from perfect strangers. The Marine Department and the various institutions of Greenock I was shown by the head officers themselves. I was a guest of their very comfortable club, and was witness to a considerable quantity of their national spirit being imbibed by mighty Scotchmen with a never-ending and " noble thirst that nothing could appease."

I was greatly edified at a visit I made to the Sugar Exchange, where an enormous business and gigantic transactions in buying and selling sugar are carried on, and all over in an hour or two. Trains in connexion with the Sugar Exchange run to and fro from Glasgow.

A vast amount of energy and perseverance is found in the industrious and honest people of Greenock and Glasgow. They are more thrifty than the same classes in Edinburgh, and display greater independence and manliness of character in all their pursuits after knowledge and advancement. At Glasgow I was enrolled an honorary member of the Royal Stock Exchange, and was witness to how business is carried on at the greatest commercial mart out of London. The Secretary of the Exchange was a brother of a friend of mine, who had risen to the highest office under the Crown in his department, and his sad death had just been notified in the *Gazette of India*. I paid the largest yards and works a visit, but took a greater interest in the gas, chemical, marine, mechanical, and other engineering works.

From Glasgow I journeyed to Edinburgh, and then along the eastern coast, through that city of contention, Berwick, and minor towns of no great importance. Some grand old abbeys, castles, and ruins are to be seen along this route, and the country here and there is interesting and pretty. The coast is bold and drear, with no great pretension. Holy Island is visible from the train. We reached Newcastle about the middle of the day, and, after a wash at the hotel, I walked to Gateshead, and called on an old friend, where I inspected one of the largest and most powerful telescopes in the world.

The following day I visited Sir Willliam Armstrong's important works, and, by the kindness of one of the firm, I was shown over every department in gunnery, and was greatly interested and edified by what I saw. The whole system of working is entirely different to what is being carried out at Woolwich, where, perhaps, with their more costly experiments, they have derived greater knowledge and perfection in manufacturing every sort and description of cannon than any private firm can attempt to vie with. As it is, great stimulus is given by Government to encourage every possible means in promoting the highest perfection in turning out the most deadly and destructive instrument for warfare. Sir William Armstrong and his able colleagues have had advantages over similar enterprising genius of other nations in this respect; and although the guns made by the firm are inferior in some respects to the "Fraser" and other more powerful pieces of artillery manufactured by the authorities at Woolwich, still they command a ready sale for the heaviest cannon they can turn out, and are patronized by all the civilized powers of Europe, and the United States Government included. No guns now are made at Sir William's workshops for our Government. The largest gun weighed 80 tons, and carried a shot weighing 600 lb., but the workmanship of the Woolwich handiwork is vastly superior. For my part, the most useful piece of artillery, either for military or naval purposes, is a lighter and more handy gun. Not so much should be thought of *size*, as rapidity of firing, with precision and accuracy. And for the Navy, the chief desideratum in attaining perfection will be *speed*, not massive armour, so much as water-tight compartments easily repairable. The *fleetest* steamers, carrying true, light, but withal destructive guns, will be found of greater service in times of emergency than heavy, massive, unwieldy pieces of cannon, which the authorities arrogate to themselves have *ne plus ultra* charms. It is like the old story of killing sparrows with round shot. But John Bull would never be satisfied unless he was trying experiments costly and laborious, and blowing his penny trumpet, allowing the world at large to profit by the result. So why should he not spend his money this way as well as any other?

It appeared strange to me that what was being executed by an English firm of mechanical engineers should be supplied to foreign powers to arm and use against us in times of nations not agreeing with our peculiar policy, when mutually they make it a matter of artillery strife.

There are many very beautiful residences in the suburbs of Newcastle, but the town itself is one of the dirtiest and most objectionable in England. Smoke, coal, dust, and grit during the summer; fogs, filthy thoroughfares, and rain in the winter.

But I suppose, after all, it is not very different to other large manufacturing towns. Newcastle boasts no good hotel, with the exception of the one at the railway station; and its locality is not inviting. The charges, too, are very high.

I visited Carlisle on my way to the English lakes, and found Hanton had established himself at the Royal Hotel, Windermere, with one or two other friends. Going out next day in a yacht, we were nearly upset by a sudden squall (squalls are frequent and treacherous on these lakes) off Ambleside. We spent many pleasant days in the neighbourhood; taking waggonette, we went the usual round, to Derwent-water, and other lakes. The scenery of these waters and mountainous drives is certainly beautiful, and greatly astonished me. I had no idea it was anything like so charming and magnificent. On reaching the hilly point which stands out on the road above Wastwater, we witnessed Scafell Pikes in a thunderstorm. Heavy, angry black clouds came rolling over white ones, and gradually enveloped all and everything as the storm swept over the low hills. The Pikes stood out boldly, with a background of storm and tempest to relieve the sombre mountain, capped with snow. Below and behind all was at peace, not a leaf stirring, whilst, in the opposite direction of the coming storm, shone forth the sun on a glorious scene of clear blue water, thickly-wooded heights, in all their rich variegated foliage at this season of the year. This calm, serene view was a strange contrast to the impending storm, which had grown in fury and force as it approached, sweeping over us. . The rain fell in torrents, heavy peals of thunder overhead were taken up and resounded again by the surrounding mountains, and the lightning alarmed the horses, so we were compelled to stop until it was over. It was a magnificent sight from so prominent and elevated a point to see the view which presented itself as the clouds cleared away, and left us in the bright sun to dry ourselves, with twenty miles before us of a drive unequalled in harmony and beauty.

Leaving the lakes, we stopped for a time at Kendal, a flourishing town of some magnitude. Kendal is a much larger place in the eyes of the inhabitants than we could possibly take in. They are a people of a very good opinion of themselves, and of their importance generally. We came in for one or two good things, and were gratified in being introduced to two of the most lovely girls in this part of England, who came here for a dance. It was amusing to watch the contempt and jealousy their presence caused their less charming sex, and the round of stories which resulted from their being so admired.

We now proceeded on a tour through England, visiting the principal manufacturing towns—Lancaster, Leeds, Manchester, Sheffield, and that hot bed of radicalism, Birmingham. Some of the reddest of the clan had gone to Nottingham in order

to try and bring in that paragon of nobility, Mr.
Bradlaugh, as a worthy representative of their
extravagant notions.   It ended in a defeat for that
gentleman.

Journeying to Chester, we branched off at
Corwen, and travelled slowly through Wales, along
the coast from Dolgelly to Aberystwyth.   Some of
the trains took only two or three carriages.   On one
occasion, the engine and a single carriage comprised the train, and we were the only passengers.
The carriage in question had three compartments,
first, second, and third class, with a place for the
guard.   The locomotives are very powerful, and
where the trains are heavy, such as between Hereford and Cardiff, and the gradients and curves sharp,
two engines are required for the ordinary trains;
and it is with no little difficulty they work their
way up hill sides, passing the most magnificent
scenery in Wales.   The beautiful scenery along the
bold, rocky heights of the sea-shore is changed for
mountain gorges and deep valleys.   The lower classes
are primitive, but honestly inclined.   They are a
practical, hardy race, not unlike some Scotch.   The
scenery, too, resembles tracts in the Highlands.   It
is singularly wild and romantic, varied and grand,
desolate and barren, rich, fertile, and densely
wooded, all promiscuously thrown together, some
fields being cultivated and bearing splendid crops
alongside stony land, uncultivatable.   In many
places we passed through English was not under-

stood by the agrarians, and their dialect was incomprehensible to us. They are a peaceful, clean, and industrious people.

From Tenby we went to Swansea, and crossed by Cardiff to Bristol, where we enjoyed ourselves for a time, Hanton returning to town, and I to Exeter, Plymouth, finally settling down near the Land's End, to write out my Reports, Circulars, and Returns I had voluntarily taken up. Having completed the whole of these to the satisfaction of the India Office, the authorities abroad, and certain journals, I scribbled, in my leisure hours, these hurried notes of my past two years. The chief events of the past months have been the startling comments made on Professor Tyndall's Inaugural Address delivered at Belfast, where the orthodox world, spell bound, received with open mouths the indisputable truth from one of the most gifted philosophers of the day. What was heresy of yesterday becomes orthodox to-day. And gradually the world is becoming truer, nobler, and purer as it heeds the words of wise and honest men. John Stuart Mill's work on religion will do much to shake the power and thraldom of priestcraft, in spite of an occasional noble Marquis passing over to Rome, or the weakness and ignorance of some of England's greatest Dukes and Lords in encouraging childish ceremonies, and extending the power of the poor old Pope. Opposed to these worthies are Mr. Gladstone's "No-Popery" tracts, clever and well written, but unworthy the notice of such a statesman and scholar, followed by an anti-everything from the bravest of the brave of bishops, the learned and mighty Dr. Colenso. With the whole orthodox world against him, this saviour of the day challenges an army of cowardly myrmidons to approach his wise teachings, but in this matter the time is not yet ripe.

Never, perhaps, has the Church of England been so scandalized, so wronged as it has on this occasion. Here are the Church's greatest divines squabbling and fighting amongst themselves about Dr. Colenso's doctrines, which have been proved by the highest court in the land to be legal and in perfect harmony with the constituted laws of the realm; and yet, in defiance of this law and order, bishops actually dare to take it upon themselves to wage open rebellion from their pulpits, and in the most unprovoked and uncharitable manner refuse to hear their brother bishop, whom they designate as an arch-heretic, and heap abuse and unchristian expressions on his holy head. It is no wonder, then, that the weak and ignorant become puzzled and perplexed when they see the men they look up to quarrelling amongst themselves, and leave the Church disgusted, either for Rome or to swell the ranks of the Methodists. Why should not Englishmen, if they are a free and independent people, listen to any scholar or doctor they like? Why should one man say, " Listen to what *I* tell you, *I* am right and infallible; everybody else is wrong, and teaching aught but mine is calculated to be very pernicious to your prospects, now and hereafter " ?

Not a little talk at this time was caused by Sir George Campbell's scheme of adopting Indian labour in England, as he considered Hindustani coolies more suited to the harder manual task in manufactories and such like places than Englishmen. I hardly think this feasible, however well it might read in theory. I am of opinion the English public are not likely to employ foreigners such as the Indians until they are more assimilated in tastes and manners to our own countrymen. Sir George has started to work too soon after his famine bout. He may have an opportunity of speaking more fully on this head when Sir Richard Temple's book of the Famine has been revised, and all objectionable parts struck out by the Viceroy, and published for the edification of an inquiring English public.

A most extraordinary circumstance took place towards the close of the year. I had been narrating a story of the late lamented Colonel Bagot and " Harry Larkins " at a large party, when, on reading the news the following morning, I was astonished to learn of the gallant Colonel's death by poison in India. The day after brought the intelligence of poor wild Larkins having met his death in a violent manner at the hands of some Yankee in the Californian district. The New York papers published a long account of one of the fastest

of men this age has produced. His life was a very
eventful one, and volumes might be published of
his extraordinary escapades and daring games in
India. He lived a life which would have brought
many a man a dozen times to the gallows. His
career abroad is too well known for me to comment
on it.

At last, Christmas has come upon us with brawls
abroad, and some misery and wretchedness at home.
Terrible railway accidents, explosions, and wrecks
innumerable, with the "Cospatrick" to head the list
of the most awful of catastrophes on record. With
all this, John Bull must keep up his Christmas, eat
his roast-beef and turkey, plum-pudding, and rich
mince-pies—drink his champagne until he has reason
to remember the week of festivities for many days
afterwards. Presents are given and received by
one and all, which is the most objectionable part
of the programme; I hardly know which I dislike
most, giving or receiving. It makes Christmas unbearable, and is, without exception, the most odious
and unpleasant task of the carnival. Paltry cards
and Christmas tokens, worthless and childish, are
sent by every one. Why make such an unnecessary
fuss at this particular season of the year? Why
should one eat more than is good for one, and drink
bad wine, which knocks you up for days afterwards?
What particular amusement can John Bull find in
making a disgusting exhibition of himself? At this
lively season he is pardoned if he says anything he

should not, and is quite justified in drinking himself foolish, and, as soon as Christmas is over, he immediately looks forward to the next with infinite pleasure and glory.

January comes round, and I get my orders to return to duty. With many sad longings, and bitter regrets, I take my departure from Southampton, wishing my dear friends and indulgent readers a hearty FAREWELL.

PRINTED BY E. J. FRANCIS, TOOK'S COURT, CHANCERY LANE, E.C.

SAMUEL TINSLEY'S

PUBLICATIONS.

London:

SAMUEL TINSLEY,

10, SOUTHAMPTON STREET, STRAND.

⁂ Totally distinct from any other firm of Publishers.

28

A WOMAN TO BE WON. An Anglo-Indian Sketch. By ATHENE BRAMA. 2 vols., 21s.

> " She is a woman, therefore may be wooed ;
> She is a woman, therefore may be won."
> —TITUS ANDRONICUS, Act ii., Sc. 1.

"A welcome addition to the literature connected with the most picturesque of our dependencies."—*Athenæum.*

"As a tale of adventure " A Woman to be Won " is entitled to decided commendation."—*Graphic.*

"A more familiar sketch of station life in India . . . . has never been written. . . . ."—*Nonconformist.*

". . . . Very well told."—*Public Opinion.*

BARBARA'S WARNING. By the Author of " Recommended to Mercy." 3 vols., 31s. 6d.

BETWEEN TWO LOVES. By ROBERT J. GRIFFITHS, LL.D. 3 vols., 31s. 6d.

BLUEBELL. By Mrs. G. C. HUDDLESTON. 3 vols., 31s. 6d.

BORN TO BE A LADY. By KATHERINE HENDERSON. Crown 8vo., 7s. 6d.

" Miss Henderson has written a really interesting story. . . . The heroine, Jeanie Monroe, is just what a Jeanie should be—'bonny,' 'sonsie,' 'douce,' and 'eident,'—having a fair and sound mind in a fair and sound body ; loving and loyal, true to earthly love, and firm to heavenly faith. The novelist's art is exhibited by marrying this gardener's daughter to a man of shifting principles, higher in a sense than she in the social scale. . . . The 'local colouring' is excellent, and the subordinate characters, Jeanie's father especially, capital studies."—*Athenæum.*

BUILDING UPON SAND. By ELIZABETH J. LYSAGHT. Crown 8vo., 10s. 6d.

" It is an eminently lady-like story, and pleasantly told. . . . . . We can safely recommend 'Building upon Sand.'"—*Graphic.*

CHASTE AS ICE, PURE AS SNOW. By Mrs. M. C. DESPARD. 3 vols., 31s. 6d. Second Edition.

" A novel of something more than ordinary promise."—*Graphic.*

CLAUDE HAMBRO. By JOHN C. WESTWOOD. 3 vols., 31s. 6d.

CRUEL CONSTANCY. By KATHARINE KING, Author of 'The Queen of the Regiment.' 3 vols., 31s. 6d.

" It is a very readable novel, and contains much pleasant writing."—*Pall Mall Gazette.*

Samuel Tinsley, 10, Southampton Street, Strand.

DISINTERRED. From the Boke of a Monk of Carden Abbey. By T. ESMONDE. Crown 8vo., 7s. 6d.

DR. MIDDLETON'S DAUGHTER. By the Author of "A Desperate Character." 3 vols., 31s. 6d.

DULCIE. By LOIS LUDLOW. 3 vols., 31s. 6d.

FAIR, BUT NOT FALSE. By EVELYN CAMPBELL. 3 vols., 31s. 6d.

FAIR, BUT NOT WISE. By Mrs. FORREST-GRANT. 2 vols., 21s.

" ' Fair but not Wise' possesses considerable merit, and is both cleverly and powerfully written. If earnest, it is yet amusing and sometimes humorous, and the interest is well sustained from the first to the last page."—*Court Express.*

FIRST AND LAST. By F. VERNON-WHITE. 2 vols., 21s.

FLORENCE; or, Loyal Quand Même. By FRANCES ARMSTRONG. Crown 8vo., 5s., cloth. Post free.

"A very charming love story, eminently pure and lady-like in tone, effective and interesting in plot, and, rarest praise of all, written in excellent English."—*Civil Service Review.*

"The book is excellently printed and nicely bound—in fact it is one which authoress, publisher, and reader may alike regard with mingled satisfaction and pleasure."—*Nottingham Daily Guardian.*

FAIR IN THE FEARLESS OLD FASHION. By CHARLES FARMLET. 2 vols., 21s.

FOLLATON PRIORY. 2 vols., 21s.

FRIEDEMANN BACH; or, The Fortunes of an Idealist. (Adapted from the German of A. E. BRACHVOGEL.) Dedicated, with permission, to H.R.H. the PRINCESS CHRISTIAN of SCHLESWIG-HOLSTEIN. 1 vol., crown 8vo, 7s. 6d.

GAUNT ABBEY. By ELIZABETH J. LYSAGHT, Author of "Building upon Sand," "Nearer and Dearer," etc. 3 vols., 31s. 6d..

GOLDEN MEMORIES. By EFFIE LEIGH. 2 vols., 21s.

"There is not a dull page in the book."—*Morning Post.*

GRAYWORTH: a Story of Country Life. By CAREY HAZELWOOD. 3 vols., 31s. 6d.

GRANTHAM SECRETS. By Phœbe M. Feilden. 3 vols. 31s. 6d.

GREED'S LABOUR LOST. By the Author of "Recommended to Mercy," etc. 3 vols., 31s. 6d.

HER GOOD NAME. By J. Fortrey Bouverie. 3 vols., 31s. 6d.

"Abundance of stirring incident . . . and plenty of pathos and fun justify it in taking a place among the foremost novels of the day."—*Morning Post.*

"Amusing descriptions of hunting scenes."—*Athenæum.*

"A clever novel."—*Scotsman.*

"The interest is sustained from first to last."—*Irish Times.*

"A really interesting novel."—*Dublin Evening Mail.*

"Displays a good deal of cleverness. . . . . There is real . . . humour in some of the scenes. The author has drawn one sweet and womanly character, that of the ill-used heroine."—*Spectator.*

"To an interesting and well-constructed plot we have added vigorous writing and sketches of character. . . . . Altogether, the novel is one that will justify the re-appearance of its author in the same character at an early date."—*Field.*

HER IDOL. By Maxwell Hood. 3 vols., 31s. 6d.

HILDA AND I. By Mrs. Winchcombe Hartley. 2 vols., 21s.

"An interesting, well-written, and natural story."—*Public Opinion.*

"For a novel of good tone, lively plot, and singular absence of vulgarity, we can honestly commend 'Hilda and I.'"—*English Churchman.*

HILLESDEN ON THE MOORS. By Rosa Mackenzie Kettle, Author of "The Mistress of Langdale Hall." 2 vols., 21s.

"Thoroughly enjoyable, full of pleasant thoughts gracefully expressed, and eminently pure in tone."—*Public Opinion.*

IN BONDS, BUT FETTERLESS: a Tale of Old Ulster. By Richard Cuningham. 2 vols., 21s.

IN SECRET PLACES. By Robert J. Griffiths, LL.D. 3 vols., 31s. 6d.

IS IT FOR EVER? By Kate Mainwaring. 3 vols., 31s. 6d.

"A work to be recommended. . . . . A thrillingly sensational novel."—*Sunday Times.*

JOHN FENN'S WIFE. By MARIA LEWIS. Crown 8vo., 7s. 6d.

KATE BYRNE. By S. HOWARD TAYLOR. 2 vols., 21s.

KITTY'S RIVAL. By SYDNEY MOSTYN, Author of 'The Surgeon's Secret,' etc. 3 vols., 31s. 6d.

"Essentially dramatic and absorbing. . . . . We have nothing but unqualified praise for 'Kitty's Rival,' which we recommend as a fresh and natural story, full of homely pathos and kindly humour, and written in a style which shows the good sense of the author has been cultivated by the study of the works of the best of English writers."—*Public Opinion*.

LORD CASTLETON'S WARD. By Mrs. B. R. GREEN. 3 vols., 31s. 6d.

"There is a great deal of love-making in the book, an element whic will no doubt favourably recommend it to the notice of young lady readers. . . . Being a novel suited to the popular taste, it is likely to become a favourite. . . . Sensationalism is evidently aimed at, and here the author has succeeded admirably. . . . Mrs. Green has written a novel which will hold the reader entranced from the first page to the last. . . . Emphatically a sensational novel of no ordinary merit, with plenty of stirring incident well and vividly worked out. . . . Florence de Malcé, the heroine and Lord Castleton's ward, is a masterpiece."—*Morning Post*.

MARRIED FOR MONEY. 1 vol., 10s. 6d.

MARY GRAINGER: A Story. By GEORGE LEIGH. 2 vols., 21s.

"A very remarkable, a wholly exceptional book. It is original from beginning to end; it is full of indubitable power; the characters, if they are such as we are not accustomed to meet with in ordinary novels, are nevertheless wonderfully real, and the reader is able to recognise the force and truth of the author's conceptions. The heroine is such a creation as would be looked for in vain in literature outside the pages of Balzac or George Sand—a noble but undeveloped character, of whom, nevertheless, we are inclined to believe that many a counterpart is to be found in real life."—*Scotsman*.

MR. VAUGHAN'S HEIR. By FRANK LEE BENEDICT, Author of "Miss Dorothy's Charge," etc. 3 vols., 31s. 6d.

NEARER AND DEARER. By ELIZABETH J. LYSAGHT, Author of "Building upon Sand." 3 vols., 31s. 6d.

NEGLECTED; a Story of Nursery Education Forty Years Ago. By Miss JULIA LUARD. Crown 8vo., 5s. cloth.

NO FATHERLAND.   By Madame Von Oppen.
2 vols., 21s.

NORTONDALE CASTLE.   1 vol., 7s. 6d.

NOT TO BE BROKEN.   By W. A. Chandler.
Crown 8vo., 10s. 6d.

ONLY SEA AND SKY.   By Elizabeth Hindley.
2 vols., 21s.

"This is a tranquil story, very well told.   There are several neat touches of character in these two volumes, and a fair amount of humour."—*Public Opinion.*

"A really good and readable novel—we hope only the precursor of others from the same pen."—*Scotsman.*

"By no means without promise."—*Globe.*

"This, on the whole, is a fairly written story.   Monsieur Jules is a worthy Frenchman whom all readers will admire."—*Evening Standard.*

"The author seems to know something of France and Germany."—*Athenæum.*

OVER THE FURZE.   By Rosa M. Kettle, Author of the " Mistress of Langdale Hall," etc.   3 vols., 31s. 6d.

PERCY LOCKHART.   By F. W. Baxter.   2 vols., 21s.

PUTTYPUT'S PROTÉGÉE;   or, Road, Rail, and River.   A Story in Three Books.   By Henry George Churchill.   Crown 8vo., (uniform with "The Mistress of Langdale Hall"), with 14 illustrations by Wallis Mackay. Post free, 4s.   Second edition.

"It is a lengthened and diversified farce, full of screaming fun and comic delineation—a reflection of Dickens, Mrs. Malaprop, and Mr. Boucicault, and dealing with various descriptions of social life.   We have read and laughed, pooh-poohed, and read again, ashamed of our interest, but our interest has been too strong for our shame.   Readers may do worse than surrender themselves to its melo-dramatic enjoyment.   From title-page to colophon, only Dominie Sampson's epithet can describe it--it is 'prodigious.'"—*British Quarterly Review.*

"It is impossible to read 'Puttyput's Protégée' without being reminded at every turn of the contemporary stage, and the impression it leaves on the mind is very similar to that produced by witnessing a whole evening's entertainment at one of our popular theatres."—*Echo.*

RAVENSDALE. By ROBERT THYNNE, Author of "Tom Delany." 3 vols., 31s. 6d.

"A well-told, natural, and wholesome story."—*Standard.*
"No one can deny merit to the writer."—*Saturday Review.*

RUPERT REDMOND: A Tale of England, Ireland, and America. By WALTER SIMS SOUTHWELL. 3 vols., 31s. 6d.

SAINT SIMON'S NIECE. By FRANK LEE BENEDICT, Author of "Miss Dorothy's Charge." 3 vols., 31s. 6d.

SELF-UNITED. By Mrs. HICKES BRYANT. 3 vols., 31s. 6d.

SHINGLEBOROUGH SOCIETY. 3 vols., 31s. 6d.

SKYWARD AND EARTHWARD: a Tale. By ARTHUR PENRICE. 1 vol., crown 8vo, 7s. 6d.

SPOILT LIVES. By MRS. RAPER. 1 vol., 7s. 6d.

SOME OF OUR GIRLS. By Mrs. EILOART, Author of "The Curate's Discipline," "The Love that Lived," "Meg," etc., etc. 3 vols., 31s. 6d.

"A book that should be read. . . . Ably written books directed to this purpose deserve to meet with the success which Mrs. Eiloart's work will obtain."—*Athenæum.*
"Altogether the book is well worth perusing."—*John Bull.*

SONS OF DIVES. 2 vols., 21s.

"A well-principled and natural story."—*Athenæum.*

STRANDED, BUT NOT LOST. By DOROTHY BROMYARD. 3 vols., 31s. 6d.

SWEET IDOLATRY. By DAMON. 1 vol., 7s. 6d.

"Love is a sweet idolatry enslaving all the soul,—
A mighty spiritual force, warring with the dulness of matter,—
An angel-mind breathed into a mortal, though fallen, yet how beautiful !
All the devotion of the heart, in all its depth and grandeur."
—TUPPER.

THE ADVENTURES OF MICK CALLIGHIN, M.P., a Story of Home Rule; and THE DE BURGHOS, a Romance. By W. R. ANCKETILL. In one Volume, with Illustrations. Price 7s. 6d.

THE BARONET'S CROSS. By MARY MEEKE, Author of "Marion's Path through Shadow to Sunshine." 2 vols., 21s.

THE BRITISH SUBALTERN. By an Ex-SUBALTERN. 1 vol., 7s. 6d.

THE D'EYNCOURTS OF FAIRLEIGH. By THOMAS ROWLAND SKEMP. 3 vols., 31s. 6d.

"An exceedingly readable novel, full of various and sustained interest. . . . . The interest is well kept up all through."—*Daily Telegraph*.

THE HEIR OF REDDESMONT. 3 vols., 31s. 6d.

"Full of interest and life."—*Echo*.

THE INSIDIOUS THIEF: a Tale for Humble Folks. By One of Themselves. Crown 8vo., 5s. Second Edition.

THE LOVE THAT LIVED. By Mrs. EILOART, Author of "The Curate's Discipline," "Just a Woman," "Woman's Wrong," &c. 3 vols., 31s. 6d.

"Three volumes which most people will prefer not to leave till they have read the last page of the third volume."—*Pall Mall Gazette*.

"One of the most thoroughly wholesome novels we have read for some ime."—*Scotsman*.

THE MAGIC OF LOVE. By Mrs. FORREST-GRANT, Author of "Fair, but not Wise." 3 vols., 31s. 6d.

"A very amusing novel."—*Scotsman*.

THE MISTRESS OF LANGDALE HALL: a Romance of the West Riding. By ROSA MACKENZIE KETTLE. Complete in one handsome volume, with Frontispiece and Vignette by PERCIVAL SKELTON. 4s., post free.

"The story is interesting and very pleasantly written, and for the sake of both author and publisher we cordially wish it the reception it deserves."—*Saturday Review*.

THE SECRET OF TWO HOUSES. By FANNY FISHER. 2 vols., 21s.

"Thoroughly dramatic."—*Public Opinion*.

"The story is well told."—*Sunday Times*.

THE SEDGEBOROUGH WORLD. By A. FAREBROTHER. 2 vols., 21s.

THE SURGEON'S SECRET. By SYDNEY MOSTYN, Author of " Kitty's Rival," etc. Crown 8vo., 10s. 6d.

" A most exciting novel—the best on our list. It may be fairly recommended as a very extraordinary book."—*John Bull*.

" A stirring drama, with a number of closely connected scenes, in which there are not a few legitimately sensational situations. There are many spirited passages."—*Public Opinion*.

THE THORNTONS OF THORNBURY. By Mrs. HENRY LOWTHER CHERMSIDE. 3 vols., 31s. 6d.

THE TRUE STORY OF HUGH NOBLE'S FLIGHT. By the Authoress of " What Her Face Said." 10s. 6d.

" A pleasant story, with touches of exquisite pathos, well told by one who is master of an excellent and sprightly style."—*Standard*.

THE WIDOW UNMASKED; or, the Firebrand in the Family. By FLORA F. WYLDE. 3 vols., 31s. 6d.

TIMOTHY CRIPPLE; or, " Life's a Feast." By THOMAS AURIOL ROBINSON. 2 vols., 21s.

" This is a most amusing book, and the author deserves great credit for the novelty of his design, and the quaint humour with which it is worked out."—*Public Opinion*.

" For abundance of humour, variety of incident, and idiomatic vigour of expression, Mr. Robinson deserves, and will no doubt receive, great credit."—*Civil Service Review*.

TOO LIGHTLY BROKEN. 3 vols., 31s. 6d.

" A very pleasing story . . . . . very prettily told."—*Morning Post*.

TOM DELANY. By ROBERT THYNNE, Author of " Ravensdale." 3 vols., 31s. 6d.

" A very bright, healthy, simply-told story."—*Standard*.

" All the individuals whom the reader meets at the gold-fields are well-drawn, amongst whom not the least interesting is 'Terrible Mac.'"—*Hour*.

" There is not a dull page in the book."—*Scotsman*.

TOWER HALLOWDEANE. 2 vols., 21s.

TOXIE : a Tale. 3 vols., 31s. 6d.

TWIXT CUP and LIP. By MARY LOVETT-CAMERON. 3 vols., 31s. 6d.

" Displays signs of more than ordinary promise. . . . As a whole the novel cannot fail to please. Its plot is one that will arrest attention; and its characters, one and all, are full of life and have that nameless charm which at once attracts and retains the sympathy of the reader."—*Daily News*.

Samuel Tinsley, 10, Southampton Street, Strand.

'TWIXT WIFE AND FATHERLAND. 2 vols., 21s.

"A bright, vigorous, and healthy story, and decidedly above the average of books of this class. Being in two volumes it commands the reader's unbroken attention to the very end."—*Standard.*

"It is by someone who has caught her (Baroness Tautphoeus') gift of telling a charming story in the boldest manner, and of forcing us to take an interest in her characters, which writers, far better from a literary point of view, can never approach."—*Athenæum.*

"The story of Camilla's trials exhibits an unusual power of delineating not what is on the surface, but what is exercising the soul under a calm outward exterior."—*John Bull.*

"The tale has both freshness and power. The Italian conspirators are well sketched and individualised, and there are some delicious descriptions of Dolomite scenery which will incline many readers in that direction."—*Nonconformist.*

"There is originality in this story. . . . . Camilla had been foolish and headstrong, but she is rather a fascinating heroine."—*Graphic.*

"The description of Tyrolese life, and all the intrigues of De Zanna and his friends, with the counter-movements of the Austrian party, are not without interest."—*Morning Post.*

"The story is written in a quaint and easy style that is very refreshing ; and there are many enjoyable descriptive passages."—*Scotsman.*

"Shadows forth much promise. The story will be read with pleasure for the freshness of its descriptions of the people and glorious scenes of the South Tyrol."—*Morning Advertiser.*

TWO STRIDES OF DESTINY. By S. Brookes Bucklee. 3 vols., 31s. 6d.

"For an early effort the work is eminently satisfactory. It is quite original, the tone is good, the language graceful, and the characters thoroughly natural."—*Public Opinion.*

"A pretty story, written strictly in accordance with the popular taste in fiction. It is a thoughtful story. . . . Possesses many elements of originality."—*Morning Post.*

UNDER PRESSURE. By T. E. Pemberton. 2 vols., 21s.

"A novel above the average standard. . . . We will not detail the dramatic end of this interesting and well-written story."—*Daily News.*

"There is humour, character, and much clever description in 'Under Pressure,' and it is sure to be read with interest."—*Yorkshire Post.*

"Mr. Pemberton has displayed keen observation and high literary capacity."—*Birmingham Morning News.*

"One of the best contributions to light literature that has been published for some time."—*Birmingham Daily Gazette.*

"The book has very considerable vigour and originality."—*Scotsman.*

WAGES: a Story in Three Books. 3 vols., 31s. 6d.

"A work of no commonplace character." —*Sunday Times.*

WANDERING FIRES. By Mrs. M. C. DESPARD, Author of " Chaste as Ice," &c. 3 vols., 31s. 6d.

WEBS OF LOVE. (I. A Lawyer's Device. II. Sancta Simplicitas.) By G. E. H. 1 vol., Crown 8vo., 10s. 6d.

WEIMAR'S TRUST. By Mrs. EDWARD CHRISTIAN. 3 vols., 31s. 6d.

"A novel which deserves to be read, and which, once begun, will not be readily laid aside till the end."—*Scotsman.*

WILL SHE BEAR IT? A Tale of the Weald. 3 vols., 31s. 6d.

"This is a clever story, easily and naturally told, and the reader's interest sustained throughout. . . . A pleasant, readable book, such as we can heartily recommend as likely to do good service in the dull and foggy days before us."—*Spectator.*

WOMAN'S AMBITION. By M. L. LYONS. 1 vol., 7s. 6d.

HOW I SPENT MY TWO YEARS' LEAVE; or, My Impressions of the Mother Country, the Continent of Europe, the United States of America, and Canada. By an Indian Officer. In one vol. 8vo. Handsomely bound. Price 15s.

FACT AGAINST FICTION. The Habits and Treatment of Animals Practically Considered. Hydrophobia and Distemper. With some remarks on Darwin. By the HON. GRANTLEY F. BERKELEY. 2 vols., 8vo., 30s.

MALTA SIXTY YEARS AGO. With a Concise History of the Order of St. John of Jerusalem, the Crusades, and Knights Templars. By Col. CLAUDIUS SHAW. Handsomely bound in cloth, 10s. 6d., gilt edges, 12s.

THE USE AND ABUSE OF IRRATIONAL ANIMALS; with some Remarks on the Essential Moral Difference between Genuine "Sport" and the Horrors of Vivisection. In wrapper, price 1s.

HARRY'S BIG BOOTS : a Fairy Tale, for "Smalle Folke." By S. E. GAY. With 8 Full-page Illustrations and a Vignette by the author, drawn on wood by PERCIVAL SKELTON. Crown 8vo., handsomely bound in cloth, price 5s.

"Some capital fun will be found in ' Harry's Big Boots.' . . . The illustrations are excellent, and so is the story."—*Pall Mall Gazette.*

MOVING EARS. By the Ven. Archdeacon WEAKHEAD, Rector of Newtown, Kent. 1 vol., crown 8vo., 5s.

A TRUE FLEMISH STORY. By the Author of "The Eve of St. Nicholas." In wrapper, 1s.

THE PHYSIOLOGY OF THE SECTS. Crown 8vo., price 5s.

ANOTHER WORLD; or, Fragments from the Star City of Montalluyah. By HERMES. Third Edition, revised, with additions. Post 8vo., price 12s.

THE FALL OF MAN : An Answer to Mr. Darwin's "Descent of Man;" being a Complete Refutation, by common-sense arguments, of the Theory of Natural Selection. 1s., sewed.

THE RITUALIST'S PROGRESS; or, A Sketch of the Reforms and Ministrations of the Rev. Septimius Alban, Member of the E.C.U., Vicar of S. Alicia, Sloperton. By A. B. WILDERED, Parishioner. Fcp. 8vo. 2s. 6d. cloth.

MISTRESSES AND MAIDS. By HUBERT CURTIS, Author of "Helen," etc. Price 1d.

EPITAPHIANA; or, the Curiosities of Churchyard Literature : being a Miscellaneous Collection of Epitaphs, with an INTRODUCTION. By W. FAIRLEY. Crown 8vo., cloth, price 5s. Post free.

"Entertaining."—*Pall Mall Gazette.*
"A capital collection."—*Court Circular*
"A very readable volume."—*Daily Review.*
"A most interesting book."—*Leeds Mercury.*
"Interesting and amusing." *Nonconformist.*
"Particularly entertaining."—*Public Opinion.*
"A curious and entertaining volume."—*Oxford Chronicle.*
"A very interesting collection."—*Civil Service Gazette.*

TWELVE NATIONAL BALLADS (First Series). Dedicated to Liberals of all classes. By PHILHELOT, of Cambridge ; in ornamental cover, price sixpence, post free.